T0047239

MARKED MASTERS

"Once again I have to hold on to my hat while we zip around Europe and land in lovely Florence where author Ritter Ames lures me in with her delightful vignette of Italian life seen through the eyes of an art expert."

– Maria Grazia Swan,
Author of the Lella York Mysteries

"Ames, with her great writing and brilliant story, has created a masterpiece of her own in *Marked Masters*. She leaves her readers doing their own research between the pages. Like Laurel, Ritter keeps the story with its rightful owner—the reader."

– *Crimespree Magazine*

"Boasting a great cast of characters, good conversations and the global background, this was a very enjoyable read and I look forward to the third book in this exciting series."

– *Dru's Book Musing*

"Well-plotted and will keep you guessing until the very end...The action is nonstop and you will find that you can't put this book down. Mystery readers will enjoy the chase and be pleased with the outcome. I can't wait to read the next in the delightful series. If you like your mystery filled with hunky spies, then you should be reading *Marked Masters*."

– Cheryl Green, *MyShelf Reviews*

COUNTERFEIT CONSPIRACIES (#1)

"This fast-paced, action-filled whodunit was enjoyable and hard to put down...it was fun to watch the pieces come together in this well-written drama. I'm looking forward to the next book in this series."

– *Dru's Book Musings*

"Funny, fast paced and just a smidge of romance. What more could you ask for? Bring on the next one!"

"A high-octane, fast-paced thrill ride of a mystery adventure that will definitely leave you anxious for the next installment."

"This fast-paced mystery had me reading far past my usual time for bed. I simply couldn't put it down because I was so drawn into the story. It's simply wonderful!"

"The book takes you on car chases, shooting, great locations around the world all in the hopes of finding a missing friend and lost artifact. I read the book three times enjoying each time."

"To save the day, Laurel takes you with her every step of the way on subways, planes, fast cars, and motorcycles all while being in danger. This book is truly a keeper, jump in a go for a ride!"

"Incredible attention to detail. The author creates a world that you truly can get lost in. The book is also a fast-paced, fun read. I'm looking forward to reading book two."

"An intricately woven tale with plenty of action and suspense. The story is crafted in such a way to keep readers guessing. The characters are well-written with smart and witty dialogue. An enjoyable read."

MARKED masters

**The Bodies of Art Mystery Series
by Ritter Ames**

COUNTERFEIT CONSPIRACIES (#1)
MARKED MASTERS (#2)
ABSTRACT ALIASES (#3)
(October 2016)

MARKED
masters

A BODIES OF ART MYSTERY

RITTER
AMES

HENERY PRESS

MARKED MASTERS
A Bodies of Art Mystery
Part of the Henery Press Mystery Collection

Second Edition
Trade paperback edition | February 2016

Henery Press, LLC
www.henerypress.com

ISBN-13: 978-1-943390-49-6

Printed in the United States of America

To all family and friends who have been there throughout the writing journey. Thank you, everyone.

ACKNOWLEDGMENTS

One of the quotes on the wall of my writing corner is by Goethe, "Be bold...and mighty forces will come to your aid."

I always keep this quote in mind when I'm writing in Laurel Beacham's point of view, because she has a job that requires strength, ingenuity, and the confidence to know others can provide backup if she calls.

As an author, I've found my own mighty forces to give me confidence while writing this series. From longtime friend and freelance copyeditor extraordinaire, Pat Wade, to a phenomenal street team who keeps me on the writing straight and narrow, and who constantly let me know they are ready for Laurel's and Jack's next big adventure. Readers, you are all my true heroes. I thank you, and I am thrilled you are always there when I call.

Finally, I absolutely have to thank my fabulous editor, Erin George, for her unwavering support to this series, and Kendel Lynn for producing outstanding covers and graphics for the Bodies of Art mysteries. Thank you both for always making Henery Press authors look better.

ONE

Two black and whites screamed to the curb, paralleling each other and blocking off any possibility of retreat. Brakes screeched. Sirens blared. My blood pressure ratcheted up a notch. The flashing lights alone set my heart pounding so hard I could swear the beats showed through my black Lycra.

One step and I bled back into the shadows of the house's side wall.

A simple pickup on a limited time frame. That's what the job had been. My objective was a medium-sized nude, which had reclined over the headboard of a blackmailer's bed for decades. A painting and headboard currently residing inside the townhouse that was the focal point of this Orlando PD team.

"He's been extorting money from my mother since before I was born," Kat Gleeson had explained earlier in the afternoon. "The blackmailer picked up the portrait at a sale after the artist died, playing a hunch it would be worth bigger bucks later. Mother received the first demand as soon as my father started in political life. Laurel, you have to help us."

A longtime friend from my Cornell years, and daughter to Senator Gleeson, R-FL, Kat called me earlier in the day, frantic to meet after hearing I was in the city. When I'd said my Miami flight was first thing in the morning, she'd turned from frantic to panicked, and I'd promised to be at her favorite cocktail bar in ten minutes time.

Now, twelve hours later, this new dilemma forced me to contemplate an alternate route inside the house for the nude painted when Kat's mother was an ingénue and the artist undiscovered. In his later years, before his final drug overdose, the once up-and-coming artist became best known for his erotic subjects and a penchant for the rock-and-roll lifestyle of the 1970s. A single moment captured in brushstrokes kept Kat's mother chronically worried and perpetually broke all these years later.

As political buzz hummed about Senator Gleeson's prospective run for the presidency, the hush-money stakes had risen sharply. The next installment hit a price Mrs. Gleeson couldn't deliver without her husband's knowledge and cooperation.

In the past few years I'd gained the reputation as the best person to call when a legitimate piece of art went missing. I'd climbed the ranks of the Beacham Foundation, from internship at the New York office during college, to field work and troubleshooting the last five-plus years since graduation, rising in the eyes of the art world as my skills sharpened and the wins mounted on my record. However, people who knew me well—or like Kat, had known me in my wilder college days—were also aware of my "special" talents, and that I was always ready to jump into a non-work venue when conventional methods fell short or were too complicated for implementation. I dubbed these pro bono efforts my "reclamation projects." Given my more visible status since a promotion a few weeks ago to head of the London office of Beacham Ltd., I knew such forays may have to be reduced in the future, but there was no way I could turn my back when someone like Kat appealed to me for help.

My prep time on this particular reclamation was understandably limited, but the facts that came back were solid— the owner was a Luddite who didn't know a silent alarm from a silent movie. An absolute anachronism today, but the attribute served him well as a blackmailer since the practice left little risk of his digital fingerprint getting lifted anywhere.

What had alerted the cops?

The head-to-toe unrelieved black I wore dovetailed into the shadows and afforded me a bit of invisibility. I contemplated the peripheral shrubbery but waited to see the officers' game plan. A peek at my watch, hidden by the hood of my sleeve, showed less than a half hour to either accomplish what I came to do or cut and run.

Car doors slammed and voices rose as authoritative tones ordered a blue scramble to search for whatever tipped them off to the location.

Another scan of the back wall showed the basement window I'd initially dismissed as too small for a final escape. But it could get me into the house as long as I sucked in my gut and visualized being *very, very small*. I also had to maneuver without being seen or heard across the white ribbon obligatory to many Sunshine State homes; the oyster-shell path that ringed the grounds around the house walls like fluorescence in the moon glow.

They drew their guns and headed for the porch. I made my move, using long-latent childhood gymnastic muscles to clear the wide, crushed path and stick a quiet landing on the tiny strip of grass along the foundation.

I pulled the penlight stashed in my bra and scoped out the basement in about 2.6 seconds. Any longer carried too much risk, but the quickly lighted view told me I'd be dropping six feet onto bare cement. That was doable.

The extended beam of a Maglite flashed from around the corner as I started feet first down the rabbit hole. When my soles hit concrete, I reached up to softly set the window back into a closed position. Then I crouched into a dark ball and held my breath. Via the locked window, I heard the cop's feet pass by, then stop. He flashed his light through the glass, across the cellar, floor to ceiling. I hugged the wall tighter and hoped he wouldn't look straight down.

"Nah," I heard him say into his radio. "There's a tiny window back here, but it's locked, and I can't imagine anyone getting through it anyway. Over."

Still, it wasn't time to sigh in relief. The mark was due home from a NASA event soon. No need to look at my watch again to know the minutes were flying. I continued to hold my breath until I heard the oyster shells crunch when the cop resumed his recon.

A cursory scan for infrared, trip wires, or motion detectors came up zero. The house was as technology-free as I'd been told. No doubt I was taking a chance going in before the cops left, but if I'd stayed outside I was pretty much guaranteed to get caught. And a ride in the back of a squad car to explain why I was dressed in black in a dark yard after midnight was not on my agenda for the evening.

The open floor plan in the living space made it relatively easy to navigate without lights. Moonlight streamed through huge windows dressed in nothing but sheers. I kept to the beige and taupe walls and the larger pieces of furniture as much as possible, using the moving shadows of the cops outside to know where and when to scoot to the next spot. The boys in blue only appeared to be doing reconnaissance, leaving me to hope for a rapid departure when they found the house secured. At least I *hoped* it was completely secure. I hadn't had time to do a whole house perimeter before they showed up.

I crept up the stairs. The landing opened to a full-wall window that overlooked the front yard. Staying back as far as possible, I watched the blue crew huddle again at the curb.

Please, please, please leave. I don't have much time left.

Just as my limbs started to cramp from standing so still, I saw one give the "move 'em out" swing of the arm, and both teams returned to their respective cars. I didn't start breathing again until I saw the revolving lights stop and the headlights turn back down the boulevard.

The master suite was where I expected, and I was probably feeling too cocky as I closed the door behind me and pulled from my pocket the sharp little tool used to extract canvasses from frames. I spun around and approached the bed—and got my next shock of the night. A gorgeous baroque frame hung on the wall over the headboard...but it was empty.

I froze. There was no backup plan for this. Where else could the portrait be?

A check of the closet and under the bed offered no answers. I started running through rooms, scanning each wall, behind the sofa and chairs. Nada.

In the study I found bookcases filled with volumes and vases, but no portraits. I circled the desk, hoping for a clue. The ultraprecise Omega chronometer on my left wrist gave one quiet beep, warning me to pull up stakes and run before it was too late.

My gaze fell on the partially open middle desk drawer, and about an inch-view of a leather-bound journal. I opened the drawer about a foot. Across the front of the journal, embossed in gold, were the words "My Women."

His little black book? Or his blackmail roster? Either way, taking it might give me ammunition to offer Mrs. Gleeson if the worst happened and the blackmailer came after her again. He'd obviously stashed the portrait someplace else. Maybe Kat spoke to someone besides me, and he'd gotten wind of a rescue attempt?

If I couldn't bring back the painting, perhaps this book could be used as an alternate method to stop the blackmail.

I needed to fly. The book went down the front of my leotard, and the drawer was returned to its partially-open position. I slipped out the side door I'd originally planned to use for entry to the house.

Vaulting the back wall wasn't even a challenge. I was so pumped I probably could have vaulted the whole house without too much difficulty.

I was behind the steering wheel of my car and digging the book out of my clothes, trying to figure out what I was going to tell Kat, when a voice behind me said, "Find anything interesting, love?"

If I could have reached him, Jack Hawkes would have been dead.

"Damn it, Jack. Don't do that." I turned in my seat and instinctively swung backhanded to try to slap the grin from his face. He caught my arm without even trying.

"A trifle nervy, aren't you?"

Jack Hawkes remained a mystery no matter how creatively I tried to corner him on personal details. Maybe some level of UK agent, likely MI-6 by the way he operated, but he treated his background as something on a need-to-know basis. I always had the feeling he didn't want to explain rather than he couldn't, and I'd learned early on to not let my guard down around people who didn't act completely trustworthy. Jack tipped the scale soundly on my distrust meter. He and I were currently teamed up to stop what may be the art heist of the century. Our single crumb of information mentioned a safe-deposit box, which was why we came to Orlando. Our legal team moved heaven and earth for Jack and me to peek inside, but we only found a combination of numbers, a pristine map of the European Union, and a reference to Miami.

When Jack and I parted company earlier, he'd said he had plans for the evening. I had no idea our evening agendas were similar, and hadn't expected to see Jack's face until our Miami flight the following morning. The sight of his broad-shouldered frame filling my backseat was unnerving enough to give my voice an edge. "I'm pissed off is what I am." I waved a hand. "It's...over. And I failed. What are you doing here?"

"Oh, a little shopping. Senator Gleeson asked me to pick up an old canvas for him."

"What?" I stared as Jack pulled an item from behind my seat back.

There it was, a gorgeous nude infamous because of the later-years reputation of the artist. Kat's mother was young and lovely, and the body of art should never have gained its now notorious reputation. "It's beautiful. A true work of genius." I should have been more upset with him, but I was truly relieved to see the painting safely away from the blackmailer's grasp.

"It absolutely is. Sorry I scooped it out already and you had to leave empty handed."

A second scream of sirens erupted from somewhere several blocks away.

"I'm guessing you went out the side door," Jack said.

"Yes."

"The neighbor to that side apparently has a predilection for night vision goggles and very nicely alerted the police to my exit right before you arrived on the scene."

"Explains why they didn't try to get inside. The neighbor saw you leave."

Jack nodded. "Goes to show we work better together than apart."

"You said you had plans. You didn't say you were after the painting, too."

"And you didn't mention it at all," he reminded.

I ignored his dig and reached between the seats to run a gentle finger along the artist's confident brushstrokes. "How did you know I was going to take this?"

"I didn't."

"Then why—"

"The senator's aide was a Rhodes Scholar, and we met when we were at university together."

"So the senator already knows?"

"Has for years. He's been waiting for his wife to bring it up but was afraid of saying anything until she spoke first. Whenever her bank account ran low, he knew she'd had to make another payment, and he would find an excuse to give her more. But he'd recognized the signs lately that things were getting out of hand, and he hired a private detective to learn the man's schedule. Tonight seemed the best opportunity to make a move, especially since we're leaving in a few hours."

I nodded. "That was our thinking too. Kat's and mine. The Gleesons' daughter and I were college friends as well."

I pulled the book from my neckline. "But I didn't leave empty handed. Found this in his study when trying to discover where the missing portrait was. I think it may be more blackmail victims. We were concerned that taking the portrait would point too much toward Mrs. Gleeson, but couldn't find any other means to stop the blackmail. I'm hoping this information defrays the risk of him doing something else to bring light to the situation."

"Like having her arrested for the theft of a painting he legally owns?"

"And used for blackmailing purposes," I replied.

"True, but proving it would bring on the media exposure everyone wants to avoid. Like you, I imagine the blackmailer counts on that." Jack turned on the dome light and snatched the book from my grasp.

"Hey, give it back."

"No, this is evidence—" He whistled.

"What?"

Jack held up a hand to silence me, then turned a couple more pages. I tried to retrieve the book, but he jumped across the seat, and my fingernails scratched the cover.

"You're going to tell me what that is, Hawkes."

"A minute, please."

Finally, he stopped shifting pages and looked up, his face a mask of disbelief. "A detailed report on human trafficking activity coming through Florida, then going out across the U.S. He's documented everything, who his clients are, what they've paid, which countries the women came from. Everything. A bit of coding, but easily worked out. This guy really is an ego manic."

"Wow." This was nothing like I'd expected when I took the journal. "So does it go to the FBI or Interpol?"

"Probably both. You drive. I'll send someone to pick up my car later." Jack pulled out his cell.

I should have called Kat to give her the high sign, but I needed to process a lot of this first. To figure out how to tell her the blackmailer had more to worry about than the loss of his moneymaking portrait, and do so without giving away state secrets. I also had to find a sensitive way to reveal her father knew about the blackmail but had kept the knowledge secret from her mother. There could be many reasons why, both sincere and creepy.

Kat and I were scheduled to meet in the airport short-term

parking in a few hours. The plan was to hand over the portrait, letting it go practically unnoticed from my car trunk to hers before we split up—me for my southbound flight and Kat to turn the painting over to her mother.

"I'd like to give the portrait to Kat instead of the senator's aide," I said when Jack hung up from his hushed-voice call to Interpol. "I'll tell her that her dad knows, but I think this needs to be a family conversation instead of one originating with an employee."

"Agreed. Is she meeting you at the airport?"

"Yes."

"We'll have a greeting party for the journal once we get to Miami. The suits are definitely interested."

I smiled into oncoming headlights and merged onto the freeway. "Our low-tech blackmailer has just become an even lower lowlife."

"And you, my love, have gained the prize that will give hundreds of innocent women their lives back."

"One nasty bad guy down, one art criminal mastermind still to go."

TWO

A few hours later—both of us changed out of our burgling black—Jack and I were sitting in the Miami airport waiting for our flight. His left forearm appropriated our shared armrest. Every time he moved I smelled the new cologne he was wearing, some kind of pleasing sandalwood scent that lingered. Dressed in his standard suit, this time brown with white shirt, he livened everything up by adding a bright-teal silk tie. The color perfectly matched his eyes, and I wondered what woman had given it to him. Jack tended to appear naturally comfortable in any setting, which was one of the reasons I had difficulty trusting him.

I saved the article I'd hurried to finish, pulled up my email to Flavia, attached the file, and hit send. The subject was one near and dear to my heart—women and art. Several months ago I'd promised a piece to the Association for Women's Advancement in Art. An old friend, Flavia Bello, ran the organization. If I'd had the money, I would be a benefactor. Instead, I happily completed the occasional article for its newsletter. Unfortunately, in the past weeks' craziness I'd totally forgotten about the article until Flavia forwarded a reminder email along with information about the upcoming fundraising event featuring women artists and subjects. I reread the invitations and sighed. Florence, Italy, this Saturday night.

Working on it with Jack around was proving to be a pain. Interminable waiting at the airport for a flight made him more fidgety. Finally he'd left my side long enough to acquire drinks and snacks, and I'd taken advantage of the blessed silence to finish up the article.

I slid my computer back into my bag, stood, and stretched. I couldn't help thinking about Kat and the conjectures and decisions she would make in the coming weeks. I planned to call and check on Kat, but it was a journey she needed to walk on her own.

The silent tears she shed as I told her were the first of many. Like her, I had a father who had deeply disappointed me. Unlike Kat's, mine accomplished the feat in a wholly spectacular manner that didn't simply deprive me of my last possibility of familial support but snatched away forever the environment I'd known from birth until age seventeen. I survived by acknowledging I could no longer count on anyone but myself, built a personal armor around my heart, and developed a trust-radar and lie-detector system the CIA would envy. Hopefully, Kat would not have to do the same.

Relax. Close your eyes. We had new things to worry about.

Tinny music emanated from the iPod of the kid sitting next to me, and I drowsily wondered at the volume the device was cranked up to—his head nodding and earbuds blasting—since I had no difficulty determining the music as Nirvana. I dozed a few minutes before jerking myself awake to glance at my watch.

Jack had been gone twenty minutes too long. His errands should have taken "seven" minutes, a direct quote, but he'd been gone twenty-seven—now eight, as I watched my minute hand move. If my watch was correct and the airline hadn't rescheduled the flight, we were due to board in little more than fifteen minutes. A phone call went to voicemail. Anyone else and I would have shrugged the tardiness off and waited for his return. Since it was Jack, though, waiting wasn't an option. If he discovered a new lead and was reconning solo—without telling me, to keep me in the dark—I wanted to find out. Now. I didn't trust the man not to shut me out of things. If that wasn't the case...Well, I needed to make sure he didn't need backup. We were supposed to be working together, after all.

I grabbed my bag and walked from the gate to the hallway. I was not going to panic. Instead, I focused on my surroundings. I smelled food, coffee, and that particular odor airports have as people move exhaustedly from one geographical space to another, a culmination of a variety of cultures and varying degrees of unwashed bodies. Jack had indicated he wanted coffee. I headed that direction, dodging a couple of bored kids playing with a tiny rubber ball. No Hawkes. With the clock ticking down the minutes, I race-walked in and out of various outlets housing magazines, newspapers, books, souvenirs, and food, eventually finding a lone wall of canteen snacks for picky customers who didn't want fresh, only processed.

Bathrooms offered the next option, both men's and women's, and I ran through each, checking stalls. The men were naturally shocked, but the women offered more vocal outrage. In the last men's stall, I found Jack's bag, contents scattered everywhere and what looked like a few drops of blood on the floor. I thrust his stuff back into the bag, carefully avoiding the blood, and headed back to the main hallway. Frantically looking in every direction, I did not want to return to the security area, and I didn't think anyone else would have gone that way either.

I turned to look back toward the waiting area, hoping to see Jack waving frantically. No luck. For a second, my gaze was drawn to a matronly woman with a huge flowered hat. An entourage of some kind followed her, all headed my way.

As they passed the water fountain, I spotted a door marked No Entry. I hadn't noticed it earlier due to a group of kids fighting over the water fountain and the fact the door completely matched the surrounding walls.

My large Fendi purse and the wheeled bags helped hide my actions from the casual observer, and, I hoped, from the standard security cameras. The locked door presented no problem. Within a minute or so, I had it open with the set of tools I carried in a hidden pocket of my purse.

I replaced the tool and grabbed out of the pack a deceptively innocent-looking instrument with a sharp edge. For extra protection.

The wide storage room held a variety of supplies on seemingly endless high shelves and no clear view. Nothing to do but run for it. I slipped off my heels and ran, holding the bags tightly to my sides as I looked up and down each aisle. I stopped suddenly as I thought I heard something. I started to call out but worried I might alert the wrong person to my presence.

Only a few minutes left before the flight boarded. I headed back toward the other end of the room, on guard the whole way, and hoped the noise was Jack.

I stepped around the last shelf and gaped. Trussed up like a holiday turkey, Hawkes was hanging by ropes from the shelf bolted to the floor, his silk tie thrust in his mouth. Under his angry black eyebrows, his teal eyes shot murderous looks my way. He mumbled something and jerked at the ropes to shake the shelf, disturbing the plastic tumblers stacked in thin see-through bags all around him. Two packages closest to him tottered violently, fell off, and burst open. The freed tumblers rolled everywhere to join compatriots, which had apparently been knocked down during the hanging.

Though relieved to see him, I wanted to laugh. I had imagined him strung up many times. I thought seriously about pulling out my phone and taking a picture, but I didn't want to risk the death my poor smartphone would likely suffer after Jack was free.

I quickly looked him over, trying to determine the source of the blood I'd seen in the stall. Other than the rope chafing, a small cut was visible at the edge of his left eyebrow. The brows pulled together in a thunderous V.

The handle of my weapon went into my mouth, to free my hands for climbing. I let the bags slide from my arms. My Manolo Blahniks were discarded next. I climbed several of the shelves and used my tool to saw at one of the ropes holding him in place. His muttering got louder. I knew I should pull the tie out of his mouth, but I didn't want the complaints to start.

The tool was sharp. Before I cut the second one holding him, I needed to cut the rope binding his hands so he could protect himself as he fell. With a bit of difficulty, I sliced through the professional knots. He jerked the tie from his mouth.

"Bloody hell, Laurel, what took you so long to find me? Have we missed the flight?"

"Get ready, the rope's about to give way." I ignored his questions as I took a final swipe.

"What do you mean—" Jack's words became incoherent as he dropped to the floor amidst the plastic ware.

His next words weren't meant for polite company as he struggled to undo the knots around his ankles. I climbed down and handed him my tool, which he ungraciously took and sliced through the rope with more expertise than I had demonstrated. He rubbed his ankles and his wrists. I could tell from the way he was moving that his whole body hurt. It looked like a small bruise was forming around the ugly cut at his brow and the shadow of another under his chin.

"I guess the blood in the bathroom was from the cut near your eye?" I used a tissue to dab at the cut. He took the tissue from me and held it tightly to his temple, then shoved it into a pocket.

He looked at his Silberstein. It hadn't been a robbery. "What makes you think it wasn't from the other guy?" he asked irritably as he held a shelf to steady himself. "Come on, we have to go. Thank God we're already checked in and the gate is close."

"Because nobody hurt could have attached you to those shelves like a string of holiday lights." I countered the earlier question he used to avoid answering what I'd asked.

He ignored me, stuffed his tie in his suit pocket, straightened his clothing, picked up his case and mine. We took off for the gate, arriving with very little time to spare.

The plane boasted the standard East Coast, in-state shuttle accommodations, crammed to the wing flaps with coach seating. Seventy passengers filled the small commuter jet, with a column of two seats on the left side of the aisle and a width of three seats on the right. The flight spent little actual time in the air compared to the eternity waiting on the tarmac. Still, I figured I could grab a quick nap and intended to do so without delay.

Our seats together were on the small side of the plane. He

wanted the aisle, and I gave no argument to sitting and scooching into the window seat. I raised to straighten the skirt of the gray knit dress I got the last time I was in Peru. It was scrunchable and one of my favorites for traveling. It also went great with my favorite heels.

Jack had charmed the flight attendant out of a Glenfiddich before takeoff and was visibly relaxed when he glanced over at me and said, "They were airport workers. Or at least they were dressed like airport maintenance with a utility cart."

A utility cart with a lot of rope. I bit my lip. "What do you think they wanted?"

"I'm inclined to think they wanted to stop us from taking the flight. They were only interested in subduing me." He flexed the hand not holding the drink. "But how did you have that sharp tool?"

"A special storage case designed for me by a German craftsman," I explained. It wouldn't hold a large weapon, yet it could escape the detection of metal detectors and appeared innocuous under X-ray. "A thoughtful favor I received recently from an old friend." Then I pointed up at the overhead compartment. "You probably should check your bag. I found the contents scattered in the stall."

Jack shrugged. "I'm not worried. Nothing in the bag for them to find."

I took a sip from my water bottle. "What would their—whoever they are—interest be in stopping you from taking the flight?"

"Or you." He took a long swig and put the glass on the tray, the cubes rattling against the plastic glass.

"Why would it have necessarily stopped me?"

He cocked an eyebrow. "Your loyalty is well-known. And you did locate me, after all."

"But I may have gotten on the plane alone if I hadn't discovered where they'd trapped you. Simply notified the desk agent you were missing."

He shot me a look that made me laugh.

"I really am glad you're all right. But I do regret not getting a picture when I had the chance. I seriously thought about it, but figured it was leverage you'd never let me use."

"Right on that count. Would you really have left me?"

"Maybe..." I let the word hang for a moment before I added, "If I thought you'd taken off to follow a lead solo again. It wouldn't have been the first time. And the suspicion did cross my mind."

Jack handed his glass to the passing attendant. "You do know I would never do anything without reason. Right? However, when going for a cup of coffee requires rescue, it proves there are no innocent errands for either of us. I'm just glad this time I'm not dead."

I shuddered through a deep breath and looked at him with astonishment. "What did you say?"

"You heard me—I'll not repeat it. I equally cannot believe anyone could get the drop on me like that."

"I'm glad you aren't dead as well," I repeated solemnly, then winked to lighten the mood. I would never tell him how true that was. It would give him too much power. "Do you think we'll ever know who's responsible?"

Jack stared into the distance. "Oh, I'm certain I'll find out." From the tone of his voice, I could tell his words were a vow.

Even before we'd taken off, I had my napping plan rolled out. I pulled on my sleep mask to firmly cover my eyes. I figured the two-seat side was best as I didn't have to worry about anyone crossing over me for the next half hour or so. The flight met capacity levels in both human and hearing volume, and as with all the short hoppers I'd traveled on through the years, the noise levels in the plane were tremendous. No matter. The steady rumble was pure white noise to me. No frills had its benefits.

Alas, my rest was not to be. We had barely lifted the landing gear when Jack's shoulder leaned into mine. He asked, "Laurel, are you asleep?"

Ignoring him should have been easy. I could have used the plane noise as an excuse if he persisted. But I knew Jack, and when he persevered I risked blowing my top due to no sleep and less patience. I lifted one side of the sleep mask, not willing to give up yet on my dream. "I'm trying, Jack. I was a little too busy last night to get my full eight hours."

"Which brings up the subject I want to discuss." He cocked a black eyebrow at me, and I was reading his lips more than truly hearing each word as he continued. "I hope this foray into crime is your first and last. The value of the theft you attempted would put a felony on your record if those coppers last night had caught you."

I moved the whole mask to my hairline so he could see me lift my own eyebrow questioningly as I reminded, "Aren't you the one who left with the masterpiece? I recall spiriting away a lowly journal law enforcement can only use to get on to a trail of human traffickers. Since it meets no chain-of-evidence rules, it couldn't be more than a misdemeanor given its market value. Perhaps you should look inward, Mr. Hawkes. I think you can keep busy enough examining your own personality flaws. But thanks for your concern."

He snorted. I wiggled the dark mask back into place.

"Still, love..." His fingers lifted up a corner of the mask. I again saw that cocky eyebrow. "You possessed more than average nerve whilst we each traipsed through the little midnight caper. You were angry but confident when we met up at the car."

"You mean when you broke into my car and stashed your loot in my backseat? Wow, now that I think about it, Jack, your transgressions are really piling up. Maybe it would be best if I not associate with you anymore. Bad influence and all."

Due to our too-close confinement, I hoped this exchange was the end of his questions. I could deflect a lot and had my personal arsenal of point maneuvers which worked against most people. Except Jack Hawkes was not most people. My extracurricular activities were known to old and trusted confidents, no further. These wrongs righted, what I deemed my "reclamations," had gone undetected for some time by all facets of law enforcement, and I intended to keep the status quo precisely as I preferred it. While I'd been close to getting caught several times, even spotted on three separate occasions, I'd never actually been apprehended or even positively identified. I'd also never before had an adversary like Jack Hawkes. Someone who learned about my exploits by getting there minutes ahead of me. Someone who from the time I met him operated under the assumption I was more than I seemed.

Well, I never said the man wasn't bright. Hopefully, flip answers and the fact he got to the painting first was enough to shut down further discussion.

I jerked the satin mask from his fingers and repositioned it one last time over my eyes. To no avail.

"Speaking of associates." Jack ripped the mask completely off my head. I glared at him as I tried to use fingers and my vague reflection in the thick airplane window glass to reduce the clown mess my blond waves likely took on from the flinging elastic. My blue eyes were a blur, but even the poor reflection showed they were narrowed in anger below my thin brows.

"Were we speaking of associates? I honestly don't remember previous conversations along those lines." I shrugged and changed my look to my patented bored face. Allowing Jack to witness any negative emotion on my part made him feel he'd scored points and goaded him into continuing for the kill. Okay, maybe kill wasn't the best word to consider in our present adventure.

He tossed the black mask into my lap. "I've been reviewing every idea I've come up with in the past week, and I cannot figure out why Moran didn't kill you or have you killed anytime between London and Le Puy-en-Velay. He could have done so many times, with ease and little risk of exposure. Even accomplished the deed himself, we now know."

"We now assume. No one's given me confirmation yet about his French alias as my vehicular knight in shining armor."

"Consider it confirmed."

Damn, I hate when he knows stuff before me. Especially when I should have already been notified.

"Is there a reason Interpol never bothered telling me?" I

crossed my arms. "Assured them you would tell me yourself, and you forgot to mention it?"

"I received final confirmation an hour ago. This was really my first opportunity."

Not exactly, but I'd let it slide this time. "You're right, Jack. But as I recall, you were the one who almost strangled me in France. Should I be concerned by your close proximity?"

"Keep this up, and I may try it again." He frowned. "I'm not joking here, Laurel. I want to know if you have something on Moran."

That was a paradox I'd been contemplating for days. My quick wits had worked overtime, but I was still walking and breathing and thinking. Even Simon was confused, lamenting right before he escaped that if he shot me, he would pay for the act later.

Jack's next question pulled me out of my funk. "Did Moran know your grandfather? They had to be near-contemporaries. Maybe he owed your grandfather a debt of honor?"

"It's possible," I said, but I had difficulty believing the theory. It was more likely my crooked father had made Moran's acquaintance, rather than my straight-arrow grandfather. Dear Old Daddy may have even owed the criminal mastermind a huge debt when he died in the Swiss avalanche. It was six months before the mangled body was found and his dentist provided the evidence to prove those lovely veneers were my father's.

Daddy Dearest owed every other blackheart. Moran's plan could easily be to spare my life to try to get a final debt repaid. Though, since I had little money, I wasn't sure what I could offer in repayment. It had been nearly a decade since my father's death, sure, but I'd never heard of a statute of limitations on outstanding markers.

After my grandfather joined my grandmama in the great beyond, my father happily fell headlong into a two-year gambling, spending, debauchery spree to end all real and imagined by Hollywood. Despite the wealth our family accumulated over many generations, by the time my father went over the wrong side of his favorite Alp with his latest bimbo, he had nearly run through the entire estate. He'd left IOUs all over Europe and the Americas. Any money that remained tied to Grandfather's estate was used to keep all my limbs firmly connected to my torso by paying off the drug dealers and mob bosses who crawled out of the woodwork to intimidate me through direct and indirect contact.

"So, has Moran had any dealings with the Beacham Foundation?" Jack asked.

"You mean besides having his plans changed whenever I find something he's stolen and get it returned to the original owners?" I replied. When Jack nodded, I shook my head. "Not that I know of, but I've only worked full-time with the foundation five years. Until I graduated from Cornell, I worked temporarily in different departments in an intern capacity, due to the fierce loyalty Max had to my grandfather's memory."

"And you, I assume, were supposed to take over the foundation."

Yes, he'd obviously been reading my file again. My voice bordered on sarcasm when I said, "Grandfather always hoped I'd take my place in the business, but that, of course, was when he held ninety percent of the stock. Once the foundation became Beacham in name and tradition alone, I'm basically nothing more than an employee. I may learn more in the coming months with my new position, but I doubt Max will change much. You know as well as I that he's keeping a pretty tight noose around my neck."

"I think you mean leash."

I shrugged. "Leash, noose, both can choke the life right out of you."

THREE

By the time we'd made it out of the Miami airport with our bags, it was well past noon. We actually arrived there midmorning, but found a full gamut of spooks in suits awaiting us, with a representative from all three law enforcement contingents: CIA, FBI, and Interpol. They huddled together near baggage claim, obviously not wanting to miss Jack and me. Like we were going to run away after calling and telling them about the journal. Still, I understood the paranoia and almost laughed at their attempt to look casual. Even as they tried to look disinterested, each one maintained a perimeter sweep of the area. Tweedledee and Tweedledum were a pair of stocky, thirty-something Vin Diesel clones who sounded like they hailed from Tennessee and New York, respectively. They were also FBI and CIA, respectively. The tall, blond guy with them, a Ukrainian, I thought, admitted to being the representative from the Miami office for Interpol.

Jack took charge and I let him. This was no place for me to try to get involved. I did take the opportunity to deposit each man's business card inside the wallet of my new Fendi bag, purchased less than a week before to replace the poor Prada that nearly died in battle during my and Jack's first great adventure. Business cards are my aces. In my line of work, one never knew when it might pay to have another specialized civil servant's direct phone line.

We ended up in one of the offices of airport security, with Tweedledum pointedly ejecting, with a few choice phrases, the much too interested local facility guard. After Jack finished his debriefing, the CIA agent stared at us, then touched his Bluetooth earpiece and started talking. The other two pulled out cell phones and sent quick texts.

The journal remained safely stored in the false bottom of my Fendi until Jack gave a nod followed by an impatient finger snap.

I stepped close to him and whispered, "Do you like that hand? Or do you want to try to snap those fingers again with your hand separated from your arm at the wrist?" I gave him my best wide-eyed expression. He had the decency to look sheepish. I thought there was going to be an actual tug-of-war when I handed over the journal. But Interpol-guy used his accent to an advantage and reminded everyone how most of the women were from his former stomping grounds. He promised to send copies of the journal to everyone by "end of the business day."

"I'd like a copy sent to me as well," Jack said. When Interpol-guy assured a file would be forwarded to Jack's email, my unease about my sometime-partner doubled. He had clout somewhere—that was obvious—but he was also comfortable lying like the proverbial rug. The problem was I didn't know how to get a true angle on our Mr. Hawkes. Incidents like this one made the challenge doubly difficult.

My stomach alternated between a rumba and a salsa by the time we finally left the security office. I'd already given up on the four-star Miami restaurants I'd been dreaming about, or trying to con Jack into paying since it required a wallet thicker than mine. There was no way to get a late reservation in Midtown or the Design District, nor in any of the high-rise restaurants that glittered above the Miami River. Reservations be damned. I was ready to find a food truck and troll for dinner like a native.

As if my brain possessed a personal Google map, I let my mind drift over the food offerings I knew wended their way on the streets behind the city's art museums, my idea of the best place to start. I would have arm wrestled Jack, and likely won, in an effort to score the first Jefe's Fish Taco or a grilled wonder from Ms. Cheezious.

We headed for the car rental outlets, and I pulled out my phone to alert Nico, my gorgeous right-hand geek. It was approaching the high season, which runs from December through April. I hoped he could score me a good room at one of the luxury art hotels. I preferred The Sagamore, but I was never disappointed when my visits ended up with a stay at The Betsy and its renovated Art Deco splendor.

"Who are you calling?" Jack whispered, locking onto my elbow.

I stopped. "Why are you whispering?" Then I stared pointedly at his hand. I thought my comment about the snapping fingers made an impression, but now I wasn't so sure.

He followed my gaze, looked up, and shrugged. He used a normal volume to repeat, "Who are you calling?"

"Nico. I need to find out where I'm staying."

"I already texted him. You're staying with me." He kept his hand cupped around my elbow and took the lead in resuming our trek toward the car rental counter. My rolling suitcase banged in irritation at the speed.

"Do you think going all alpha like this improves your odds?" I asked him.

The airport public address system came on announcing flights, and I practically had to read his lips. "What odds?"

"The odds I'll continue to cooperate with you," I said. Then the PA ended, and I added quietly, "You tell me nothing. You try to take over. You expect me to follow docilely in your wake. You snap your fingers at me...When are you going to get that isn't going to work with us, Jack?"

The suits still trailed behind twenty feet or so, and I saw Jack cut his eyes to look over my head. He raised one finger. Then he ducked his head closer to mine. "Our Orlando trip netted much less than was hoped for when the intel came through on Simon's safe deposit box. Nothing but a number, a map we could get online anywhere, and a few scribblings that pointed to Miami. Despite Nico's best effort, he has yet to figure out the purpose of the number, and I can't find any clues on the map. While he's pursuing different angles, we need to work the Simon trail and see what links your old beau has to Moran. To get the kind of information we need, we're going to have to play the wealth card. A yacht trumps a luxury suite every time, and we have one at our disposal. Does the opportunity to dine and sleep aboard a yacht meet with *milady's* approval?"

"Ass."

"Is that a yes?"

Outflanked again. My hand itched to slap him. "Yes. It's a 'yes,' damn it."

Bringing Simon up in that context was Jack's ace to shut me up, and we both knew it. At the close of our last mission, we learned that Simon Babbage, my short-time ex-lover, now archenemy, had apparently also worked with master criminal Devin Moran. Or Philippe Aubertaine, the name I'd been given when I unknowingly met him in France. And probably another half-dozen aliases. I was still trying to process the traitorous Simon with the ex-lover Simon. Not that I wanted him back—at least not as a lover. I wanted him in the kind of handcuffs that never made a man smile. We were still evaluating the fallout to determine how long he had been a traitor during his ten years as head of Beacham London. But personally, I could see a pattern between my losses to Moran during the eight months of Simon's and my affair. I'd worried at the time I was losing my touch, and often consulted with Simon as a mentor about my plans and the subsequent disappointments when I lost another round. Now I knew Moran had an unfair advantage.

On a search Jack and I undertook for a historic jeweled sword, Simon disappeared with a bundle large enough to transport such an object, or any other art treasures we didn't yet know about, and the thief hadn't been a blip on the radar since. I wanted to hit him very, very hard where it hurt the most—his freedom and his wallet.

As we neared the car rental company, I ducked into the ladies' room, and by the time I came out, slightly more refreshed, Jack stood at the counter flirting with the cute car rental brunette. Too much to handle on an empty stomach.

"Jack," I called. When he looked up, I pointed to my phone

and then to a corner about twenty feet away. He nodded, understanding I needed to check in with my office.

"What's up, boss?" Cassie, my assistant, grinned at me on the small screen.

She knew I hated when she called me boss. I'd known her since college, and she and I were learning the ropes in running the London office of Beacham Ltd. together. Not all the kinks were worked out yet, but she was turning into a phenomenal analyst and researcher in the field of missing art.

I frowned out of habit and said, "I think Jack's working on a dinner date, but he has to make sure I get fed first."

"Really?"

"No. He's working on getting us a rental car, and the counter help is a young Jessica Biel wannabe. You know what that means. Jack has to flirt, and every woman thinks a British accent sounds sexy."

"How do you feel about that?"

"Huh?" What kind of question was that? "I feel annoyed, naturally. We have work to do, and he's wasting time flirting. Last time he finagled an Aston Martin. All we need is a plain sedan—"

"Never mind. I was only making conversation." Cassie laughed then turned professional. "I got news from Max today you're not going to like. All expenses you incur have to come through me."

"What?"

"He got the bill for his AMEX Black."

I sighed.

"You knew this day was coming."

I nodded. I have a problem with budgeting—as in, I have no real clue how it's done. Fortunately, my man-of-all-talents, Nico, is a master at getting into any computer. When my funds ran short at a critical time when I needed to globe trot, Nico hacked into our boss's credit card history and tacked all necessary expenses onto Max's account. But if Max realized the charges were for my benefit and mandated this fiscal timeout, what did he do to my favorite secret weapon?

"Cassie, did Nico—"

"Don't worry. Max tried to chew him out, but Nico pretty much ignored all of it. He was here in the office to Skype with the New York office anyway, and Max took the opportunity to vent his spleen. I think Nico thought it was humorous rather than humiliating."

"Which means Max now feels humiliated instead of vindicated."

"What can I say? It's Nico."

Right. And he knows that Max knows everyone in the world would offer my perfect techno-wingman a job the minute he decided he'd had enough of the Beacham Foundation. Which would also be the day I had Max drawn and quartered. At some point, the man had to learn to leave the fieldwork to the experts and give us the support we required.

From the corner of my eye, I saw Jack wave a set of car keys.

"Gotta go, Cass, but a couple of final things. First, I'm assuming Nico is still on the payroll."

"Yes. Absolutely. And flouting every screaming command Max made during the Skype session."

"Good. Now for my second question. Have you found out anything about the number Jack and I found in the safe-deposit box in Orlando?"

For security purposes, my team was working alone on this new discovery. Jack was convinced there was a mole in one or both of our organizations, though we hoped anything on the Beacham side ended with Simon's defection. Given the possible scope of the heist based on intelligence learned so far, we decided to keep everything at a minimalist level. Cassie and Nico received regular updates and helped with research. But even they would not know everything. We couldn't take any chances. We didn't want to risk tipping off a mole anywhere.

Equally, I wasn't taking any chances with Jack. Information I gained on my own would be parceled out on a need-to-know basis too. Without asking him, I knew he would be doing the same. We might be partners, but we weren't very good at working as a functioning duo.

"Sorry, but no," she said. "Nothing on Nico's end yet either. At least, nothing he's made me aware of."

I already knew Nico had come up with nothing, at least if I believed Jack. Still, I wanted the confirmation from Cassie since I didn't know why Jack seemed to be running my source as if Nico was his own. It was one thing to share my resources, another to abdicate all authority. "Okay, we'll talk later. Maybe we can conference on Skype this evening."

"I'll get a message to Nico and see how his schedule is running," Cassie said.

Jack cut the distance between us with several long strides, his patience obviously at an end. One more question before he got too close. "Have you found any more missing art on the bad USB drive? Anything else pointing to Florida, since we've now been led here because of the bank box?"

"Nothing yet." Cassie's image shook her blonde, hot-pink-tipped hair and looked down like she was keying or making a note while she talked. "But I have an idea on how to get into the corrupted areas. I'll let you know if I find anything interesting in the next few hours. I'm hopeful."

"Great. I have to go. Talk to you soon." I ended the call as Jack entered my personal space.

"Anything?" he asked.

"Max is out for blood over my finances, but what else is new? Got the car?"

He dangled the key ring tagged to a steel-blue Mercedes 350 Cabriolet ragtop.

"A convertible, Jack? Really?"

Yet when I saw it a few minutes later, I had to admit it was gorgeous. I didn't put up any fight when he opened the top to the sun.

"Dig around in your catchall of a purse and fetch something to hold back your hair. The windblown look is devastating on blondes of your age." He grinned, knowing full well I recognized he was pushing my buttons. Successfully, as usual.

He was also right about my bag. I still had the lovely gold-on-white Hermes scarf Cassie lent me for camouflage on a Chunnel ride. Though how something so expensive could make one incognito in such a setting was unbelievable in the extreme.

Yet in the current situation, riding in an expensive car, heading for an expensive part of Miami Beach, and playing the part of an expensive playmate to Jack, the coin-and-chain printed scarf was perfect. I slipped it over my hair and tied it under my chin, Lauren Bacall or Kate Hepburn style. Then I added big sunglasses. For a split second I could imagine my grandmother looking down at me—from wherever she and her old cronies played their nonstop bridge rubbers—with love in her eyes and a smile on her pale-pink lips, nodding in approval. I looked the part and was now completely wind resistant.

Jack grinned, and I had little doubt he was thinking exactly as I, despite never knowing my grammy. There were moments when he and I connected in ways I didn't understand.

We were on the road and checking out the early street scene as we headed for Miami Beach and the water. The day was fast approaching the trolling hour, and later when the streetlights came on avenue by avenue, we'd see the hipsters converge, merge, and urge each other into sleek bars and trendy restaurants. We were on the cusp of the evening's magic moment when the marathon clubbing and dining commenced. The fact it was a Thursday didn't make much difference. The scene would have been familiar any other night of the week too, but weekends naturally heralded even bigger crowds and wilder spectacles.

I wanted food.

"Jack, can we stop somewhere for a late lunch." I looked at my watch.

"Soon. I thought we'd check out Wynwood first."

Wynwood was once an industrial district. Thanks to the art crowd, it had been transformed into their personal Mecca and was known for the monthly gallery walk. But, alas, a flick of my phone told me tonight did not show the gallery crawl on the art scene agenda. So why were we headed there? I raised my voice to be heard over the street and wind noise. "Got a tip I should know about, Jack?"

"In a moment. Want to check out a source," he shouted back. "See if we can find any connection to Simon."

It hadn't been that long ago Frommer's too often commented in their Miami guides about how the city lacked any reputation as a cultural center. Thankfully, reputations were made to be reversed. The beach city's artistic street cred had changed in a progressively upward movement during the last few years. With the milder winter climate, Miami started playing host to international events and created liaisons with other esteemed art fairs. And the Miami cultural reputation made its slow but steady rise.

So I was not surprised Jack already had a potential lead to follow, and I mentally reviewed the Fendi's stash of costume jewelry in case I needed to upgrade the bling of my ensemble. A couple of blocks farther on our journey and the city's design district opened up. The city was changing in a good way.

Yet the set of Jack's jaw told me wherever we were headed in the art scene was not likely all glitter and lights. Didn't surprise me, but didn't make me happy either.

When I noticed how the silver Honda behind us kept making every turn we did, well, the knowledge pushed happiness even more distant. In my peripheral vision I noticed Jack straighten, and I knew he'd spotted the car too. Not that I doubted his observation skills for a second.

FOUR

I wanted to make a joke, ask Jack if he needed me to drive, say that I could lose them. But the gravity of the situation wasn't lost on me. The Honda was coming up fast. I didn't dare to turn around and look. I stayed hidden by my seatback and continued to study my side mirror. The expression I read of the guy riding shotgun increased my anxiety. A second later, he raised his right hand to the dash. Sunlight flashed on the metal object he held.

Jack must have seen the same thing in the rearview. I watched him grimace and hit the accelerator as if we were in a Ferrari. In fact, as I scrabbled to choke the door handle in a death grip, he even said, "God, I wish I had a Ferrari right now."

"I take it they were fresh out at the rental counter," I yelled back.

"Actually, no. I thought it would look too retro-*Miami Vice* and Michael Mann, and chose classy instead. Thought you'd prefer it." He kept his face forward the entire time he spoke. No smirk, no wink. But I watched a nerve twitch one time at his temple.

I wasn't sure how to respond. How I even wanted to try to respond. With my left hand, I dug in my purse to find my smartphone instead. I wished we had the top up on the car, but was not going to suggest Jack slow down to do so.

Regardless of the number of times I'd visited the city for one art event or another, I didn't usually drive in Miami. Rather, I was picked up and delivered wherever I needed to go. Given the always-changing cityscape and Jack's current Le Mans maneuvers, I was quickly and hopelessly lost. I had just brought up my phone's street map app when Jack slammed on the brakes and jigged right. The phone rocketed out of my hands and onto the floorboard. I'd find it later. No way I was letting go of the door.

I didn't bother asking Jack if he had a plan. The set of his jaw said he did—even if he didn't.

No matter. As fast as our real-time views changed, my screen app probably couldn't have kept up. Buildings were a blur, and I heard sirens in the distance. Jack moved to the left turn lane as the arrow changed from green to yellow. The Honda remained inches from our back bumper. Jack didn't slow in the turn for the light that turned red. As our car filled the intersection, he grabbed the hand brake and pulled an almost perfect Rockford one-eighty sliding-round move. Our Mercedes barreled back the way we'd come, speeding again in the traffic-free lane. The Honda wasn't as quick. Traffic anticipating the green came in behind us and cut off our pursuers.

"Keep driving." I stared into the mirror to give a blow-by-blow. "They're trying to back up and follow us, but they're blocked in by the oncoming traffic."

I didn't know if Jack's driving panache was due to beginner's luck, survival, or specialized training, and figured it was probably a measure of all three. I patted his leg in encouragement. He smiled. Then he had to burst my euphoria, yelling over the wind, "I'm glad we could slow them down a bit, because from the sound of their motor when they were behind us, I think they have a lot more horsepower than the Honda's factory specs."

A few seconds later, his prophesy came true. The Honda resumed its tail, not even trying anymore to pretend it wasn't interested in us. I looked back and met the gazes of the two twenty-something males through the Honda's windshield. Though we all hid behind sunglasses, there was no doubt who the two behind us thought was the prey in this situation. They were in this for keeps. I wondered how long the adrenalin and testosterone cocktail surging through all these alpha males' veins would hold out. And if we would escape before someone had a stroke. Or worse.

The wind pounded my ears and jazzed my pulse up several more notches. But it's all fun and games until someone pulls a gun. A hand snaked out of the passenger window of the Honda.

"Jack! Gun!" And the first shot screamed over my head.

The young thug was either a lousy shot or simply trying to scare the shit out of us. As far as I was concerned, the latter was a fait accompli. It wasn't going to get us to stop, however. Jack's jaw tightened. His lips looked like one thin line.

"Hang on," he yelled.

Like I'd have even let go if I could.

Still, when he took a kamikaze opportunity to use an almost nonexistent break in oncoming traffic to zip at the last second into a tiny, nearly passed mouth of an alley, my heart practically left my body.

Amid the cacophonous crescendo of angry horns and panicked brakes, I experienced centrifugal force strong enough to give me an idea what a facelift felt like without the benefit of anesthesia. We went up on two wheels, then landed hard when my side again belly flopped to the asphalt. Was there a way to get whiplash without being hit? If so, call me the poster girl.

The Mercedes fishtailed dangerously close to each side of the alley, clipping a dumpster with the right rear bumper and nearly sideswiping the concrete facades of the buildings until Jack fought and regained full control. I had no idea if we were going the right way down the narrow one-way crevasse, and I kept my eyelids squeezed shut and prayed. I didn't know the ethics of praying when breaking the law to save your life, but a second later Jack shot out the other side and hung another hard left. I opened my eyes when I felt the sun's heat again hitting my face, and looked to my right to see the light winking across the water of Biscayne Bay. I began breathing again.

"How in the hell did you keep from hitting something?" I grabbed my head with both hands. "How did you ever get onto this busy road, making a left no less, without causing a pileup?"

"One of us must have a guardian angel." He grinned.

"Well, I'll admit I closed my eyes and prayed."

"Me too."

My jaw dropped. "You what?"

"Just kidding." He laughed.

Okay, it may have lightened the moment, but we both knew we had to get off the grid soon. Jack made three more quick turns, but since our pursuers apparently missed their first opportunity to blast through the alley with us, they either had to reconnoiter after overshooting the opening or had given up the chase. I was betting on the former, since the gun convinced me they were prepared to go to whatever lengths necessary.

"So, who were they?" I asked when Jack finally slipped the Mercedes into a public parking garage.

"That's the million-dollar question, I'd say." He riffled his long fingers around the top of the steering wheel, almost as if he couldn't believe it was still in one piece. I understood the feeling. Then he mused, "Couldn't be Moran, since the pair in the Honda seemed to have no compunction about killing you."

"Or I'm not Moran's favorite anymore." I frowned. Back to the question of why Moran spared me the last time. And while the location and vehicles were different, I had to admit there were similarities between this incident and the shooting by the motorcyclist in France. As well as our escape under gunfire on the streets of London. Both were believed to be Moran-commissioned jobs. Was this incident similar because Moran was behind it? Or to make us think he was? "It wasn't the Amazon this time though. Or Weasel and Werewolf."

"No," Jack agreed. "A couple of blokes who looked like every other young man in Miami. Nothing remarkable."

"Except the gun."

"There is that. Made an impression, I take it."

"Forty-four Magnums usually do."

"Thank your guardian angel he had that cannon. He likely wouldn't have missed if he'd been aiming with a lighter gun." He slipped off his Ray-Bans and pulled out his phone. "In the meantime, I think we need to add insurance in case there were people with videos that could identify us to the authorities."

"No doubt there were people taking videos."

"A fact which makes me deliriously happy at the moment."

"You want us picked up by the cops?"

Jack smiled and finished his text. He turned and said, "Luckily, the U.S. Senator whose family is in both of our debts after last night's little exercise is a representative of the whole state of Florida. Not just Orlando."

Why didn't I think of that? After giving myself a mental palm slap, I asked, "So, you're going to have your buddy get the senator to keep our names off the police blotters?"

"Yes, and if a video does surface to help positively identify the guys or the Honda, I want to know that information too." His phone chimed, and he read the text, then turned it my way. *On it. Ur covered. Will send DTs gained l8r.*

"Which I'm translating as his promise that if he gets any details later, you will receive them too."

Jack nodded.

I chewed my lip, thinking. "How did the guys in the Honda pick us up? This is a new rental car. No opportunity for them to add a tracking device. And I didn't notice them following from the airport. Did you?"

"They could have the car rental agent on their team. Most rentals are GPS tracked now, especially luxury models. But that gets complicated since they didn't know which company we would use. Hell, I didn't even know which company I was going to use." He shook his head and raised his phone, looking a moment at the screen. But he returned it to his pocket without using it again, then said, "My guess is one guy stayed in the car at Miami International, ready and waiting to move, and the other went inside and shadowed us from the arrival gate. I imagine our meeting the suits whetted their interest and concerns even more. As we all left the complex, they likely hung back at enough of a distance to tail us until they could pick their spot to drive us off the road to kidnap or hijack or..." His voice went almost to a whisper. "Or kill us. Who knows?"

The volume of his words went up a smidgeon, but his tone remained deadly. "When they realized we spotted them, they moved in close and improvised. Almost always a mistake."

The semi dark was getting to me, and I removed my sunglasses to study Jack's face in the forty-watt lighting. I didn't know what to think, but I had a question I wanted to ask. "Were they after both of us? Or one of us?"

"What difference does it make?"

"If both," I reasoned, "then it relates to the project at hand, and it means we're getting closer even if we don't know what we're getting closer to. If they wanted one of us, then it may be something out of one of our pasts. And if that's the case, we might need to split up. To make sure the other person doesn't get hurt in the crossfire, and give us a better shot at reaching our objective if we become compromised."

Jack didn't say a word. He simply stared at me long enough that I felt my pulse rising again, and not in a good way. I reached down to the floorboard, trying to break his focus by moving to retrieve my cell phone. The ploy worked. He slammed the gearshift into reverse, and we cruised for the exit.

A half hour later, Jack pulled into a side lot of the prestigious Browning Gallery, a small but world-renowned terra-cotta landmark with its distinctive 1920s architecture and gilded Art Deco design touches. In the open spaces around the gallery, activity bustled as crews set up for an annual art fair scheduled to open the next day.

The gallery was decked out for the fair and members-only party. Notables from corporate and various government interests would be on hand for the important event. This event had reached the point of being truly international.

The preparations reminded me of the opening extravaganza for the gallery's Browning Art Studio that I attended more than a decade ago, when I was in my teens and my grandfather still made appearances at such occasions. My heart ached a little from the memory.

I hoped to look in on the studio before we left, to see if it had changed much in the interim. I remembered the space as a fully contained facility, able to meet the needs of most artists. In the years since that opening, an artist-in-residence program was implemented and continued to receive great buzz.

Despite the banners and party prep going on in the foyer, my pulse calmed as we moved through the streamlined décor. The Deco era was probably my favorite, though I loved the way baroque tastes color many European buildings. I followed Jack down the taupe-carpeted hallway leading to the administrative offices.

"Jack Hawkes, as I live and breathe," a sultry voice spoke from an open office door. Seconds later, the scent of Obsession filled our personal space, and the bronzed figure of Melanie Weems embraced Jack before he could fend her off. Not that he tried very hard, what with that damned flirty grin and cocked eyebrow and all.

"Melanie, love, how have you been keeping yourself?" he asked.

I recognized his tongue-in-cheek tone, but she obviously never picked up on it. So she complied by running fingers across his cheek and answering with a low chuckle. She was nearly as tall as Jack, thanks to killer gold Louboutin heels high enough to hurt my feet just looking at them. This woman and I had a long history, and it wasn't a good one. It had to do with a "mean girls" incident she implemented during a college internship that ultimately got a very good curator fired. Oh, and the subsequent wardrobe malfunction she experienced at a gala museum affair a few days later, which she blamed on me but could never prove.

I'd heard she'd made director at the Browning but hoped I could avoid her while we were in Miami. Surely, she wasn't his source...

"Oh, Jack," she breathed the words. "Keeping myself? You told me once that I was fabulous. Am I not still fabulous?"

Yeah, her intentions were blatantly obvious, and unfortunately Jack seemed to have forgotten why we were at the museum in the first place.

"Melanie...glad you had time in your calendar for us," he finally said.

She slowly rotated on one heel and pretended to see me for the first time. But she was trying too hard to hold her expression. "Us?"

He pulled me closer. "Melanie, I'd like to introduce you to Laurel Beacham of the Beacham Foundation."

"We've met—" I started.

"Before she had to fall back on getting hired by her family," Melanie said, cutting off my sentence. I held my breath and looked bored. I'd been the target of many backstabbers in my time. I had no problem backing away from this. She placed a hand on my arm. "So good to see you trying to build something out of all your family's embarrassment." I subtly moved my arm away from her hand.

I smiled. "And it's wonderful the museum could overlook the discrepancies on your resume. They must have been desperate for a director."

"Excuse me—?"

"Ladies," Jack said. But he looked at me, shooting a warning glare I read as an order to behave. Maybe he needed something from her. Well, I would if she would. But I didn't say that out loud. Instead, I smiled again and took a step back, pivoting to get a better view of the Picasso hanging behind her desk. I wished it was a print, but I knew better.

"Love your office, Melanie. Glad things have worked out well for you."

No, she didn't believe me. She did sheath her claws, though, and that's all I truly hoped for. I turned and smiled at Jack. "I didn't realize you two knew each other. Wonderful that you have friends here in Florida, Jack."

"Oh, we're more than friends," Melanie purred. I think she would have coiled her body around his if it wouldn't have come off as totally unprofessional. "Remember the lovely weekend in Austria? Those unbelievable comforters on the bed, duvets filled with mile-high goose down?"

Oh, for Pete's sake.

"Look," I said, moving farther away with my words. "You two conduct whatever *business* you need to attend to. I want to check out the studio while I'm here. Jack, why don't you come and collect me when you're ready to leave?"

I was still starving, and I wanted to make a comment about that too. What I didn't want to do is try to digest food if Malicious Melanie tried to join our little dinner party.

"But, Laurel, I—"

"No, Jack, it's fine. I'll leave you to this and find my own way to the studio." I turned and sped down the hallway, calling over my shoulder as I escaped, "I'm pretty sure I remember where it is. Don't worry about me."

I wanted to laugh. Too delicious a revenge to exact on him. Still, if he didn't extricate himself from the female octopus soon, I refused to get involved. Instead, I planned on taking to the streets to hunt down a food truck. Where was this freaking yacht he'd mentioned? Didn't all yachts have chefs? They'd have to feed me if I boarded the vessel and said I was Jack's guest, right?

"All I need is a damn slip number. I could find the harbor and fall prostrate at the chef's feet to prove how famished I am." I turned a corner, and floor-to-ceiling windows replaced the wall. I looked outside and all other thoughts flew from my mind.

A pair of twenty-something young guys in hoods, one muscled and the other rail thin, jumped into the cab of a flatbed wrecker. There was no writing on the driver's door, but the window framed the skinny guy I'd last seen shooting at us out of the passenger window of the silver Honda.

Sitting like a lovely parade princess on the high bed of the wrecker was our Mercedes 350 convertible. The first thought that raced through my mind was *thank God we didn't use my credit card.*

FIVE

Food is not an obsession with me until I can't get anything to eat. When things reach that point, food becomes the only thing I can think about. A sticking point when police officers want you to describe car thieves and your mind is totally absorbed with imagining the perfect grilled cheese sandwich from Ms. Cheezious and whether you want a cup of soup to go with it. Since I was feeling a touch crabby by that point, the crab sandwich had already crossed my mind. Until I thought about adding tomatoes. Tomatoes made me think of Italy, and prosciutto, and creamy provolone on a thick country white bread. My mouth watered. And to wash it all down with a nice glass of prosecco. Surely, there was a wine bar nearby.

"Miss...miss."

The officer reeled me back into the present where there was no food, no wine, and no real leads about who had stolen our car.

"Officer, I'm sorry. I've given you all the details I can. Both had dark hair and short haircuts, one beefy, one thin. No visible tattoos. Young, probably early twenties. They were the same pair we'd noticed earlier following us in a silver Honda sedan. We got the partial license plate, which Jack already gave to you." I shrugged and turned my head, using the opportunity to sweep my gaze around the perimeter.

Preparations for the weekend art event proceeded efficiently, though I caught several workers cutting their eyes our way to try to figure out why the police were onsite. Dozens of white tents dotted the area around the gallery, with a galley zone and bleachers marking one border, and chairs ahead for VIP seating. Like all events of its kind, beyond the premiered art and award accolades, major points of this weekend gala were about fundraising, allowing politically connected speakers their turn at the podium, and letting the rich, beautiful people see and be seen by their peers. I understood—I was one of them once, and that much money meant constant security. I'd need an entrance card if I wanted to mingle with those gaining spots in the red chairs, and there was little likelihood Melanie would provide me with the open-sesame lanyard I needed. But if there was a means of getting a handle on where Simon was now, this was the perfect venue. I understood why Jack decided to drop in, though it was looking more counter-productive by the second.

I turned back to the officer. "I'm sorry I can't give you more information, but if you have more questions—"

He shook his head. "No, I'll file the report and get the car theft division working on this one. We'll call if we find anything."

"Well, I hope you find our luggage," I said, waving a hand between Jack and myself as I added, "All we have are the clothes on our backs."

"I'm sorry, miss."

"Thank you."

He gave me a brief nod and a half smile, then moved back toward his squad car. Jack was on his cell and in deep conversation, likely to the car rental place and trying to get replacement wheels. I wanted to strike off and find dinner, but another look at the tents made me pull my own phone from the Fendi.

It was near midnight in London, but Cassie answered on the first ring. I gave her a brief synopsis of current events, then told her why I'd actually called.

"I need you to contact the foundation office in New York and get someone to send me tickets to this weekend's Browning outdoor art extravaganza. The foundation probably received the tickets months ago. They should be in a file somewhere."

"You don't think someone else is going to use them?" she asked.

"Doubtful. But if they are, tell New York I absolutely must have at least one pass in my hand tomorrow morning. I need to be able to get into all the VIP areas with no questions asked. If I have two passes, I can get Jack in anywhere too. But he probably has his own way in. It's not critical for him to use Beacham invites."

"I'll get right on it and call or text you back."

"Oh, and if you hear from Nico, have him call me."

"I think he's in New York."

Perfect. What I needed to hear. "See if he can bring the passes down to me. I could use him this weekend."

We rang off, and I flagged down the nearest construction guy. "Is there a food truck nearby?"

"Saw a Jefe's truck round the corner a few minutes ago. Might try checking the other side of the gallery."

"Thank you."

So my choice was made for me. The guy was right. Even before I rounded the building and the truck came into view, I heard the exuberant music over the rest of the street noise. This would serve as a start on quelling my hunger. I grabbed enough fish tacos and fresh carnitas to be sure Jack wouldn't filch any of my share, added a couple of beers on the way back, and arrived at his side as Lady Bountiful. In the same instant, he jabbed an angry finger into his touch screen and made an overly negative groan.

"No car?" I asked, holding up what I'd determined was his share of the food and putting it down between us as he continued to do whatever he was doing with his cell. I scarfed down my own food in world record time, finishing off with a deliciously cold one.

He sighed and scooped up the tacos and carnitas, setting the beer on the low wall running along the side of the building. After he chewed and swallowed several mouthfuls, he answered me. "The car rental company is working on it. I'm not sure they don't believe that the theft wasn't actually our fault. Telling them the coppers are already working the case didn't seem to change any minds either."

"They're probably right." I took a small bite, then shrugged when Jack gave me a shocked look. "What?" I asked. "It was the guys from the Honda. They'd already been on our tail. Taking our car was their plan B."

"Or..." He glared at me. "They are Miami car thieves who already had an order for a car exactly like the one we rented. And the fact that they stole our car has nothing to do with the reason we're in Miami."

I shrugged again. "Believe what you want. If I were the rental company, I would blame us. I don't believe in coincidences. But if your theory turns out to be true, it points to why flashy cars may not be the best choice when you're trying to stay under the radar."

"I was trying to fit in with the crowd we need to talk to."

"Yeah, keep telling yourself that, Jack. The fact no one we're going to be interviewing will likely see us in the car kind of blows holes in your story. And even if they did, they'd know we flew into the city and had to rent a car."

"Says Miss I-Have-To-Buy-Designer-Everything."

"What I wear is something everyone *will see*. And unfortunately, all of it is now gone with the car."

His jaw dropped. "Bloody hell. I didn't think about that. I'll make a call and get us some clothes."

"Good. I hoped the yacht you mentioned had emergency clothing on board beyond bathing suits. Where was it located, again?" I still wanted to know how he knew Melanie, but there were too many people milling around to ask.

Jack laughed and took a swig from his beer bottle. "Like I'm going to tell you. The only way I know you won't give me the slip is if I keep from telling you the harbor slip number."

"Cute play on words. But what's to stop me from grabbing a cab, finding myself a nice anonymous hotel somewhere, and running my own game here?"

"Nothing, except you don't have the ready cash to do that. And the best chance you have to get in last minute to the VIP section is to get me to convince Melanie to give you a pass."

"Do you have a pass?"

"It will be waiting for me tomorrow."

"Then maybe I'll let you mingle with the hoi polloi, and I can go shopping for replacement clothes."

"Again, you have no funds."

I did a slow burn. "What makes you think you know everything?"

"Because I know everything." He offered up his best superior smile.

Deep breaths. Don't show anger.

Had Nico turned on me? When did he and Jack get chummy? My budget freeze wasn't public knowledge until Cassie told me today. I couldn't believe either of them would be traitors...But there was one person I could believe would talk much too freely.

"Max called you and said to keep me on a short leash for both finances and intel, didn't he?"

His smile broadened. I had my answer.

"That lousy, cheap bast—"

"Laurel, is that you?"

I turned to the sound of the voice and recognized Tina Schroeder, a throwback to my childhood. One of the few whose family hadn't turned their backs on me, because the older Schroeders ran all the angles. Younger than me by a few years, her shining brunette waves were pulled back off her classically beautiful face. Long, graceful limbs, a figure to die for, and a killer tan completed the cover-girl perfection. I saw her here and there; she'd partied on the same yacht Simon and I were guests of while we were still a couple. I had a fleeting thought to pick her brain, to see if she knew anything about Simon's latest activities or sightings. Unfortunately, the girl was about an inch deep when it came to mental processes.

Her history always reminded me of a latter-day Anne Boleyn, but it was her mother, Phyllis, who did the pimping instead of her father. Tina was born gorgeous, and her family didn't just live above their means, they jumped both feet into a money pit. Twice, Mama Schroeder secured "suitable engagements" to billionaire octogenarians for her lovely twenty-five-year-old daughter, but the engagements ended days before nuptials could be exchanged—one due to death and the other to the groom-to-be's family stepping in and getting great-granddaddy ruled mentally incapacitated before Tina could become a Mrs. and get added to the will.

I introduced Jack.

"I know your name from somewhere." Tina gave him her wide-eyed look and shook his hand. "Maybe from Debrett's?"

I couldn't help it, I snorted. Jack immediately started choking. Peerage, right. The girl couldn't help but husband shop. Putting my arm around her, I hugged Tina and carefully maneuvered her away to let Jack recover on his own.

"It's great to see you, Tina. Do you work for the Browning Gallery now?" I truly was curious as, based on the competition alone, I couldn't believe Melanie would hire her.

I wasn't surprised when she shook her head, the brunette chignon wound so tightly it gave me a headache to look at her. "No, I'm assistant to the event planner. Phyllis got me the job."

No surprise there. "Be sure and give your mother my regards."

"Oh, please call her Phyllis. She's decided to divorce herself from the title of mother."

Jack was still close enough, standing slightly behind and to the side of Tina. That remark started an eye roll I felt I could use. "Tina, think you could take a break, and we'll go find a cup of coffee or something? Don't want to miss a chance to catch up with you."

She smiled at me. "That would be great." A frown crossed her lovely face. "I have to be handy in case I'm needed." Her brow cleared. "Let's go to the refreshment tent."

Wow, thinking ahead. I was impressed. "Sounds great." I turned and called to Jack. "Why don't you double-check on the replacement car or get us a taxi. I want a few minutes with Tina."

I could tell he was biting the inside of his cheek and trying to contain his grin. No harm in a brief catch-up conversation, and she really was a sweet kid despite her family's greedy nature.

As we walked toward the tent, one of the workers shot off a great wolf whistle. Tina turned away stone faced, obviously on orders from her mother—I mean, Phyllis—not to fraternize with hourly workers. But I smiled, accepting the compliment, as I glanced over my shoulder to see Jack's reaction. Nothing. No smile, no frown. But he was watching. I decided to take it as a good sign.

"We don't have a cappuccino machine," Tina apologized. The white canvas flap was tied back for easy entrance. "But the brand is pretty good if you like standard ground roast."

Since I was interested in information rather than refreshment, I would have been happy with pure ground mud. Light filtered by the canvas tent gave everything a soft glow, and the shade reduced part of the heat. A huge fan blasted from one end. We got our cups, and I steered her to seats in the far corner.

"Tina, I don't think I've seen you since last summer in Nice. But you're really looking great." Jimmy Choos made her firm legs look outstanding. She carried herself straighter and with greater confidence than before, and her cheekbones showed more definition. I figured Phyllis had her working with a trainer. "Do you like this job?"

She shrugged a narrow shoulder, her black Diane von Furstenberg wrap dress moving infinitesimally to show a hint of cleavage. "I guess. Phyllis thinks I can make good contacts this way."

"I imagine she knows better than anyone." I smiled to make my words sound friendlier than their hidden meaning, but I needn't have bothered.

"Oh, absolutely. She's a pro at making connections. She conferences with me three times a week to help me maximize my potential."

Yeah, right. "Look, Tina, I was wondering if you've run across Simon Babbage in the past couple of months. Maybe spoken with him at an event?"

"Simon?" She scrunched her forehead. "I thought you two had a thing for a while. Are you trying to hook up again?"

"No. I mean, yes." I stopped and took a deep breath. "What I mean is, yes, Simon and I had a bit of a fling." Okay, a nearly-a-year fling. "I'm not trying to get back together with him, but I would like to find him."

"I thought he worked for Beacham."

"He's parted company with the foundation."

"Oh." She scrunched her forehead again. I had to wonder how long she'd be able to do that before Phyllis started pumping Botox in to manage any future wrinkles. She smiled and asked, "Do I need to give you the snuffbox, then? Or does it belong to Simon?"

"What?"

"He sent a snuffbox a couple of weeks ago and asked me to hold it for him. Said it was related to Beacham, and he had a buyer in Miami. He wanted the snuffbox in the city in case the buyer wanted it before he could get over here to deliver it in person."

This was not what I expected. "What does the snuffbox look like?"

"Seventeenth century, gold with inlay—"

"Stop." I held up a hand. Ohmigod, it had to be the same snuffbox I was supposed to get in Italy when everything began to go wrong, but how did Simon get it, and did he kill our courier? We had thought he was only connected to the sword. But now..."Yes, you need to give the snuffbox to me. Is it at your place? Can we go now and pick it up?"

She looked at her Rolex. Probably a knockoff, but a good one. "I have a meeting in a few minutes. I really can't be late. And I have plans tonight. But I can bring the box tomorrow. Can you meet me here at ten o'clock? I have to monitor the VIP desk."

This close and I'd have to wait? Could this actually be the same snuffbox I was supposed to have picked up in Italy the night this whole escapade started? The night I found the first body. The night I met Jack for the first time. The artifact he was supposedly chasing to stop an international heist we were currently still pursuing. It had to be. "Look, if we could—"

A shout on the other side of the canvas stopped me.

"What the hell are you doing there? Eavesdropping?" a baritone voice bellowed. "Get back to work or you're fired!"

I jumped and headed for the nearest opening, trying to see who had been listening to our conversation. No one was between the two tents when I got to the other side of the canvas wall. Frustrated, I headed back to try to convince Tina to skip her meeting. Again, no luck.

She was a figure disappearing in the distance. "Tomorrow, Laurel," she called. "I'll meet you at ten o'clock and have the package for you." She picked up her pace and disappeared in the crowd of activity in the final phases of set up.

To my right, well within hearing distance of Tina and me, I saw Jack. He had his phone to his ear as he glared at me.

SIX

I sank back into a chair near the tent opening, stretched out my legs, and eyed Jack. With the phone now glued to his ear, the uncompromising gaze directed toward me promised retribution. For what, I had no idea, but I didn't particularly care either. There was a lot to consider, and none of it included putting him "in the know."

Several workers walked by with supplies. I waved at Jack and waited for him to come to me. Whatever he was up to at the moment, I had too many things on my mind to risk getting sidetracked. I rapidly ticked over what Tina said and what it truly meant. One part of me wanted to skip the yacht Jack booked us on and find my way *alone* to Tina's condo. I would have suggested a catch-up sleepover, but she'd vanished too quickly. There was a lot I needed to learn, and getting the information from Tina would take time and finesse. Not because she was holding back, but because she had no idea what she actually knew.

Surely Tina still lodged in the Brickell Key. No way Mommy Dearest would let her leave such a prime locale for catching a billionaire. I'd attended a forgettable party there, but the view from Tina's apartment still came immediately to mind. The septuagenarian age of the neighbors she and Mommy hunted as possible candidates also came to the forefront.

Top urban neighborhoods in Miami were often rated for their walkability. The area still known as Brickell used to be known as Millionaires' Row in the early twentieth century and was now called the Manhattan of the South. The neighborhood was a go-to place for the up, the coming, and the arrived. Full of financial, residential, and investment properties set right on the Gulf.

I saw Jack shove his phone in a pocket and walk my way. His face unreadable.

"Any luck?" I asked. I stood as he drew near, even raised my eyebrows to punctuate my bright question. He shot back an even darker look. Either his phone conversation hadn't gone according to plan, or something else had happened while I was out of sight in the tent. "You weren't happy when I left to talk to Tina, but you were at least in a decent mood. Now you seem on edge."

I could almost see the waves of excess energy ripple off his body, and his face suddenly went from tense to incredibly tired. I instinctively reached out and touched his arm. He moved his free hand to cover mine.

"What is it, Jack?"

"Nothing. Everything." He shrugged, then pulled me aside as two workers came up lugging a huge piece of plywood. We walked on to the front of the gallery, until we were well away from the overtime setup.

"Were you on the phone with the police? The car rental place again?"

He shook his head. "It's time to regroup, and I think the best place to do that is on the yacht. Neither of us has had enough sleep, we've almost been hijacked, and our car's been stolen. We can't talk here, but we do need to talk. I think a luxury ship on the open water is where we need to begin our conversation."

Personally, I didn't like the reference to open water, but he had a good point. If he had gotten any information from Melanie, it wouldn't pay to tell me in such a public setting. And the ride to the yacht, and whatever other activities before our debriefing, would give me the chance to figure out what I wanted to tell Jack about Tina and the snuffbox. I'd play fair if he would, but past experience told me that wasn't going to happen unless I had treasure to trade. Jack didn't outright lie. Well, yes, he did, actually, but I was getting pretty good at spotting when he tried. I didn't want to think about why that was probably important, but I knew I needed to sometime soon.

"Should I call a cab? Or do you have a better idea?"

"A brilliant idea that involves a hired car sent by the yacht. I called, and the captain said he would dispatch the vehicle straight away." Jack looked down the street and took a step closer to the curb. "In fact, I believe it's here now."

Seconds later, a Lincoln Town Car slid silently to a stop right in front of us. Jack had the back door open before the driver could do his duty, and moments later we were cruising again down the Miami streets, this time cocooned in caramel smooth leather comfort and sipping the sparkling dry prosecco I'd dreamed about hours before. It was tempting to believe things were looking up, but every time I had thought that lately, something unexpected fell from the sky instead.

As we settled into the seats, I looked out the tinted windows and saw again the tent Tina and I had escaped to. It reminded me about the eavesdropper. "Jack, when you were on the phone and I was with Tina, did you notice a couple of guys come out from the backside of the tent? One shouting at the other?"

"You're joking?"

I shook my head.

"Laurel, there were people yelling at each other the entire time we were there. The place is a madhouse."

"This would have probably been a foreman yelling at a worker."

"No...I..." He closed his eyes and shook his head. "Why? What would have been different?"

I could have told him then. But I knew the harbor wasn't far, and I wasn't sure how much, if anything, I presently wanted to tell Jack. I hedged. "While we were in the tent. It sounded like some kind of altercation on the other side of the canvas. Wanted to make sure no one was hurt."

"Not your problem."

"Yeah, I guess I have more than enough to worry about already."

The rhythm of the Town Car made me drowsy, and that coupled with the wine was enough to push me over the edge to sleep soon into our journey. I woke when Jack gently shook my shoulder. "We're here."

He offered a hand to help me out of the car. It was near enough to full dark that the harbor was lit up like Disneyland. The docks were full, every slip taken. Though winter was approaching, the balmy Miami temps meant these hardy crafts wouldn't have to wear winter covers through the season and would be operational for all the upcoming Christmas and New Year's blowouts. But in early fall, the scene boasted nothing more than a couple of booze cruises starting up from their slips.

I'd always loved sailing and had spent many a sun-drenched day crewing for my father as soon as I was old enough to tie a decent knot. A connection Simon and I had shared. That alone should have warned me about the man. Should new warning bells be sounding for Jack, too? I knew it was wrong, but I couldn't help generalizing about men and sailing. Well, any experiences reminding me of my father.

No. A yacht is different. You can't vanish alone on something that big.

A brisk, damp wind whipped across the cold water and slapped my hair against my face. I brushed the strands from my eyes and looked around. The lap of the water against the posts and planks even relaxed my jangled nerves. The car pulled away. Jack and I made the boards thump as we strode down the main deck. I smelled fish and sea creatures in the brisk air. A couple of spectacular yachts sat at the end of the far dock. There were larger boats off in the deeper water, and I asked Jack which one was ours.

"Out there."

Out there was a fairytale sight of the kind of sinful extravagance I truly loved. The kind that reminded me of life before my grandfather passed away. A sleek vessel, all black and brass and sensuous curves to reflect the light from the harbor area. It appeared to be four-tier, but before I could assimilate any more information, Jack halted at a cigarette boat moored along the edge of the planks.

"This will take us the last leg of our journey," he said and offered a hand to help me step in, something I was grateful for, given the gently bobbing gangway.

Even before he started the engine, the muscle of the forty-plus-foot missile spoke to me. I recognized the Mercedes-Benz emblem and knew the boat operated in the neighborhood of thirteen hundred to fifteen hundred horsepower. A lot of speed for a simple shuttle ride. I wanted to grab the controls myself and push the phantom thing to its limits. "Jack, could I—"

"No, I'm doing all the driving this time."

I guess he still hadn't forgiven me for the motorcycle ride through London during our previous adventure together. No matter. It took what seemed like seconds for us to reach the yacht. As its strong steel masts grew closer, I was able to focus between the two Jet Skis hanging at the stern to read the lettering that gave the boat's name and home berth:

Folly Roost

Great Britain

"Interesting name," I murmured as Jack held my waist to help me mount the ladder.

"Interesting owners," he replied.

I took a moment to shoulder my purse higher so I could look down at him to ask, "Employers or friends?"

"Countrymen who were happy to extend an invitation to someone working on Her Majesty's behalf."

Oh, aren't we the noble-sounding one, Mr. Jack Hawkes. I wanted to say it out loud but knew to hold my tongue.

I'd been to Florida many times, but this was only the third time since college I'd been out on the Gulf. My father used to go deep-sea fishing, and I tagged along if Granddad's yacht was involved.

It was a long climb, and when my foot finally hit the deck, I knew why. I'd been on my share of yachts, but this was by far the biggest and looked to be the most modern. Clever brass lanterns hung from various posts on the main deck, obviously electrified but giving that *getting away from it all* air as the yacht still offered to take everything along too.

From the nearest of several upper decks, a small dingy hung ready, yet lashed securely, above my head. I took note. One never knew when one would need to make a quick and untimely escape. As Jack joined me on deck, I heard a radio crackle and turned to see a man in a white uniform striding our way.

"Morgan, good to see you," Jack said, striding closer with his hand outstretched. "And we are grateful for your sending the car."

"My pleasure."

Jack made introductions, and then Captain Morgan waved toward the middle of the boat. "Margarite has dinner waiting for you in the saloon. She's making sure you have clothing and supplies in your rooms, so everything is as you need it to be." His radio squawked again, and he took his leave with a wave.

Jack set his hand to the small of my back and directed me toward dinner, which I was grateful to the captain for arranging. The car was terrific, but food was my siren call. Having coffee for breakfast and nothing but the light food truck lunch several hours past the noon hour, I was ready for a good dinner. My *escort* led me up the stairs and into a grand saloon.

Spectacular, spacious, and simple. I'd been on a few yachts in my time, but the Folly Roost cleared the field. My eye was drawn to a portrait on the wall opposite the pulpit, or pointy, side of the vessel. My feet moved toward that interior wall as if of their own accord. I followed their lead, my gaze held by a painting I recognized in its gilded frame as the *Woman Dressing Her Hair*.

"Lovely." I wasn't sure I'd even spoken the word aloud. I was too focused on the long, full locks, the refined hands holding the brush, and the subject's ivory complexion. Then I noticed something near the spotlight and moved in for a closer look.

"Yes, it's a fake," Jack said from behind my right shoulder. When I turned to look at him, he added, "A good fake, I'll grant you. Nevertheless, a fake. The original was stolen decades ago, and this copy is but a reminder of the kind of masterpieces that are out there and kept from the public." He stepped forward and brushed the bottom edge of the painting with a gentle fingertip.

"While it might not be the original artist's work," I said, still searching the brushstrokes as if to will it to be real, "it truly is a lovely item within what is likely a gifted artist's body of art. Despite the fact the artist's skill was used to create a forgery."

Jack offered me a twisted smile and turned back toward the center of the saloon. "Shall we dine?"

"Thought you'd never ask."

A buffet had been set up on the aft side of the saloon near an exquisite mahogany dining set. Most yachts I'd sailed on used the narrow pulpit corner of the boat as a build out for an elongated booth seat, much like one huge sumptuous window seat, and used the seating with a couple of extra chairs for all dining. In the Folly Roost, the designers built-out the space to include a luxurious champagne-colored crescent-shaped seating, as well as a full eight-setting table and chairs covered in the same fabric. A uniformed waiter stood in attendance, and another waiter approached with a wine bottle. At Jack's nod, the second waiter popped the cork and set the bottle down on a nearby table. The wine was left to breathe, and the waiter moved across the room to acquire two glasses.

The smell of food made my stomach rumble. Jack laughed. "I'm glad you're hungry, Laurel. Chef prepares food you'll be talking about for weeks."

"So you're often a guest here?"

His smile vanished, and he gave me a look both steady and a little disconcerting. "I make it a practice to afford myself of all luxury at every opportunity."

Those words were a silent message, I knew, and I would be thinking them over again.

The first waiter offered plates and helped serve from the

buffet. I started with a celery heart wrapped in prosciutto and topped with a tart cheese sauce, the aroma of which sent my taste buds salivating.

"I hope this will please your palate," the waiter said. "If not, please ask and it will be provided."

"I'm finding everything I need, thank you," I murmured, too focused on the food to speak any louder. Jack appeared even more famished than I and loaded his plate almost to the overflow point.

"Is there anything else?" the first waiter asked me.

Just at the point of shaking my head, I realized there was something he could do for me. "Could you turn down the lights in the room for a few minutes? I'd love to see the starlight over the bay."

"Good idea." Jack took my plate and handed both to the waiter. "Please set these at the table, midrange, and lower the lamps." Then his hand was again at the small of my back and guiding me toward the long sofa and the intersecting windows with their panoramic view.

In the darkened sky, I could see thick clouds to the south. "The stars are lovely right here, but we may still see some of the tropical storm remnants by the end of the weekend."

"It's not supposed to get past Cuba," Jack murmured. "But this still is hurricane season. It's quite optimistic of the Browning to stage an outdoor event this time of year."

Several catty remarks nearly escaped my lips. Melanie was never the sharpest knife in the drawer, but her tongue certainly was, and since she was Jack's friend of sorts, I didn't want anything negative I said to get back to her. I did have to wonder about his taste in sources given her innuendo about their past. But the way Jack responded said he might not have the same memories, or at least feelings, about the incident. If we were going to use his contacts, I wanted to know they could all be trusted.

A number of smaller vessels crisscrossed the boating channels, lights bobbing on the crafts at bow and stern, and several more at midpoints on the larger crafts. All too soon the beauty of the night was overcome by the hunger pangs we experienced from smelling the food waiting for us. Candlelit tapers sat in crystal holders on the table, and the flames wavered like fingers calling us over, their reflection in the wine almost enough to entrance me in the moment.

I scooted onto the cushioned chair by my plate and crossed my legs to the side. The waiter had set Jack across from me, each of us in the middle of the long sides of the table. I was surprised, wondering why Jack didn't take the head position instead.

Sad to say, we attacked our food with classlessness derived from pure hunger and fatigue. We didn't even try to talk over our dinner despite the perfect proximity we had for conversation. And we made little more than monosyllabic noises of assent when the waiters replenished our glasses or offered to bring over dessert.

Finally sated in a way I don't think sex had ever accomplished, I let my gaze rove over the darkened room. I was about to ask about a Picasso on the wall behind the buffet when the door breezed open and a Sophia Loren lookalike entered the lounge. Jack rose from the chair as she entered. She wore heels and a clingy black dress that hugged her curves in all the right places. Her smile stretched from Venice to Rome.

She offered that smile to me, along with a "*Buonasera!*" But she hugged Jack and kissed and patted both of his cheeks. He made introductions for us, and as I moved out from behind the table, Margarite surreptitiously looked me over then gave Jack a tiny nod. "It is a pleasure to meet you, Laurel Beacham. If you need anything while you are aboard, you need only ask. Anyone can help you or will locate someone who can do so. Please, you are our guest."

"Thank you." I shook the hand she extended and noticed the firm grip. The woman was likely late fifties or maybe even sixties, but she wore her age well and obviously kept in shape. I took her to be a female majordomo on the yacht, and she had probably run things for the family for decades. Jack's next words confirmed my thoughts.

"Margarite is the best friend any traveler can have, Laurel."

The woman almost preened under his compliment. "I don't think even the captain is truly in charge when Margarite is around."

She slapped his shoulder playfully. "Oh, Jack Hawkes, you will get me into trouble. Shame on you."

"It's very nice meeting you, Margarite." I couldn't contain a yawn any longer and hid it behind my hand. "Oh, I am sorry. I don't want to inconvenience you, but if you could show me to my room, I would appreciate it."

"But of course. Everything is ready."

"Laurel." Jack's voice carried that warning tone. "We need to talk, you and I."

I yawned again, this time cupping both hands, hiding most of my face. The second yawn was a fake, but I truly was sleepy, and I squinted my eyes to give it everything I had. "Jack, I'm exhausted. We'll talk tomorrow when both of us are much fresher."

"Your friend is correct." Margarite took my side. "I can see the fatigue on your face as well, Jack. Let Renaldo get you a cognac while I take Laurel to the sleeping deck. You will have plenty of time to talk tomorrow."

"But the event—"

"Is at ten," I said. "You and I are both still functioning on London time, and we'll likely be up with the sun. We'll have plenty of time to discuss our options."

His eyes drooped slightly when I mentioned time zones. Margarite waved for me to follow, and Jack offered no further objection.

SEVEN

"You have an en suite." Margarite crossed the lovely aqua-and-cream stateroom to open the door I would be using shortly for the shower I desperately needed. The queen-sized bed drew me like a magnet. I couldn't remember when I'd been so tired. While putting off my talk with Jack until morning was my standard plan to determine what I wanted to reveal, tonight it had been a necessity. I didn't want to think about how easily my brain would spill things I wanted to keep to myself. Then Margarite threw me a curve.

"I knew your mother, you know."

It was fortunate for me the bed was right there, or I would have probably landed on the floor when my knees gave way. "No, I didn't. Jack never said anything."

She moved to the small desk and straightened the wild riot of fragrant colors that rose from the crystal vase. "I was a few years older than she, but we had much fun." Her hands stopped fussing with the flowers, and she turned to give me a devilish grin. "We could get into trouble. One time we spent the whole day on the beach in Nice. Your grandfather had a fit when he learned we'd both been topless. Luckily for me he liked me, or he could have gotten me fired. He shook his finger at me and said, 'MJ, don't you ever do that again.'"

I remembered my grandfather talking about a beautiful Italian girl he called MJ. The room spun for a moment. "Did you work for my family?"

"No." She shook her head. "I worked for one of your grandfather's business associates. But when I was treated badly by the man, your grandfather helped me get into business school. Once I graduated, he helped me to get a job. Now I live aboard this yacht and take care of all of its business."

"Who owns the Folly Roost?"

Margarite acted like she didn't hear my question and crossed to the closet. Behind the louvered doors was a veritable boutique specializing in clothing sized around my figure. "I had things sent from a few local stores. Jack gave me an estimate for the size. He is pretty good in such things. All that observation training, you know."

"No, I really don't. How long have you known Jack? Did you work for his family?"

She laughed and shook her head. "Not really. But he was around often and was a most precocious boy when I first met him."

"And he hasn't changed one whit."

My remark made her laugh all the harder. She said, "Oh, you do know him well. I had such a feeling."

"A feeling about what?" This conversation was leading me in circles, and I didn't think lack of sleep was completely at fault.

Her smile softened a touch, and she walked over and took my hands. "Trust him. Trust yourself. I know what I say is true. You each have what the other needs."

"What are you talking about?"

She patted my hand. "Sleep. Your eyes are barely open. Here." She walked to the dresser and removed a full-length silk charmeuse gown in soft ivory. A matching robe lay draped over the upholstered bench at the end of the bed. She put both pieces in my hands. "Go, stand under a warm shower, change into these, and sleep. You need to be well rested."

With this cryptic advice, she sashayed to the door, flashing one last grin before she disappeared into the night.

Three a.m., and after a few hours of shut eye, I'd awakened even though my cabin and bed were incomparable. Normally I would have reveled in a long slumber, but I had things to do and needed to use every opportunity. I moved almost in a dreamlike state, not really feeling awake or asleep, and scooped up the robe I'd replaced on the footboard bench. From the Fendi, I pocketed my tiny, powerful flashlight. Then I slipped quietly from the deliciously cool air of the cabin and into the sultry atmosphere. There were storms brewing out on the horizon. I could feel them. But I hoped they'd stay away until we accomplished whatever we needed to ultimately do in Miami. I remembered the snuffbox then and smiled knowing it would soon be in my hands, and I might discover any secrets it held.

The narrow deck was empty. I leaned over the smooth railing to stare at the moon lazily reflected on the slowly undulating black water. My movements were deliberately measured, like the sea below.

I wanted another look at the *Woman Dressing Her Hair* in the main saloon, but I didn't want anyone observing to be aware of my interest. Nonchalantly, I strolled the deck before moving toward my destination. Like any guest who couldn't sleep, I would pour myself a drink to help coax my mind to relax. No one needed to know about my special interest. Especially Jack.

The saloon was almost pitch black, the curtains all closed. I located a sliding switch near the doorframe and pulled the lights up to a couple of watts from dim. I knew what Jack had said about it being a forgery, but I wanted a chance to verify my own thoughts. Something was familiar about the brushstrokes and tickled an idea in the back of my mind.

Within a few minutes I'd confirmed for my own interests that what Jack said was true, but I couldn't remember what my subconscious still seemed obsessed over. Eventually, the information would surface. I had just returned the tiny torch to my pocket when I heard a startled "Oh!" from behind me.

"Please excuse my intrusion." Margarite gave me her broad smile as she moved closer. "I walked by, saw the lights on, and thought Ernesto had forgotten to extinguish them."

With a wave toward the painting, I explained, "I couldn't sleep.

I came in to take another look at the paintings and see if I could find the wonderful cognac I was too sleepy to enjoy earlier."

She laughed and moved to the bar. "Excellent idea. The best way to get back to sleep, I say. Is the room comfortable for you?"

"Absolutely. No complaints at all." I accepted the small snifter she passed to me, then watched as she poured another for herself. She was still in the dress she wore at dinner, and nothing about her looked slept in. "When do you go to bed, Margarite?" I took a sip. Heaven.

Once again, she laughed. "I am...oh, what is the word? Insomniac. That's it." She set her glass back down on the bar top and waved her hands as she spoke. "I sleep a few hours here, another few there. It all adds up in the end."

The liquid slid effortlessly down my throat. "This cognac is excellent. Everything about Folly Roost has been superb as far as I can see."

She picked up her glass, raised it high above eye level, and swirled it near one of the recessed lights. "This is the owner's private collection. He keeps it especially for his valued guests."

"Who owns the Folly Roost?"

At that second, the captain burst in. "Oh, good, you're here. We received your call. He's holding for you."

"Please excuse me." She slid her glass back to the middle of the bar. "I've been waiting for my son to call. I must go to the bridge." She slipped her hand through Captain Morgan's arm. "Thank you for coming to notify me." And they disappeared out the door.

I finished my cognac and rinsed the glass under the faucet behind the bar. I wandered past the Picasso, but my heart wasn't into examining it any closer. It looked like the real thing, and the fact Jack pointed up the other as being a fake right away, without mentioning the Picasso, made the probable answer lead my feet back to *Woman Dressing Her Hair*.

Something. Something. But what? Those brushstrokes. Whose were they? Why do I remember them, and what am I remembering?

The effort was too great. I was trying too hard, and the answer wouldn't come as long as I persisted. Besides, fatigue was coming back suddenly in great waves. I hadn't had enough sleep, and the liquor on top of the exhaustion was the final push.

By the time I made it back to my stateroom, I was nearly operating on autopilot. I'd left my lamp on and oriented my feet toward the bed. Then I remembered nothing else.

EIGHT

The next morning dawned overcast, the distant clouds of the wee hours now settling comfortably in the Miami environs. I was ahead of Jack getting to the saloon, despite the fact it was after seven already. I couldn't remember when I'd had a better night's sleep, and discovering the beautiful fawn-colored linen suit in my closet—and finding it a perfect fit—pushed me into the delirious zone on my happiness meter. I'd even decided to tell Jack about the snuffbox, let him know we could be at the end of our journey in searching for the microchip that supposedly held details of what could soon be the greatest heist in the art world. We also might reasonably have the chance to halt all preparations in their tracks.

I felt like the cat that ate the canary—cliché, I know, but apropos. Out the windows, I watched the sun move higher in the sky, and heard a speedboat zoom away from close by. It may have even been the boat Jack and I arrived on the previous evening. The motor sounded familiar anyway. I imagined the speedy craft made many ferries back and forth for supplies, as it obviously had yesterday to return with all the clothes Margarite stocked in my bedroom suite.

In an instant, I realized exactly how much I'd missed this life and how I planned to relish this mini-return. The world was a glorious place when Laurel Beacham was rested, optimistic, and eating eggs Benedict on a yacht nicer even than the one Granddaddy used to own. I was in my element and invincible and ready to offer Jack an "in" into my happy space.

"Ah, I knew you would be early." Margarite swooped in with a smile and a yummy mimosa in each hand. "Here, we'll share some early girl talk."

My plate was empty, and my hand was full with the lovely flute. We clinked glasses and each took a sip.

"I didn't think I'd finish breakfast before Jack even made it in here." I laughed. "Guess that final cognac was precisely what the doctor ordered for total relaxation."

Margarite waved a hand. "No, no, Jack left on the launch a few minutes ago. He said he would meet you at the Browning event."

The glass slipped from my fingers and shattered across the tabletop.

As one of the waiters cleaned and someone else brought me another filled glass, I went through the motions, said the right things, but was still trying to figure out what I'd heard a moment ago. Jack left. Jack left without me. And without talking to me before he departed. Despite the fact he was the one gung-ho to make plans and trade information the previous evening.

I wasn't sure what it all meant, but I knew he'd lost his opportunity to learn about Tina and the snuffbox. I intended to hold that secret as close as I could when I had the item in my hand within the next few hours.

The appeal of girl talk vanished then too. I smiled a lot and made conversation, but neither my heart nor my brain was truly in it. Jack was long gone, and I waited until I heard the return sound of the high-performance boat before I asked, "Is that the launch now? Would they mind returning to shore right away? I have a few things to take care of this morning."

"No problem at all." Margarite rose. "I'll tell them you'll be ready momentarily."

"Give me five minutes."

While she left to inform the crewman, I flew to my room and returned any items I'd taken from my Fendi, then scooped up yesterday's clothes. Everything looked the same. I admit to wishing I could stay longer, and not simply for the luxury. This desire was partly due to wanting to tap into Margarite's knowledge of

Beacham history. To be completely honest, I would have loved to talk with her about my mother. Having lost my mom when I was barely four, it was other people's stories that kept her real to me. Still, if wishes were horses, yada, yada...I wasted no time taking my leave.

At the ladder, Margarite did nothing to stop me, didn't even try to slow my progress, but her expressive brown eyes said she was disappointed somehow. Equally as likely, the roots of her "look" may have hinged on that last *reveal* she'd offered before she left my room the previous night. I needed to think about that when I had the time. Still, the mission came first, and while I had no idea if I was the cause of her disappointment or the result, I didn't take a moment to ask. Nevertheless, I continued to wonder.

Minutes later, I was the solo passenger on the black launch as we drove into the wind toward Miami. The water was choppy and inhospitable, as if it knew reinforcements were coming and didn't have to play nice anymore. Sheer speed swept my hair back and away from my face, and the momentum seemed to sweep the cobwebs from my brain at the same time.

I contemplated how Margarite fit in with Jack and/or his family. If she'd known him since childhood, they had a history. A history that might include her making sure something was slipped in my wine the previous evening, so my exhaustion could be enhanced and allow Jack to slip out without me come morning light.

Yet, this idea begged the question as to what he could be up to at such an early hour and why he needed to go alone. Unless Melanie gave him a lead he hadn't shared, we were still waiting to see what Nico came up with before proceeding. At least, that was the plan as far as Jack and I had discussed. My connecting with Tina had been a fluke—well, not completely, since the girl never failed to use art events in her husband-trapping plans. But he could not have known when he drove us to the Browning Gallery that I would encounter Tina in her new career endeavor. And he couldn't know what she told me unless he was the person eavesdropping.

But that didn't make sense. The shouting definitely had to be between coworkers at the site.

As I stood waiting for my cab beside the harbor master's office, I contemplated my next move. It was too early to show up to the fête. I wondered if Nico was in town yet. A second later I knew for sure.

"I just got off my flight from New York" was his proffered greeting when he answered my phone call. I could picture his stern look when he added, "And no, I have nothing yet on the numbers. They seem to be a complete enigma."

"My first question was actually to ask why you'd suddenly decided to buddy up with Jack."

He said a few choice words in Italian before responding. I was relieved he did his cursing in his mother tongue, as I didn't need more reason to be angry at Jack, and Nico's words could have fueled my temper.

"Why would I align myself with him?" Nico asked, the Italian accent still strong in his tone. "He's in Max's pocket now."

As I suspected. Who needed confirmation when instincts won every time? "Sorry, Nico. Things have gone sideways too often lately, and it's left me off-balance." Then I told him the facts relating to the resurfacing of the fabled snuffbox. "I'm supposed to pick it up today, but my cab should arrive any minute, and I plan to shoot over to Tina's condo and try to get it ahead of schedule."

"You don't think it still has...well, you know."

Yes, I did know. And I appreciated his discretion. "My first thought would be no, but Simon is nothing if not an egotist. If he was actually selling what was hidden inside, instead of the snuffbox, and that's why he wanted Tina to hold it here in Miami, the object could still have what Jack purports it was drafted into transporting. At least, it's my hope."

A yellow cab pulled up to the curb at the end of the harbor master's office and honked. "There's my ride. I'll meet you at the Browning event after I see Tina, then we can decide if we want to guard the snuffbox as a team or send you back to London with it ahead of me. You do have the foundation's passes to get us in today, right?"

"I live to serve."

"I'll take that as a yes and not sarcasm." I smiled. He really was good at what he did. I wanted to talk to him about *Woman Dressing Her Hair* when we had the time. There was something...The thought wouldn't come forward. I probably needed to get Cassie on it. As I opened the cab's back door, I added, "I really appreciate the way I can always count on you, Nico. You do know that, right?"

"Let me guess. Cassie told you how Max yelled at me."

"Yes, but—"

I didn't get to finish my sentence. Nico laughed and broke the connection.

The driver was at least seventy and grizzled to the point of almost appearing a caricature. His day-old growth of gray whiskers, Chicago Cubs cap, and gravelly Windy City accent let me know I had a veteran cabbie behind the wheel, even if we were well over a thousand miles from Wrigley Field. A couple of flips of my finger on my phone, and I had the Bricknell address to Tina's condo. I recited the cross streets for the cabbie.

The morning drive was expectedly bad, but the driver knew his shortcuts and verbalized all of them around his unlit cigar stub. "Yeah, I gave up smoking these stogies years ago," he said, gravel still in his voice. "Now, I chew on them."

I knew I would be pushing at that mental picture all day.

Despite the traffic snarls and snafus, I finally saw Tina's skyscraper in the distance. Yet the first view I had of her building was not an optimistic one. Several police cars and an ambulance tied up the front street parking spots. I pulled out my phone again.

"Hi, it's Tina. I'm busy having fun or shopping right now. Either way, promise I'll call back if you leave your name and number. And even quicker if you're inviting me to a party." The giggle that ended her voicemail message made me catch my breath. The levity didn't bode well with my reservations.

It had to be a busy morning for her. She was probably driving and couldn't get to the phone. Or on another call and couldn't switch over. Or she could be in a dead zone and her phone hadn't even rung for her to hear. The dead zone thought was enough to send a shiver up my spine. Okay, maybe I needed to quit lying to myself and acknowledge what my gut was screaming to me.

"Stop the cab. And wait for me. Please."

"Look, lady, I can't double park with all these cops around."

I kept my eyes trained on the boys in blue and swirled a finger in the air. "Keep circling the block. I'll jump back in, I promise. I'll pay the extra fare."

The cabbie's words arm-wrestled their way around the cigar. "Gimme what's already on the meter."

"But you'll wait for me, right?"

"Yeah, yeah," he growled, then pulled on the brim of the cap.

The ambulance pulled away at that moment, but the lights and siren remained off. Several officers were watching as I exited the cab, and I wished I hadn't worn slacks so I could distract them with a flash of thigh. Instead, the Fendi and I put on our most confident attitudes and headed for the elegant glass and brass-plated entrance to Tina's condo building. Grandfather always said people perceived whatever one projected, and at that moment I wanted to project the mien of someone who wasn't expecting the worst. Getting into the lobby was easy, but all further progress stopped at the elevators.

"Ma'am, do you live here?" asked a man in a dark suit, his badge clipped to his belt and peeking out behind the right flap of his suit jacket. Detectives onsite already. This didn't look good.

"No, Detective, I'm here to see a friend. We made plans yesterday to meet this morning." Too much info. Slow down, Laurel. Keep with one sentence answers.

"And your friend's name?" He poised a pen over his notepad.

I reminded myself about perception, and flashed my best *I'd love to talk, but I'm really in a hurry* smile, and said, "Tina, Tina Schroeder."

His dark gaze hit me like a sudden laser. "Please step over here for a moment." He introduced himself as Detective Roblo and led me to the corner farthest away from the doors and elevators.

Yep, as I'd feared. The worst.

All the gory details aside, Tina was found about thirty minutes before in the alley behind the building. A probable victim of robbery, according to the detective, but I felt a shiver when he said her throat was cut. Okay, that was one gory detail. I bit my lip to keep from blurting out how her death was like the fat man in Italy. I did not want to get into that with Miami law enforcement.

"Was anything of value taken, Detective?" I had to know.

"Yeah, the thief grabbed her purse and ran."

And I was pretty certain the snuffbox was part of this supposed thief's loot.

"But why kill her? Was she...violated?" I knew my questions were natural, and I wanted to appear absolutely genuine. Well, my grief was, after all. I really had liked Tina.

The detective put a comforting hand on my shoulder. "No, there was no evidence of anything sexual."

Which would have been a relief if it didn't make her subsequent murder seem much more unnecessary in a simple snatch-and-run robbery. Still, I was grateful for the information. "Thank you." Tears stung my eyes.

He took my contact details. At this point I wasn't sure how long Jack and I would be in Miami, but I told the detective I was leaving after the day's art event and I was in Miami to attend as a representative of the Beacham Foundation. Apparently my grandfather's name still carried enough cachet to offset the mess my father did to it in the greater Miami/Dade area, because the detective raised his eyebrows when I showed my ID, and he quickly waved me on.

My cabbie, on the other hand, chose the opportunity to move on to greener pastures, since he'd required my green before I'd left the vehicle. One of the uniformed cops called for another cab, and I waited at the curb debating my options. I wasn't sure if I should go on to the event and get in during the confusing early setup or do some nosing around here first.

A black Lincoln Town Car slid noiselessly to the curb in front of me, and the back door opened. Jack stepped out. I didn't know whether to let my anger speak over being left earlier, express my gratitude he'd shown up when I was still shaken by the news of Tina, or walk quickly away because I was more than a little apprehensive about where he'd been during the time frame of the murder. Not to mention the serendipitous way he showed up soon afterward.

Irritation and apprehension moved to make my decision. "No, thank you. I have a cab coming." But this was Jack. He'd had more than enough chances to kill me and leave my body hidden in places it would have never been found. While I was fairly certain he wasn't a murderer and there were things I needed to say to him, this was not the time and a closed car was not the place. At least, not until I had ample opportunity to mull things over. Things like, why did Jack happen by this place right now, and where had he been previously?

"Laurel, don't be obstinate. Get in."

"The cab is already on its way. I don't want him to drive all the way down here and have no fare. Cabbies need respect too."

"In this neighborhood, he'll be quickly dispatched to another fare. Never fear. We barely have enough time to get to the Browning event, and I must still charm Melanie into giving you a pass."

"I'm not—"

One of the uniformed officers took note of the idling Town Car and interrupted with, "Sir, you're going to have to move along."

Jack shot me a warning look. "Laurel, we'll discuss this en route."

I complied. A Beacham was taught never to create a scene unless it was completely necessary. And despite my doubts about Jack's honesty, I couldn't force myself to go against my social training in this instance.

The buttery soft leather was as inviting as ever, and Jack offered a cup of coffee from the carafe.

"Thank you."

I'm always amazed when served with a china cup and saucer in any kind of limo. We've become a society of to-go cups and disposable everything.

"So, why are you here?" Jack asked. "Didn't have your fill of coppers yesterday when the Mercedes was stolen?"

"Could ask you the same question." I purposely kept my eyes on my coffee as I spoke and only looked up after taking a sip. "Why are you in this neighborhood?"

"I had a meeting," he said. "You didn't mention anything yesterday about taking a jaunt to Bricknell before the art festival."

"I assumed I would have an opportunity to do so when we met for breakfast, but you had other plans." His face colored when I said that. Interesting. "Didn't think I needed to be informed about your plans, either, Jack? Who did you meet, and did you learn anything new?"

He muttered something I didn't catch.

"What was that?"

"Never mind." He crossed his arms over his lovely Tom Ford jacket. It was new, and Margarite obviously knew his size as well. I could have left it at that. Except I couldn't.

I was about to add another of my two cents to the situation when Volcano Hawkes sputtered and blew.

"You cannot use any reason, can you, Laurel? We're trying to keep our investigation quiet, then you find whatever state of affairs is the most dangerous to you personally, and that's where you hare off to. Someday, someone isn't going to be there to grab you before it's too late. Someday—"

"Now, just a minute, bucko." Where did he get off? "I don't know what you think you know, and maybe you already know everything, but when you picked me up, I was going to meet Tina. You know, Tina, the girl I talked to yesterday. I was trying to meet with her for coffee before heading to the fair. And if you hadn't slipped away at dawn and left me on the boat, you might have been invited too."

Okay, none of that last bit would have happened, but I had a head of steam and needed enough words to vent it.

Jack was undaunted. "All the police at the building didn't tip you off that your idea wasn't the safest one you'd ever devised?"

"There was an ambulance. Someone could have had a heart attack or fallen down the stairs."

"Police aren't normally called for either of those types of occurrences."

"My God, you sound like Max." My boss could be insufferable at most times, but his leaps of logic could reach Olympian lengths. No way I could tell Jack about the snuffbox and Tina's connections to it and give him more ammunition to hurl my way. I should have come clean in the beginning when he could jettison his anger on the fact the snuffbox had once more likely disappeared. As it was, I had to play this out to its logical conclusion.

"I had no reason to think the activity at the building entrance impacted my seeing Tina in any way. She was the picture of health yesterday. The ambulance didn't even play into my thoughts." Then the walls of the car started moving in on me, and the gravity of what had happened. I heard my cup and saucer clink onto the floorboard but hadn't realized I'd let go. Instead, I suddenly realized I'd slid down to lie on the leather seat. "If I hadn't gone, I wouldn't know right now that she's dead."

A second later Jack pulled me to his chest, and all the tears I'd trapped inside my heart broke for freedom. He handed me a handkerchief. Yes, an actual monogrammed hanky, and for a brief instant I lost myself in the incongruous thought of how few I saw anymore with men under sixty.

Then I bawled. He stroked my hair, moving his hand slowly to my back and soothingly down an arm, a leg, about any place he could reach.

What made me finally stop sobbing was the fear my makeup was likely ruined, and we were mere blocks from the Browning. A mirror confirmed the worst. I'm not shallow. I'm practical.

Worse, as I panicked and made a quick fix, Jack turned from Mr. Sympathy to a warped version of Henry Higgins. But instead of chastising me on diction, he tried to keep my attention by lecturing in the "for your own safety" vein. When he finally said, "I'm sorry about your friend, but you have to understand you cannot wander into—"

"You know, Jack," I interrupted. I scooted as far away from him as the interior allowed. "A minute ago you were acting like a gentleman." I balled up the hanky and threw it at him. "A real gentleman. You almost fooled me. But an actual gentleman would never have left this morning without me. And if it was absolutely necessary he did, said gentleman would have told me he was leaving, then taken a cab for himself and left me this Town Car."

"I don't see how that makes any difference."

Neither did I, but no way I would admit it to him. "That's why you'll never be a gentleman, Mr. Hawkes." I roughly tugged the Fendi near my side, turned my back to Jack, and focused on my mirror. I did sneak a couple of looks at him, but he crossed his arms and stared pointedly out his side window.

I salvaged enough of my face until I could get into a bathroom. At the moment, I needed to set my own agenda. A plan guaranteed not to include Mr. Jack "Panties in a Twist" Hawkes. I may not have known who killed Tina, but the art fête would be a good place to ask questions. I owed it to my friend, and equally I owed it to myself to try to find the next link in the quest of the snuffbox. It had been my responsibility to retrieve it in Italy, after all. The entrance of Jack and his major art heist conundrum had no bearing on my original mission.

Someone was playing dirty, and if I'd been with Tina this morning, I might have shared her fate. The thought made me kind of feel like shivering again.

"Laurel, you're going to have to trust me." Mr. Silence broke his self-imposed détente. Boy, did he pick the wrong time to talk again.

"Trust you? Trust you? When you take over and decide where I'm going to stay, when I'm going to eat, and when I'm allowed—or not allowed—to leave? Put yourself in my place, Jack. Would you trust me if the roles were reversed? Or would you be concerned that a whole multitude of nefarious people have control-issue tendencies, and I might need to be careful around *everyone,* including you?"

"Nefarious."

"I didn't want to pigeonhole you, so I threw your evil tendencies in with the multitudes."

He grinned, and I had to slide my hands under my thighs to keep from slapping him. The man kept pushing me. Soon. Soon, when I didn't have a driver as a witness.

Regardless, I think Jack knew what I was thinking because he leaned closer and pulled at my wrists until he could take both my hands in one of his. I looked away, and he used his free hand to twist my chin back around to look at him. "I have a few nefarious tendencies, but none that need concern you. I simply want to keep you safe, and you tend to do everything in your power to keep me on the verge of a heart attack."

I opened my mouth to speak but found a huge lump in my throat instead. I thanked my lucky stars when the Browning filled the view through the windshield. As the car pulled to the curb, I had an out, and my voice returned.

"I talked earlier to Nico. He has a pass for me. See what you can find out from Melanie and company, and I'll work any sources I have who show up today."

"I don't know—"

"Don't be silly, Jack." I stretched out a foot to the sidewalk as the driver opened my door. "I'll be in public view all day with Nico to watch my back. You'll be in more danger associating with Preying Mantis Melanie."

"Remain in public view at all times."

"This is my element, sir." I anchored a hand on one hip and waited for him to join me on the pavement, while hoping he hadn't realized my words were not really an assurance. Couldn't help it. I had to give myself wiggle room, and lucky for me Jack didn't seem to recognize the evasion for what it truly was.

"Good." Jack fastened a button on his jacket as he resumed full height. There were going to be a lot more women noticing Mr. Hawkes than the art at the festival. Thank goodness I was immune to his charms.

The driver closed the door and returned to the front seat. The car glided silently away, making me remember another question I'd forgotten to ask. "Why did you even rent the Mercedes? Why didn't Margarite or the captain send the Town Car for us? Then we would still have our luggage because the driver would have stayed behind when we entered the gallery."

"Precisely why I didn't. I couldn't predict where our path may lead last night, nor how long we might have been held up at various places, and I didn't want the poor chap bored out of his skull."

Uh-huh, with satellite television and radio in the vehicle, and personal phones that can do practically everything short of time travel. Jack may not have been able to recognize my evasions, but I had become a pro at spotting his attempts at same. No matter.

"Next time?" I raised my eyebrows.

"Definitely." He nodded.

NINE

Nico was obviously following the GPS signal on my phone, because he was at the curb and waiting when we pulled up. It didn't take much coaxing to get Jack to hand me off to my associate and go investigate on his own. I think Mr. Hawkes had already had enough of me for the day, and I can't say I didn't share the feeling.

My right-hand geek was dressed in summer-weight Armani and looking good enough to eat. "Nico, I swear I'm going to lose you today to one of the gallerinas."

His beautifully sculpted black brows rose closer to his curly hairline. "If it does not happen, I will feel I've wasted my time coming today."

Hand to my heart, I said, "I feel slighted."

He snorted. "Until the first of your many admirers comes up to reacquaint themselves with the beautiful and talented Laurel Beacham."

"Thank you for mentioning beautiful, but only you know my true talents."

"Not all your talents." His smile was nothing short of a leer and made me laugh. Oh how I'd missed his humor in the past week.

He already wore a pass around his neck and pulled another from his pocket. "They were in the file, exactly as you told Cassie," Nico said, draping my pass on its gold lanyard over my head. "I also have this for you to carry with you at all times." He handed me a flat packet, deceptively lighter than its appearance implied.

"What is it?" In that weird way crowds develop, we were

suddenly surrounded by people, and I felt almost claustrophobic.

"Your personal escape hatch. Keep it in your purse," Nico said. "We'll talk about it later."

"Okay." My curiosity was aroused, but I knew better than to open something when Nico said to wait. I pointed toward the gallery. "I need to use the restroom for a second. Why don't you circulate, and I'll find you in the tents."

He nodded, then moved to join the surging crowd, his dark curls disappearing into the throng.

It was quick work to make my face once more presentable. The patch-up I did in the car had been enough to cover. Having a few moments alone in the ladies' room helped my appearance and boosted my self-confidence. Long ago, I'd recognized the value of stealing a few minutes alone to breathe, and this day was no exception. However, all good things come to an end, and when Melanie stepped through the door, I realized it was my cue to depart.

"He's out of your league. You know that, don't you?"

My hand was on the pull bar. I was almost out the door. I told myself, *Leave, don't look back.* Then my mouth started moving, and I turned to face her. "Melanie, I don't take anyone's leftovers, least of all yours. If you think you have any chance with him, go for it. But I honestly believe he has better taste."

She raised her throwing arm as I ducked out the door. An instant later I heard her lipstick case shatter when it hit the tiled wall where I'd been standing.

In the tents and enclosures, we could hear the wind, but Mother Nature wasn't slowing down this party. Champagne and caviar flowed like water, and I grabbed a mimosa from a circulating waiter. The glass was a prop. I needed to keep a clear head today to see what I could learn about Tina's death and where the snuffbox may now have traveled.

"Have you seen the event planner?" I asked one of the gallery employees circulating among the guests.

The woman, whose name tag read Kendall, pointed to a

glassed-in corner at the top of the Browning. "Last I saw of her, she was heading for the top of the building. There is a small set of corner offices where she can keep a birds-eye view on things as she makes phone calls and fields questions. You might check there."

Overnight, the courtyard had been covered with a high dome top to protect the artwork from the direct effects of the sun. This was the New Artists area, and I would be back to check things out, especially since crews were pumping in cool air via several strategically placed portable AC units. The now probable storm was making the day sticky already, though it wasn't even noon.

As I again approached the Browning's front door, I turned to scan the crowd on the off chance I would see Jack or Nico. Neither man came into view, but as the old saying goes, "A good time was had by all," or at least the event was in the process of getting that appellation. Beautiful people were laughing, mingling, talking, and drinking as well as eating. Inside, a small band played a mix of chamber and Latino music in the main lobby, the sound faint but pleasing.

I waved away another waiter, this time sporting a kind of artichoke heart hors d'oeuvres, and pushed through the crowd to the Deco railed staircase. Everything on the ground floor was new art, much by established contemporary artists and a good number by new fledglings who had somehow come up with the entrance fee, and still more who had been asked to participate. None of this was going to get me any answers about my friend's death or a seventeenth-century snuffbox, and it wasn't worth my time unless new information surfaced. I hoped Jack was making progress in our joint mission, because I'd pretty much put all thought of it aside as my plans shifted toward coordinating horizons that included this new murder.

The stairs were covered in a custom runner, unpadded to keep people from tripping. The pattern of the carpet was that of lush flowers and vines, blending well with the Deco motif of the building. I wondered at how the Browning justified the cost of this kind of extravagance. I didn't have to see the backing to know the exquisite rug was handmade. It might be worth Cassie's time to check on the Browning's finances and donors. Can never be too careful or too well informed.

I didn't plan to storm the castle, so to speak, but moved ever upward in a casual yet efficient manner. The second floor housed the beginning of the Browning's art collection, and the works stretched to the fourth floor as well. The elevator was going to get a workout that day. At the point of rounding the curve in the staircase, I glanced over to the queue for the single elevator, a device as slow as any utilized in this type of setting, and figured the wait at the end was probably now past two in the afternoon.

The fourth floor also held an artists soundproofed studio. This was the space I had planned to check out yesterday, but a certain set of car thieves thwarted those good intentions. I made a pretense of interest, to lend credence to my seeming exploratory jaunt before I headed to the top floor. My true destination. Instead, a woman in a severe black suit with a cell phone to her ear nearly bowled me down on the stairs. The phone flew out of her hand and arced over the railing, executing a nosedive before exploding into a handful of pieces as it hit the parquet floor.

"Damn!" The woman moved past me to recover the plastic and electronic pieces. I recognized her as the person who had signaled Tina when we'd left the tent the day before, and assumed I'd found my quarry.

"You're the event planner, right?" I walked back down to the fourth floor.

She gave me a weary nod and a wary look, most likely over her limit on complaints and problems already.

I offered my practiced handshake. "Laurel Beacham, of the Beacham Foundation."

"You're based in New York." The Brooklyn accent was still strong in her voice, and I knew she was either commuting in her business endeavors or was a recent transplant to the Florida sun. The basic black business outfit she wore put an even stronger point on my assumption.

"Well, I'm based in the London office." I stooped to retrieve a small square piece that probably covered the back of her phone. She scrambled to pick up the rest of the scattered parts. "But I've been in Orlando and wanted to stop into the event today while I was kind of in the neighborhood. You've truly done an outstanding job."

The woman smiled and suddenly showed her vulnerability. "I'm Alice Lawson. I can get you a card—"

I had already pulled one of mine from the Fendi and offered it to her. "You can mail one to me here. Or email me a JPEG file. I'll forward it along to the events planner in the New York office."

"Oh, I will." She unceremoniously shoved the pieces of her phone into a too-small pocket in her skirt, making the fabric bulge. I handed over my small contribution.

She thanked me, and I moved on to what I really wanted to ask her. "I was here yesterday in the late afternoon and ran into a friend of mine. Tina Schroeder. She said she worked for you, but I haven't been able to find her today. She was going to meet me earlier about an item she was passing along from a friend. Do you have any idea where I could find her?"

Alice's face turned as pale as the marble statue on the floor behind her. She stuttered, "No...Tina...Tina failed to show this morning. Probably got bored." She attempted to laugh, but the effort came off as lacking. "You know how she is."

Now the big question, what made her so nervous? The fact she thought she was hiding Tina's death from me? Or because I'd said the girl was bringing something to give to me today, before she was murdered? I probably shouldn't have taken the risk of saying that last bit, but I'd wanted to see what it got me. I figured this was the kind of thing Jack had been warning about earlier.

I waved a hand. "Oh, no matter. It was just a perfume sample a friend wanted me to try. Starting a new business and trying to beat the bushes for customers, and friends are the first asked to try the new scent."

Alice seemed to relax a fraction, and she faked a laugh as she said, "Yes, we all have those kinds of friends. Don't we?" But her dark eyes still held a hard look.

"Isn't that the truth?" I put a hand on her forearm to imply solidarity. "You've saved me looking all over for nothing. I'm sure you need to get back to work."

"Nice meeting you."

"You too. And remember to send me your business card." I smiled one last time at her, then quickly made my way back down the stairs. The third floor was full of experimental art, my least favorite. I headed to the second floor, drawn to the area featuring Sebastian, an artist who'd been well established for the past fifty years. It was rumored he still lived somewhere in Italy, but no one had seen him for decades. A few people quietly walked and talked in the area, but most on the floor stayed engaged with the art. There was nothing second class about this gallery.

The oversized landscape of a Tuscany vineyard was exquisite. Done in oils, the work reminded me why I'd gotten into this business. Daydreaming over a picture had been my modus operandi as far back as I remembered. For that fragile second, I was lost in the Tuscan countryside, searching for the elusive Sebastian. A voice near my right ear startled me.

"Does it speak to your heart?" said Anthony Berintino, otherwise known as Tony B. He stood too closely behind me and was clad in confidence and a thousand-dollar Italian suit. He was such a stereotypical hood, I didn't know whether he had no imagination or actually set the bar for every other low-thinking thug with visions of grandeur. Long suspected of being connected to some of the "families" and the acting front man for a dozen corporations, Tony B had never been convicted of or even charged with anything in the twenty or more years his name had been active.

Slick, cool, with a powerful physique and a smile that dropped women at thirty paces—and there had been plenty of those over the years—I knew he was always in evidence at Browning celebrations. I'd also noticed him and Melanie with their heads together when I was checking out the line to the elevator. Nothing had changed recently. The man was one of the reasons my grandfather had started disengaging himself from the Browning right before he died.

In his early forties, Tony B's confidence matched his physique, and I knew he was building a reputation few people discussed. And as long as no one discussed it, he felt free to increase his influence through monetary gifts and celebrity attendance at events such as this one.

Looking past Tony B's shoulder, I saw his too-thin, too-blonde wife of fifteen years also present and holding court nearby, but as usual they worked the room separately. I had run into both him and his long-suffering bitch of a spouse many times over the past few years, usually at the most prestigious events. I had even sat next to him at one of the less prestigious, and ultimately more infamous, parties held on a private yacht anchored on the Strait of Gibraltar. We'd had to stop our host from diving headfirst into the dangerous waters because he'd had too much to drink. He had "wanted to swim naked with the fishies." As I recalled, Tony B had been the one most often getting the poor man refills.

"Tony B, it's lovely to see you." He moved in for a hug, but I stepped back and offered a hand.

"You look terrific, Laurel, but fawn really is too understated a color for you. Think about a bright red or a peacock blue next time."

Now I'm getting fashion tips from a thug. Great. "Thank you for noticing. I've been at a slight disadvantage with limited luggage this trip."

He smirked, then pointed toward the painting I'd been studying. "I see you like Sebastian."

I turned and pulled the Fendi closer as I processed possible options to get away from him. "Yes. I love his work and the legend behind his life story."

"Women and their romance." He leaned closer. "I have a couple of Sebastians of my own. In my office. I'd love to show them to you."

Come up and see my etchings, little girl. Okay, maybe not, but that's how his offer made me feel. Regardless, I'm nothing if not diplomatic. "Gee, I'd love to, Tony B, but I'm only here for part of the day. Breezing through to add a touch of Beacham interest to the celebration."

"Really? That's funny, because I heard something different. My mistake."

There was the warning shiver again. Who recently spoke to Tony B about me? Melanie or Alice? And why? Did he have anything to do with Tina's murder? I could have asked if he'd seen Simon lately, since I knew they were acquainted in the past. But common sense told me to get out of there quickly. "Well, it was good seeing you, Tony B. And thanks again for thinking of me." I excused myself and headed back to the lobby level to regroup. The man was never a person to be trusted, but something about the way he said what he had made me doubly uncomfortable.

I texted Jack and Nico and asked them to meet me outside the ladies' room. While I waited inside, I rummaged through the Fendi for Cassie's Hermes scarf. I still loved the suit, and would always take Margarite's clothing suggestions over Tony B's, but this was a festive event, and a little extra color couldn't hurt. I did a quick twist maneuver with the scarf and connected the ends in a loose knot. The golds and burnished brown in the Hermes were a perfect complement to both my hair and the linen suit.

In a couple of minutes, an old-money matron wearing blue silk and dripping diamonds pushed open the door and asked, "Are you Laurel Beacham?"

"Yes."

"Well, there are two nice gentlemen out here who asked me to see if you would please come out."

"Thank you." As I pushed past her, she entered the restroom. I scanned the hallway, looking for either of the guys, but was instead grabbed by each arm and muscled farther down the hall and away from the crowd in the lobby.

I twisted to try breaking free, but their holds tightened. "Wait a minut—" And that's when the goon on my right lifted the portion of the Hermes that lay across my bodice and pushed it into my mouth.

"Keep quiet, and everything will be fine."

Obviously the diamond-clad matron didn't know a gentleman when she saw one.

TEN

We exited the building at the loading dock, where a big black Mercedes sat idling. One of thugs grabbed my Fendi and pawed through it until he found my cell phone. He took the phone, dropped it to the pavement, and smashed it with his size thirteen shoe. I couldn't scream, so I wiggled and fought. I was not getting into that car without a struggle. My heel ground into the instep of the goon holding my right arm. But my self-defense move didn't matter. They shoved me and my purse into the trunk and slammed down the lid.

No phone, trapped in the dark in what felt like a mobster's car, and Jack and Nico had no idea where I'd gone. Hell, I didn't even know where I was going. Or why. Or who had the balls to kidnap me in broad daylight.

I wasted a few moments looking for the trunk latch release cable It had been disabled. While the Mercedes trunk was good sized, it isn't surprising I quickly felt cramped and claustrophobic.

Nonetheless, I counted myself lucky I was awake and all in one piece. As I quantified the situation, I used the opportunity to remove the scarf from my mouth and take it off my neck as well. Call me paranoid, but all of Jack's talk that morning, chastising me for continually putting myself into harm's way, was hitting home. I couldn't take credit for this current predicament though, as I had little choice but to move with the Danger Twins.

I squeezed the slippery fabric, telling myself being proactive was better than nothing. After all, having something knotted around my neck left me vulnerable for an easy throttling.

Conversely, holding the fabric in my own hand meant I had my own silky noose ready if a chance defensive move presented itself. The fabric might be beautiful and softly elegant, but I knew from experience that silk was deceptively strong, like my own backbone, and I intended to use both if pressed into another corner.

The car took enough short-block turns to hinder my keeping a running tally in my head. Besides, I didn't know Miami well enough for it to matter. When the engine went silent about twenty minutes later, I had no idea where we might be. I hoped it wasn't a dead-end road near a cemetery.

The more gracious goon, the one who only shoved my scarf in my mouth, opened the trunk lid and grunted in a way I interpreted to mean "Get out."

They resumed the tag-team escort, and I realized we were in an underground parking garage. I began to realize where I was going and why.

"Laurel, what a pleasure to see you." Tony B greeted us when the Danger Twins shoved me into his office. He took in my appearance in one piercing comprehensive glance. "I'm sorry we had to do things this way, but I heard you were asking about Tina, and I wanted a private place to give you the bad news."

"Tony B, I appreciate that, but I already got word. You really shouldn't have gone to all this trouble." I glanced back at the Danger Twins. I summed up the situation quickly and decided I needed to take the offensive. Let Tony B believe I considered all of this the fault of his over-enthusiastic goons not understanding his orders. "Your men take their commissions seriously." My upper arms felt bruised, and I played it up for all it was worth, rubbing my muscles as if to assess the damage, and I warned, "You do realize your people stuffed my own scarf in my mouth, manhandled me out of the gallery against my will, and stuffed me into a car trunk? *Your car trunk. To your office.* By any stretch of the imagination, I could level a charge of assault, battery, and kidnapping. Surely you want to apologize and put this all right again."

He walked around the massive desk and leaned against its

dark wood front panel, his posture stiff and tone of voice menacing. "How did you hear about Tina?"

"Why...from the event planner. She said Tina took off. Quit, I assumed." With my words I saw the steel tension leave his body. He smiled slightly and waved a hand for his henchmen to leave us.

He motioned me into one of the visitors' chairs, and I sat, holding the Fendi in my lap and keeping a bit of space between us. He shot me a glance, letting me know he recognized what I was doing. He poured scotch from the decanter on his desk and held out one of the glasses. "Please, let's have a drink together," he said.

I didn't want to mix alcohol with this scenario. I needed to stall and figure out how to get rid of the liquor. Not much else I could do though. I took the glass. "To what are we drinking?" I asked.

"We're celebrating. A long-lost item has returned to my possession after a series of events conspired to keep it away. Or, should I say, a series of people," he mused as he sipped his drink, then produced the smile of a shark going after a school of fish.

The snuffbox I was supposed to pick up at the *castillo* last month. Until I'd found my mustachioed contact dead and the snuffbox missing. How had Tony B gotten involved with it? Rapidly, I replayed the history of the snuffbox as I knew it. Neither Tony B nor his organizations fit in at any point. Was he the one responsible for the mustached man's death? While Tony's name was associated with a lot of high-powered, albeit often shady, dealings in the art world and various other activities, I hadn't heard the word murder associated with him. Though most of the "transactions" he'd involved himself in often produced rumors about innocent people taking the fall for Tony B's rogue actions. In his own mind, I believed he considered himself a power-broker and a fixer. Those of us who knew him well recognized he was actually more side-tracker and social-climber. But he could have hired someone to kill the Greek, and even if everyone knew the guy who confessed hadn't actually carried out the murder, the Italian connection was still there. The confessor could have covered for one of Tony B's compatriots who did the deed and needed protection.

I set the glass on the desktop and stood up. "Would you excuse me?" I smiled. "As you can tell, I'm a smidgeon worse for wear, and I'd like to visit the powder room." He pointed, and I headed toward the executive bathroom.

"By all means, proceed," he said smoothly. "But please leave your bag here."

"Oh, but—"

"The bag stays here, Laurel. I want to speak with you, and I don't want you getting in touch with someone who will interrupt our conversation."

I couldn't help it. I slammed a fist against my hip and said, "One of your underlings already stomped my phone in the alley. I couldn't get in touch with anyone short of sending a message in a bottle through the sewer system."

He nodded. "Very well. I will also see that your phone is replaced."

As I hurried to the bathroom, the sound of his low laughter followed me.

I rolled a towel to set at the bottom of the door to help hide any sounds I created and let my gaze rove over the lavish room. A Jacuzzi took up a corner, as well as a toilet and bidet. There was a small shower as well as a closet filled with more Italian suits and shoes.

One of the other things I'd learned on the yacht trip circling Gibraltar was Tony B's wife couldn't hold her liquor either, and she was one of the bitterest harpies I'd ever met. Not that I blamed the woman. Her husband openly flirted with anything in a skirt, and once when I'd helped her to the couple's stateroom and poured her into bed, she'd mumbled something I hoped would be useful in the present situation. In a slurred cadence she'd sung the words, "The bastard doesn't know it, but I know his safes are in his toilets."

Naturally, I didn't learn where in his restrooms, but with the size of this space there was plenty of room to hide one. I started with the obvious and checked the medicine cabinet for a trip button to make the whole unit swing away from the wall. Then I moved to the toilet tank. Another minute and I had the shoe shelves silently rolling out of the way, and found the tiny ribbon marking where to pull to remove the carpeting.

The safe was a standard model I had cracked many times thanks to wonderful training received from an Irish thief. I was surprised Tony B didn't have anything high-tech, but he wasn't really known for having a love of gizmos. I'd heard him say many times if he "couldn't eat it, screw it, or intimidate it, what's the use?"

As the safe opened, I held my breath. I ran my hand through the papers and cash and searched a small velvet bag containing a few pieces of not very good jewelry. No snuffbox in sight. I closed everything, feeling momentarily defeated.

If Tina was killed today, the snuffbox was still in Miami. And if Tony B had it, it had to be in this office building. It had to be here. Maybe he had another hidey-hole.

I moved to the shower, and that's when I noticed the flaw. The recessed soap dish was flush on one side but out a fraction of an inch on the other. I tugged, I pressed, I prayed. And when I was about to give up, I removed the bar of soap and the unit moved soundlessly toward me. Damn, it was weight activated.

Ignoring my fear of spiders, I reached blindly into the dark opening and had to swallow a squeal when my fingers closed on the object I knew was the snuffbox. I hurriedly wrapped it in my scarf and then hid it in one of the secret pockets of the Fendi. I flushed the toilet and turned on the tap, taking the opportunity to wash my face and hands. Those were comforting moves designed to give me time to swallow my excitement, and keep Tony B from becoming aware of my true intentions. I needed to figure out how to get out of this mess.

There was a bottle of imported Swiss lotion on the counter. I smoothed some on my face, and the smell reminded me of my mother. I shut the memory down and stared into the mirror. I had to get out of here and back to the Browning. Or find a way to contact Nico and Jack.

Still in the exact position where I left him, Tony B reached again for the scotch. "Come on, Laurel, drink up. I can't think of anyone I'd rather celebrate with. I find it very fortuitous you are here with me. How's Max?"

"Same. Tight, frustrating, and determined to have his own way."

"Oh, yes. I think most of us are extremely determined to have our own way. Don't you agree, Laurel? You wouldn't have reached your level of, shall we say, success in your field, if you weren't single-minded and bullish about your recovery process. Or convinced your way was the right and only way."

I picked up my glass without sitting but played along. "I'm not sure I know what you're implying. I work for my family's foundation, and this latest incarnation finds me heading the London office."

"My mistake." He smiled and rose, the glass in his hand. "I'm interested in what you think of a work I'm relocating. Would you accompany me?"

I followed as he opened a door to what looked like a study and wondered what this Neanderthal would be doing with a study. Heavy drapes blocked the sunlight. He flipped a switch, and a wall sconce came on, perfectly positioned to illuminate a small yet spectacular landscape unmistakably the work of the artist Sebastian.

For five decades, Sebastian's paintings and prints had graced art galleries and museums and been used to raise money for a variety of causes, mostly connected with improving the lives of children. His earlier works centered around portraits, although he had also ventured into landscapes, particularly those concerning the Normandy region of France and the Tuscany region of Italy. Paparazzi had searched all over Europe for him to no avail. It was believed he lived a reclusive existence, continuing to paint, though no one had proof one way or the other.

We approached the painting. About three paces away, we both stopped and stared. The foreground held a lovingly cared for lily pond and the land around it. In the distance a house appeared deserted, waiting for its owners to return home. As with all of Sebastian's work, it looked as though the painting somehow glowed with a vibrant light. Hundreds of critics and art fans had speculated on how he achieved that effect in his work, and hundreds had been frustrated. Equally frustrated were all the artists who attempted to duplicate his style.

We remained silent and appreciated the painting.

"Beautiful," I breathed, awed by the variety of feelings Sebastian's art always produced. I may have seen his work already that day at the Browning, but one could never see too much of sheer genius. "I don't think I know this piece."

He dragged his gaze away from the painting with what appeared to be difficulty. "It's never been displayed. It's always been in the hands of a private collector."

"It looks like it's from Sebastian's earlier period."

"It is. Painted over thirty years ago."

"Is this the possession you recently recovered?" I asked, playing along, continuing to stare at the brushstrokes.

I could almost feel the cruelty in his smile. "Oh, no. I acquired this many years ago from the original collector."

Reluctantly, I turned away from the painting and looked at him. The debonair playboy good looks definitely had a sadistic, sinister slant. Or maybe it was the focused lighting.

Fun time was over. Time to go. I didn't know what Tony B was up to and didn't want to find out.

"Thank you for allowing me to see such a master. I'm afraid I'll have to be going. Duty calls as usual. I have a plane to catch, but I'm sure we'll run into each other again soon."

"While I appreciate your diligence and haste to get back to work, I'm afraid that will be impossible." I took off walking back to his office, heading for the exit out. With impeccable manners, he waited for me to precede him into the office.

"I'm not sure I understand," I prevaricated. I needed to keep the situation from escalating.

He reached out and took my right hand. I used every ounce of self-control I possessed not to jerk away from him. He said, "I told you it was fortuitous you appeared when you did. I heard you were coming to Miami and hoped we would run into each other."

I was puzzled and knew my face showed it. He smiled. "I don't mean to sound mysterious. I have something else to show you. Come back into the room with the Sebastian. There's another connecting room we can access inside. I have a painting you wrote a piece about several years ago, and I've been waiting for a chance to get you and the painting together ever since I read it."

Periodically, when something caught my interest and I wanted the public aware of an injustice, especially those injustices I could physically do nothing about, I gathered research and wrote op-ed pieces for the *New York Times* or the UK's *Guardian*. Unsure as to which article he was referencing, I asked, "You've got a painting I wrote about?"

"Yes. While you're in town, I wanted you to see it did indeed still exist."

How did he know I was coming to Miami? "Talk to Max about my itinerary? Or do you have another mole in Beacham?"

He laughed. "Oh, nothing so clandestine, believe me. I ran into him in Baltimore Wednesday afternoon, and he asked if I was still interested in investing in the Browning. I told him I already had. That's when he told me you were in Orlando for a short time and headed to Miami in the morning. With that information, I made it a point to do everything in my power to see you today. To correct some misinformation that appears to have upset you. Far be it from me to cause distress to a woman as beautiful as you, Laurel. Your passionate plea for the loss to the world of such important artwork piqued my interest as well as melted my heart."

Interesting and creepy. "Is there a reason we can't do this another time? As I said, I'm over-scheduled at the moment, but I'll be in Miami for several days—maybe—"

Who knew at this point?

"I apologize if this is an inopportune moment, but since you're here now, I feel I must insist upon the right to take advantage of your presence."

I had no doubt the Danger Twins were standing sentry on the other side of the door. Maybe if I reminded him of the risk.

I pulled my hand free and said, "I don't want to sound ungrateful, but continuing to hold me against my will is a federal offense, Tony B. A felony. You've always been careful to keep your hands clean. Can't we please do this the next time I'm in town? The weather is turning ugly, and I want to get to the airport before I miss my flight."

He retrieved his glass from the desk and savored a long sip, his pleasure at the taste of the liquor obvious. Everything he did had a sensual feel to it. *Ick.*

"I didn't plan the day this way. You're without wheels, and I had a car available to bring you here. Nothing that could be considered kidnapping."

Except, of course, that I rode in the trunk.

He continued. "Unfortunately, your actions preempted my plans." He took another sip, his eyes never leaving mine.

I preempted his plans? I felt thunderstruck. "You're the one who took the Mercedes. You know we were shot at, right?"

"I understand it was quite a wild chase."

As he talked, I made a mental survey of the contents of my Fendi and glanced around the room. If I couldn't go out through the door, there had to be another way.

He smiled. "I've watched you for years, Laurel. I've known Max a long time. We've often talked about our sleeping beauty, referring to you. You maintain such a cool businesslike front, but when you're writing about what you perceive as an affront to the world of art, your words contain so much passion."

I tried but couldn't stifle a small sense of betrayal. Max had talked to this letch about me? More than a few times? Something didn't fit. Would Max really discuss me with him? He knew how my grandfather felt about Tony B. Granted, Max didn't know the Tony B stories I'd heard. Another problem with people in the office not understanding fieldwork.

My shoulders straightened. I'd had enough. Time to take the offense. "I'm not sure I understand where all this is going, and frankly, I don't care. I've never had a high opinion of you, but now what small good opinion I did have has tanked. I'm leaving."

I headed for the door. I grasped the knob as a knock sounded. Tony B reached around me and opened the door, his hand gently grasping my elbow to move me out of the way. I hadn't even heard him come up behind me.

It was Danger Twin number one. "Can I be of any help, sir?"

"No," Tony B answered. "We're on our way to look at the second grouping now."

Danger Twin number one closed the door, and I heard it lock. Tony B grasped my elbow again and pulled me back toward the room housing the Sebastian. "You really do want to see this."

I really didn't, but recognized a power play when I experienced one. And hoped if I cooperated I would either be released or find a way to free myself.

"I've been looking forward to this ever since I heard you were coming to Miami."

He seemed to have an honest grin on his face for the first time. He led me through another door into total darkness.

"Wait a minute—"

"No worries, Laurel. I don't want to ruin the surprise." He let go of my arm. After a soft click, three lights came on across the opposite wall, illuminating three portraits.

I stared as a light bulb went off in my head. I covered my mouth with my fingers. I didn't want to make a sound. Sebastian's *Juliana*, Weaver's *Greensleeves*, and Gilmaier's *Retribution*. *The Portait of Three*. I never dreamed I'd see this trio together again.

I tore my gaze away from the pictures and stared at Tony B. He stared right back at me, his expression triumphant. He broke the thick silence.

"I had to show you. After I read your article, I felt as though you understand what I felt when these first came into my possession. They are magical, are they not?"

My gaze returned to the three. Painted at different times in history, the artworks had been loaned to a museum as part of a retrospective on the changing faces of women. The three came to the museum from the same source, a company named The White Pelican. Their owner had insisted the three be displayed together, and I could see why. Each portrait, while emphasizing its own merits, also complemented the one next to it. The *Juliana*, a larger piece, tied the others together and was mounted on the wall between them.

They had been stolen over fifteen years ago, on the opening night of the exhibition from La Galleria del Giardino della Vita in Florence, Italy. At that time, the privately owned museum specialized in exploring topics related to all things human and had begun to make a name for itself, when the art was stolen. The owner of the museum, as well as the owner of The White Pelican and all the other donors, were investigated, as was every guest attending opening night, but no connection was found and no arrest ever made. After the theft, the portraits became known as *The Portrait of Three*.

While art theft is fairly common, and everyone was insured, for the next year a string of bad luck seemed to follow the museum owner, Andrea Tessaro. He eventually killed himself, creating more speculation that the owner knew more than he let on. Again, nothing was proven.

My interest? I'd been twelve and attending the opening with my grandfather. Bored with the speeches and toasts, I'd wandered off and found myself in front of the exhibit of the three, fascinated by the works. I fell madly in love with *Juliana* and wished with every fiber of my being I could be her. The painting revealed a woman in love, emphasizing her beauty, her love, her humor, her extraordinary light. The darkness portrayed in the other two paintings, one a woman of sadness and loss, and the other, a woman caught up in anger and revenge, provided a trio of women's emotions from the high to the low.

Enraptured by the paintings, I'd highly resented the intrusion when a young male voice asked me what I was doing there. He insisted I return to the main salon until the ribbon cutting that signaled the opening of the exhibit. Naturally, I argued and told the tall young man to go away. As our voices rose, a security guard arrived and escorted us back to the salon, me dragging my feet and staring back at *Juliana* longingly. The boy triumphant and smirking.

The pictures must have disappeared immediately after we were removed from the hall by the guard. The obnoxious boy and I were the only ones at the opening to see the exhibit before it was stolen. A huge loss to the world of art.

Stolen paintings often never surface again for public viewing. Instead, they disappear into private collections, often for generations. While insurers compensate those affected by theft, they do nothing to restore the art to the rightful owners.

In that one night, all chance for anyone to enjoy the three masterpieces in their perfect state together disappeared as though the paintings never existed. Singular photos of the works never compared to the display I witnessed of the three all as one setting, in their true form. These priceless paintings, secreted in this hidden room of Tony B's office, were exactly as I remembered. Especially the *Juliana*. No childhood perspective had colored my memories. I wished my grandfather could be there. We discussed many times the ramifications of stolen art, and I'd tried as many times to explain to him the magic of that exhibit in the gallery setting—in their perfect showcase. My eyes grew damp. I ignored the tears and spoke, "If you read my article, then you know how I feel about stolen art."

"I do," he returned softly. "But I didn't steal this exhibit. I acquired it much later."

"You knowingly acquired stolen property."

"You're missing the point, Laurel. I didn't focus on that aspect of your article. I focused on the obvious passion you had for this trio of paintings. You must have been a child when you saw them, yet it made a lifelong impression on you. I knew after reading I had to let you see them again."

"I could report this to the authorities," I insisted.

He laughed. "You could. But one never knows when something bad is going to happen to a friend. I have many connections. Also, if you did report to the authorities, I'd know and would simply remove the paintings. In fact, I may have them destroyed if the pressure is strong enough."

I closed my eyes against the certainty in his voice. I wouldn't risk the paintings, and he knew it.

"Would you like to remain in this room for a few more minutes?"

I nodded. He brought over a chair and left the room. I heard the door lock behind him.

ELEVEN

As much as I wanted to steal the paintings or just stand and bask in their beauty, I knew I needed to get out of there. I couldn't trust Tony B to let me go. Between his veiled remark about the snuffbox and this revelation, I knew about murder and theft on a grand scale. And even with the Danger Twins in custody, Tony B's lawyers would have a difficult time disassociating their client from my allegations.

The room had been carefully constructed to maintain proper temperature and humidity. There were no other doors or windows. Tunneling through the air-conditioning system seemed my singular option. The air vent was on the far wall and up near the ceiling. I made a few mental calculations, then from my Fendi-full-of-goodies, I extracted a small flathead screwdriver and scooted a nearby ugly brown chair closer to the potential escape route. A few quick turns of each screw and I could see inside.

The space would be tight but worked in my favor, since I didn't think any of Tony B's muscle team could follow. One problem. While I needed to reach the vent, I didn't want them figuring out right away how I escaped.

Necessitating precautions. I moved the heavy chair back to its original place. I would balance on the upholstered arms to reach the vent. At least that was the plan. Balance would be key, but the chair was heavy, probably to hold the big guys who used this room, and likely offered enough counterbalance for my purpose.

Although it used up several precious minutes, I took a few additional precautions. I put the loose screws back into their holes in the vent cover and pulled a strip of super adhesive squares from my purse. These were the adhesives I used in my extracurricular activities when I needed to affix motion sensors to tip me about prospective hazards. I hoped the strong squares would help shield me from the real and present danger I knew would come soon.

Each adhesive was placed on the vent side of the frame, at each point of a screw. The adhesive had to hold the now cockeyed screws in place to hide the holes, and hopefully act as a temporary way to attach the frame back over my escape hatch. Thinking about that phrase made me wonder about the packet Nico had given me hours ago and how he'd used those same two words. There was no time to investigate, but hopefully he'd have the opportunity to brief me on it later, as promised.

I slid the frame into the vent, backside up as it lay on the tunnel floor, and pushed back enough to give myself a landing zone at the entrance to the opening. The strap of the Fendi went around my neck, leaving my hands free as I crawled through the aluminum maze. It took more effort than I'd planned to balance on the chair arm, and the purse did threaten my center of gravity. I took a few deep breaths. This was no more tricky than some of the jobs I'd successfully accomplished but riskier than most. In those cases I'd faced being unmasked for my efforts and called a criminal instead of a "reclamation angel." In the present circumstances, I likely risked losing my life. I knew too much, and even if I didn't yet understand what I knew, Tony B knew that I knew it, which made all the difference. He could lie about replacing my phone all he wanted, but I wasn't fooled. Someone killed Tina, and since he had the snuffbox, I had to assume Tony B had blood on his hands in a significant way.

Worst of all, I had to accomplish the feat without making any noise. One clunk, a single thump, and I could have My Favorite Thugs barreling through the door.

I mentally calculated height and trajectory from my tentative stance on the chair arm. I steadied myself and mentally prepped for the leap and swing toward my possible exit to freedom.

At the last minute, I stopped and slid off my heels. I risked cutting my foot on the exposed metal rim, but barefoot and able to grab with my toes seemed worth the gamble. The stilettos went into the Fendi, the heels not quite making full clearance.

I knew I'd taken too long when I heard laughter emanate through the wall from the other side of the room. Time for action.

Leaning in, I grasped the framework as tightly as I could, then jumped from the chair, and swung my legs up and through. Made it. Now to hide the evidence. Since I was feet first and on my back, I had to move over the vent cover without being able to look at it. A couple of the adhesives caught me, but overall things went well. I twisted carefully to keep my movements quiet.

Lock picks doubled as an extension of my fingers, helping me reach and lift the vent cover by running the picks through the skinny rows of vent openings. I used my versatile tools as a kind of handle device to guide the cover back. Then I used the picks to pull back on the cover and at the same time put as much pressure as I could against the adhesive to get it to at least look screwed into the wall.

Finishing with seconds to spare, I didn't have room enough to turn around. I crawled backward into the tunnel. I checked over my shoulder to view my options. At the first intersection, I was able to adjust to crawl naturally. About the same time, I heard the cursing from behind me. Distance was now at a greater premium than silence. I moved faster.

On the opposite side of the building, I found a stash of what appeared to be cocaine near a loose vent cover. With a couple of kicks, I had the cover off. I dropped into an empty office and scrabbled behind the desk. I started to grab the phone to call Nico, willing to take the risk a switchboard light somewhere would give Tony B my location, but a surprising thing happened. My Fendi started to hum.

When I pulled out the packet Nico gave to me earlier, I found a burner phone on one end. I ducked down behind the desk and answered.

"Where the hell are you?" Jack bellowed. "We found pieces of your phone behind the gallery. Nico said I could reach you at this number."

"Shh," I whispered. "I'm in Tony Berintino's office building. I was kidnapped by two of his thugs and brought here. I'm going to try to make it to the roof and use the fire escape to get away. Get Nico to track my location from this line and meet me on the street under the fire escape."

"All right, but be careful. The wind has really whipped up. Are you sure you don't want us to send in the police?"

I thought about the snuffbox hidden in the Fendi and knew I needed to get away ASAP. Cops could take too long, especially with the kind of influence Tony B may control. "No. No cops. If you aren't there when I get down, I'll run to the nearest busy public place I can find."

"Nico says we're two minutes from your location."

"Good. I'm heading for the roof now. Good-bye."

"Laurel!"

"What?" I whispered back.

"Just...oh, God...be bloody careful."

"This wasn't my fault, Jack."

"It never is."

I cut the line before either of us said any more. There wasn't time to waste. I slipped out of the office and into the hallway, ducking into recesses whenever I heard voices. I pulled a dental mirror I kept in my bag and used it to check around corners before I took the risk of moving. When I passed a fire extinguisher cabinet and alarm, I thought for a second about pulling the red bar. But doing so offered to give away my location without providing any additional insurance. I'd already told the guys not to send police. Having a team of firefighters storm the building meant the same risk. Tony B could call me a trespasser and have the Danger Twins back him up. I'd get arrested and he would walk out of this mess without a scratch.

Danger Twin number two almost caught me once, but I

slipped into a supply closet he'd searched a minute before, and that's where I struck gold. A diagram on the narrow wall showed I was a short jog away from the stairs to the roof. I slid back out of the door and used the dental mirror to watch both Danger Twins enter separate hallways and disappear from sight.

The door was six feet away. I ran, still barefoot, and twisted the lever to open the door. There was no sound as the door opened, and I slipped into the stairwell, but as I pushed against the door to hurry the hydraulic closer, a high-pitched squeal sounded.

I left it closing on its own and flew up the stairs, hearing my pursuers thunder down the hallway.

The weather was wicked as I broke through the exit to the roof. I felt like I'd entered a wind tunnel and had to lay against the door to get it latched again. A dozen steel rods lay discarded six feet away. I dove for one and shoved it under the doorknob of the roof access mere seconds before the thugs hit the heavy door. I bounced my weight on the bar one more time for luck. The knob wiggled in obvious anger but could not be turned.

I ignored the risk to my feet and did a quick jog around the perimeter, matching my pace to the pounding rhythms my enemies made trying to reach me. The fire escape was a no-go. Tony B called in reinforcements. A van sat below the final drop. Worse, I saw another hood climb from the driver's seat with a long iron hook and watched him grapple the lower of the raised rungs to pull down the fire escape ladder. I called the guys.

"Jack! Nico!" I yelled into the cell phone, hoping one of them could hear me over the wind's roar. "I'm on the roof, and they've completely cut me off. I'll try to stop the guy coming up the fire escape, but I need you to get below to cut off the others if they circle back to the van."

"No, jump instead," Jack yelled over the speaker. "I'll be on the south side."

"I can't jump a dozen stories!"

"Use the chute," Nico said.

"You packed me a chute?" I was touched.

"Of course he did," Jack said. "It's in that packet he gave you today. We each have one. You're no use to us crippled."

Okay, now things were back to normal. "Thanks, guys."

I again pulled the packet from my bag and hurried to the far end of the building. It was a mini-chute, fine for nice days but not for the current gale force. I didn't weigh enough for this wind shear. I'd be tossed around like a blond leaf.

My gaze returned to the pile of discarded rods. Heavy rods.

I pulled the snuffbox free of its silken wrapping, then returned it to the hidden pocket. The Hermes scarf went tight around my right pant leg at the ankle, and I tied a secure knot. Then I unbuttoned my slacks and shoved as many of the long steel pieces as I could down the leg. The scarf held everything. A splayed bungee cord skittered across the roof. I snatched it, used the line to tie the other pant leg, and repeated the process with the rods. Fastening the slacks again was a challenge, but I prayed the experiment held for the short-term.

Hook Man shouted as he cleared the roof's parapet. I dropped off the other side of the building.

Free falling can be both dangerous and exhilarating at the same time. When you're dropping between buildings in a heavy storm, the angry clouds turning everything as dark as evening despite the clock showing midday, common sense would tell anyone to be afraid. But be seconds away from possible death or dismemberment—and jumping with a makeshift plan is the only option—the needle on the reality scale makes a definite slide to the exhilaration end of the spectrum.

I hung onto the metal rings that kept my small fluorescent yellow parachute steady as I dropped toward the pavement. The wind pushed me far off target. Nonetheless, Jack had the car, this time a Mercedes sedan, beside me as my feet hit the asphalt. Nico's strong arms pushed me into the car's shotgun position, which was good since I could not bend my legs at the knee. He dove into the backseat. I reclined my seat back as far as possible and simultaneously slammed the door. We screeched through the next light before I'd barely taken a second breath. I looked over to the driver's side. The dash lights illuminated Jack's profile, showing an expression as stormy as the weather outside.

At that moment, I knew there were layers of Jack I might never learn.

After Jack's secrecy that morning I'd planned on slipping out of Miami with only Nico in tow. With Jack having aided in my rescue, on the other hand, there left little I'd be able to do to shake his shadow. Might as well show him my prize.

"I found something in Tony B's office," I said, extracting the snuffbox. "This look familiar?"

"Is that—" Jack cursed as he almost hit another car. "How? Is there anything inside?"

"Simon sent it to Tina," I answered as I shined my tiny flash onto the snuffbox and found it empty. "No, there's nothing inside."

"Your friend Tina who's—"

"Dead. Right."

"Who's dead?" Nico asked from the backseat. I gave him a quick synopsis. He whistled.

Jack dodged another truck, then asked, "How did it get into Tony B's office?"

"I think you know the answer to that."

"You have no proof he killed her, right? Just supposition."

I shrugged and played the light over the maker's mark that appeared on the bottom of the object. "His goons broke my phone. I couldn't call for help. Then they transported me in the trunk of their car. A big black Mercedes, by the way. Can we please not use this brand of car for a while?"

"Your point is valid. We'll go with Audis or BMWs next time," Nico responded. "You see anything on the snuffbox?"

I passed the small treasure between the seats so he could have a look for himself. "Check out the marks, then stash it in your backpack. Check it out better when we get to London. Now though, take a moment to look closely at the marks. There's something off about them, but I'm not sure what."

He took my flashlight and within seconds said, "It's a fake. Created by a counterfeiter in Florence. I know the mark well from my research. Either Simon switched this one with the original, or Max's initial source on the piece is bogus."

Florence. Italy again. My original rendezvous to pick up the snuffbox was in Italy, and now this Florence connection after I'd found the missing article with Tony B. What did it mean? Well, I knew one thing for sure—we weren't going home to London until we made an exploratory detour to check out this new connection.

"Are you thinking what I'm thinking?" Jack asked.

"We are, if you're thinking that we'll find some answers with a side trip to Italy."

"That's exactly what I'm thinking."

As Nico zipped the snuffbox into his pack, I asked, "Can you get the three of us on the first flight to Florence?"

"Already on it," he said, activating his phone. "Destination the Aeroporto di Firenze-Peretola."

TWELVE

Airport restrooms were never my favorite places to change clothes, but at least they provided privacy and access to mirrors and water. The Fendi went onto the hook of the lavatory door as I regretfully removed the linen suit. The lovely outfit lasted less than a day in my care. Not that it was my fault, but the designer threads really weren't made to double as protective clothing in a great escape. The Fendi already looked road weary as well. Maybe I needed to find a designer who worked in Kevlar for all my clothes and accessories. The one amazing survivor was Cassie's Hermes scarf. My grandfather may have worn Rolex, but he always owned Timex stock and quoted the catch line of its ads, "Takes a licking and keeps on ticking." Forget that old watch commercial—good silk is the stuff that can really take a licking.

At least I had my gray dress from the day before, tightly rolled up in the bottom of my bag. Thank goodness for sturdy knits, even if the dress and I could both use a good shower. Nothing but those dratted air dryers hung on the wall. I used the insides of the linen jacket to scrub my hands, legs, and feet. My poor feet had taken the brunt of the landing since I was barefoot when I skidded to the ground. The pockets on the linen jacket had been useless for holding anything but served as perfect padding to go between my scraped heels and the Manolo Blahniks. Finally, I shoved the remaining material into a trash receptacle, gave the Hermes scarf a good handwashing, and tied it on the strap of the Fendi to dry. A quick cosmetic redo left me once again feeling more human. Nothing like a confident shade of red lipstick to straighten a girl's backbone.

The guys saved me a seat at the gate, but Jack was pacing when I got there.

"What took you so bloody long?"

Ah, he cared. Or it bugged the alpha male when he wasn't in complete control. Naturally, I assumed the second option.

"Well, I hope the time I spent was worth it." I smiled. "I'm trying to look less like a bag lady."

He reached for my hand, and I shied away when he touched my scraped palm. After examining the skin, he said, "Let me see if the boarding clerk has a first aid kit."

"No need." Nico dragged his black backpack from the seat beside him and rummaged around until he found adhesive bandages and a small tube of antibacterial ointment.

"Thanks." I took the items and sat in the chair that originally held the backpack. "I probably need to slather this ointment all over my feet, more than on my hands."

Nico shrugged. "Feel free. It is yours."

I started with my hands and got Jack to set the bandages across the worst of the scrapes. Then I found a couple of cotton balls in the Fendi and applied the rest of the ointment to my feet. I think Jack was afraid I was going to ask him for a foot massage, because he suddenly found a reason to leave.

"How about if I go and find us coffee?" He didn't even wait for a response and took off trekking down the concourse.

I tried unsuccessfully to get comfortable in the plastic seats in the regular waiting area of Miami International. We'd made a group decision on the way to the airport to stay away from the airline club lounges. That was likely the first place Tony B would send spies to look for me. I reminded myself survival was preferable to deep upholstery, and the tingling of my feet and hands at the moment helped reinforce my resolve.

Nico bumped my shoulder with his to get my attention.

"What?" I asked.

He never took his eyes from his phone as he spoke. "I will be trailing off when we hit London Gatwick for the transfer to

Florence. I have a few things to check out. Call if you need me, but I am not much for fieldwork, you know."

I did know. As instrumental as Nico was in helping with my recent rescue, since the cell phone and chute he gave me truly saved my skin, actual involvement in the nuts and bolts of a recovery was not something in which he usually participated. "Still, I'm glad you didn't give me the event pass in Miami and leave."

"I try never to leave things half finished."

"Just know I appreciate you."

"I do." He raised his curly black head, and his dark brown eyes shifted from the screen. "But given what did happen during the event, I am not crazy about putting you on a commercial jet to Florence right now, with Tony B probably checking all flights out of Miami. And I don't want him connecting you with Jack. You said the museum director knew him. That they have history."

"Yes."

"And the museum director is cozy with Tony B. She's probably already mentioned that you both arrived in Miami together."

"Again, yes. We need to stay under the radar. We've already boycotted the lounges. What else do you suggest?" I asked.

He pressed his screen a couple of times, then typed a text message before he answered. "I think it would be a good idea for you and Jack to arrive separately in Florence."

"You think he'd go for that?"

"Absolutely not. Here is what I have planned." He pressed another button, then his head jerked in the direction Jack had disappeared minutes before. I looked at the screen and realized he had a tracker on Jack. Sneaky.

Nico fired off a string of quiet curse words, then spoke rapidly. "He's on his way. Listen carefully. Your ticket and mine are booked together under a Beacham account. Jack's ticket is on a separate revenue stream to keep Tony B from putting all of us together. When we hit Gatwick, I leave, and you'll be met by a scruffy rock-and-roll roadie who is going to take you to a private jet. If Tony B checks, it will look like you stayed in London. The heavy metal group Whyte Noyse is performing in Rome, but they have a private party plane chartered that will drop you at the Florence Peretola Airport en route."

"Sounds loud." I loved rocking out to the ear-bleeding cuts on *Nyght Noyses*, but I'd heard many things about the group, and none sounded any quieter than their music. There went my chance to grab any sleep as we skipped through time zones. "But it does sound much safer. How did you manage it?"

"Their English publicist, Patricia, loves my body." His grin was almost evil.

"She's not the only one."

"Who's not the only one?" Jack settled back into the chair beside me, offering us a choice from a trio of cappuccinos.

"One of Nico's conquests. He's leaving us in London to stay on her good side." I winked at Nico. He frowned and turned back to his cell phone screen. I twisted in my chair toward Hawkes. "Any plans once we get there?"

"I'm working some sources," Jack said. "While we're cramped on a plane for fifteen hours, it will give Cecil and Max ample opportunity to work their lines of communication. They should at least have something for us to see once we reach our long layover at Gatwick."

Cecil was Jack's boss, the counterpart to my pain-in-the-ass Max. I'd never met Cecil, but from the negative murmurs that repeatedly escaped Jack's lips, the two superiors seemed of the same penny-pinching type. However, no one could hope to reach and sustain their level of responsibility without making connections along the way. I counted on those connections to make a difference in our present situation.

Jack leaned around me to address Nico. "Wasn't there anything more direct?"

Nico shrugged, never taking his gaze or his thumbs off his phone screen when he answered. "Best I could do in a rush. Can't get to Florence Peretola except from Gatwick. Flight out of Heathrow would have been faster, but you would need to go to the

Galileo Airport and have the longer commute in from Pisa. Thought this was better. Plus, gives you both time to get clothes at home before the next flight."

"Bloody hell, there is that." It appeared Jack was getting both tired and cranky.

I glanced down at my own outfit, wrinkled from being worn all of yesterday, stuffed in the Fendi when I left the yacht, and pulled out for another go after ruining the lovely linen suit playing Rat in the AC Maze and then Rocky the Flying Squirrel. The burner phone was in my hand to call and ask Cassie to put me an assortment of clothes together, until I changed my mind and let the cell drop back into the Fendi's dark depths. I didn't want Jack hearing our discussion, and I had no idea where she should meet me at Gatwick.

"Nico, can you text Cassie for me and ask her to bring a rolling bag with a good selection of clothing? I don't know what I'll need in the next few days, but since I'm back to recycling yesterday-wear, I can use everything. Be sure and give her a good idea on where she can either leave the bag for me or meet me. Right?"

He lifted his chin when he realized what my words implied. "Got it. I will add a phone number in case she needs it."

"She has your number," Jack said.

"Not the burner number, remember?" I knew Nico meant the number of either the publicist or the roadie. Something Jack didn't need to know. But his question reminded me. "Ask her to bring me a new corporate cell phone too, to replace my smartphone. Have her key in the list of 'gotta have numbers'. She has the list from when I borrowed her phone last time."

Nico nodded as his fingers flew over the touch pad.

Minutes later, they called our flight. I didn't think it was an accident Nico had us scattered throughout the plane. He may have even picked our flight for this reason. I enjoyed a first-class seat, but he and Jack had to stick it out in coach. Jack tried to sweet talk the attendant into an upgrade, but the flight was overbooked as it was, and we were just squeaking in. I turned off all gadgets, stowed my gear, and settled in for a nice quiet ride across the Atlantic, hoping for a little shut-eye along the way.

My seatmate was even more antisocial than I felt. He threw his bag into the overhead compartment, then removed his suit jacket to place it carefully on top, grunting something I perceived as a hello. I offered a tight smile, regardless of the meaning. He sat down, crossed his arms, closed his eyes, and seemed to feel the world had disappeared from his dimension. I couldn't have been more pleased. Outside, the storm was gathering quickly and the winds growing stronger. I hoped our pilot got us to cruising altitude quickly to avoid the sudden drops that happened on flights like this. I needed a distraction.

"Do you happen to have a copy of today's *Guardian*?" I asked as the attendant passed to close the drapes between our section and coach.

"I'll check in a sec."

Everyone thinks they have to bring their own reading material, or make do with what's in the seat pocket ahead of them. Laurel Beacham Travel Tip Number One—never touch anything left in the seat pockets. *Ick*. All those horror stories that sound like someone's imagination, they're not only true, they're worse. Thank goodness for travelers who hand magazines and newspapers to flight attendants as they leave. I really wanted to see tomorrow's *Miami Herald*, but since that wasn't possible without a time machine, I figured I may as well try to catch up on news from London.

The takeoff was rocky, and the initial climb as I expected, but the attendant did find an almost complete *Guardian*. I forced myself to concentrate on the pages. News from London was typical: another royal brouhaha with dodgy news outlet illegally hacking phones and Twitter feeds, and Parliament was in the middle of more familiar shenanigans—same old, same old. I scanned the details to be able to make polite cocktail talk at parties. Also to make sure I didn't offer the wrong quip if I ever ran into one of the guilty parties. That's the real purpose of staying current with the news.

Ah, but here was something interesting. An international real estate ad offering a luxury palazzo apartment. Sixteenth-century Florentine architecture, and in the shadow of the Pitti Palace. I knew Nico was working on accommodations for us, and while this was likely out of my price range, I wondered if Max could pull a few strings to make me an elegant squatter while the apartment was still in the "showing" state. Or not, since I wasn't too pleased with Max at the moment and his inability to keep my working locations confidential. It might be worth schmoozing my contact at Sotheby's to see if he could run interference for me with its international real estate division. Lots more goodies than rare art were handled by prestigious auction houses these days. I folded that page of the paper, then shoved it into the Fendi. When the flight attendant came around with our lovely filet mignon dinner on real china—I think coach had chicken in heat-and-eat trays, poor Jack and Nico—I passed along the remainder of the newspaper for the next traveler.

Dinner was fine. Even my seatmate roused himself for the three or four minutes it took him to inhale the steak and a bourbon. As he drifted back to sleep, I devoured a surprisingly elegant chocolate dessert and contemplated stealing the one still sitting on the sleeping lug's plate. Even I wouldn't give up chocolate for sleep. But I saved my stealth talents for another venue. Not because I didn't want the brownie fudge concoction, but because the attendant came by and picked up his dishes seconds before I made my move.

The beauty of eastward travel is the way the journey erases time zones along the way. In our case, the five hours between U.S. eastern daylight time and London. When traveling after noon, it means darkness comes even more quickly. My eyes dimmed long before the lights were lowered. The attendant offered a real pillow and blanket—I did love first class—and I was set.

* * *

"Laurel, wake up."

I felt like I was swimming out of cotton wool. When I finally got my eyes nearly open, Jack sat where sleeping lug had been snoozing. Nico stood in the aisle looking nervous.

I stretched to look around but saw everyone else still seated in the dimly lit cabin. I leaned back against my pillow and felt my eyes close.

"Laurel! Wake up. You have to see this." Jack's voice hovered just above a whisper, but the urgency of his tone snapped me out of my slump.

"What? Are we landing?"

"We're a couple of hours away. But Nico pulled security footage from the Browning event. You need to watch this." Jack queued up the video.

"How did you get—"

"No questions, Laurel. Look at what Jack is showing you." Nico pointed to the screen, then crossed his arms. "I was trying to find out when Tony B left the event. I saw who he was talking to as you were taken away."

"Yeah. This guy look familiar to you?" Jack held the screen closer to my face. I watched the Danger Twins drag me for a second before we disappeared out of the frame. In the top half of the screen, I saw the clutch of "beautiful people" mill around in the lobby, their mission to see everyone and be seen by the same. Jack tapped a fingertip at the upper right-hand corner, and I finally saw what they meant. Tony B buttonholed a younger man, laughing and slapping the fellow on the shoulder. His skinny bitch of a wife walked over and pointed in the direction where my image had disappeared a minute earlier. My Favorite Felon leaned in then and whispered something in the other man's ear. That's when I got my best look at who Tony B exited the building with a moment later.

The other guy was Rollie. Devin Moran's grandson and heir apparent to the mastermind's criminal empire.

THIRTEEN

Our party broke up when my fellow first-class passenger returned from the bathroom and wanted his seat again. Nico took his phone and trekked back to coach. I assumed Jack would do the same, but no.

I heard a ding sound overhead, and the Fasten Seat Belts sign flashed back on.

"Look, mate." Jack stood and pulled out his wallet, counting out a bunch of bills. "I'll pay you to trade seats with me. What will it take?"

"I don't want to change seats," my frumpy fellow passenger said. His voice was so deep I almost couldn't understand him. "I want first class. I bought a first-class ticket. And I'm staying in first class."

The guy slid back into his seat and Jack tried once more, but I could see the effort was fruitless. My lug was there to stay. I held up a hand. "Jack, see if one of your neighbors will change with me, and I'll—"

The flight attendant interrupted us. "I'm sorry, sir, but the captain has turned on the seat belt sign. We're hitting turbulence, and you need to return to your seat."

Jack deflated for a moment. I gave a crooked smile and shrugged. He swept his gaze in a semicircle, and I knew he was going to try to bribe another passenger. Which told me he really wanted first class more than he wanted me in coach to talk. But the attendant pulled rank instead. "Sir, I really must insist you go back to your own seat immediately."

The plane waffled right then, and Jack fell against our seat backs. He took the opportunity to tell me, "We need to talk about this. Figure things out. Do some planning."

I nodded. But while a jillion thoughts shot through my brain, the one that seemed to set up residence was the message Moran had tried to kidnap me again. I'd gotten away before thanks to quick thinking, the rush hour crowds in the London Tube, and an innocent businessman who would likely forever stay clear of women in high heels. More importantly, this time Moran's hired help didn't seem as averse to actually getting rid of me.

Had Rollie been in the office while Tony B kept me trapped? When I met Rollie a couple of weeks ago he'd seemed like a really nice French guy. Later, I learned he was not the innocent he appeared to be at first glance. So what did I think now? Besides what an idiot I was for not seeing through his persona?

Truthfully, I felt frozen. Like someone had tased my brain. Rollie had actually been there onsite when the kidnapping occurred in Miami, talking to Tony B as it all went down. Obviously things were stepping up somewhere in the game plan. We were either getting close or Moran saw us as a growing risk.

This new information also meant it was going to be damned difficult getting away from Jack at Gatwick. I needed to take every advantage I could. Rollie and Jack already met, and I had little doubt Moran knew who Hawkes was in detail. But us being together again—in Miami, then London, then Florence—would confirm we were still working new angles of the same job. A job whose outcome hopefully meant the fall of Devin Moran's empire.

An hour later, the plane touched down, and I was out of the fuselage and off the plane long before the guys had a chance to waylay me. Oddly enough, I could thank my anal seatmate for the perk. Though he wouldn't accommodate Jack earlier, he allowed me to slip around him when he held up the line moving forward as he again donned his suit jacket and withdrew his bulging carry-on from the overhead compartment.

I texted Nico to explain to Jack. We needed no scenes in an airport, and I had no doubt after the Rollie footage that Jack would be even more determined to play my bodyguard. I could give him my logical ideas on why splitting up was even more critical, but he wasn't going to buy it unless the idea came from his brain. Too late.

As promised, a scruffy type who was bearded and disheveled in well-worn jeans and a black leather vest, and pretty much met everyone's stereotype of a rock-and-roll roadie, stood a few feet past customs with a sign reading L. BEACHAM. I waved to show him I'd arrived and queued up at the shortest customs line.

While some of the contents of my bag usually elicited a few interesting questions, I sailed through this brief search and interrogation unscathed. Traveling light had its benefits.

The roadie held up a large wheeled bag I recognized as my own and said, "A pretty lass with pink-tipped hair left this for you."

"Yes, that was Cassie."

"Okay then. Let's roll." He tossed my bag like it weighed nothing, and the luggage landed in the back of a waiting golf cart. I assumed a full bag of luggage was nothing after manhandling huge electric amplifiers and stage boards. He waved me toward the passenger side, and I hopped in beside him. I turned back and saw Jack run into the customs zone just as we zipped toward the exit. I untied the scarf from my purse strap and covered my head. A second later I'd added my sunglasses. I'd have to take them off to climb the stairs to the plane. But since it was a rock group's charter, my disguise could easily be chalked up to a publicity-shy celebrity instead of my wanting to stay incognito in case any of Moran's watchers manned the airport.

The roadie gave my new look nary a glance. I was really beginning to like this guy.

"I'm Clive, by the way," my escort told me, holding out a callused right hand as he used his left to steer the cart out of the building and onto the tarmac. "Patricia said you're a good egg and you won't grass all our secrets to the press."

"I thought grass was when someone narced to the police. It

works with the press too?" When he frowned at me, I quit my musing. "Sorry. Whatever. Yes, I'll keep anything quiet from the press. They've never really been my friends either."

Well, some were, but I didn't think Clive wanted to hear me dither on. And his opening up with this line made me wonder what kind of drug use I might witness on the plane. Not that drug use would surprise any of the press. I would have thought the group's image actually required that kind of thing broadcasted. "Look, as far as drugs—"

He held up a hand as we neared what appeared to be our jet. I don't know one private plane from another, but the musical cacophony coming out of this one pretty much spelled out Whyte Noyse to me.

"Here." He handed me a pair of earplugs and leaned closer so he wouldn't have to shout. "Wear them until we take off. I'll make introductions after we're in the air."

Okay.

The earplugs were cushy, and when in Rome and all of that... He grabbed my luggage bag from the back. I had to get myself up the ladder before Jack had a chance to spot me on the tarmac. Thanks to the long transatlantic flight and the time zone difference, dawn was struggling to peek out over the horizon. I needed to get into the noisy plane as soon as possible. Yes, the thought sounded crazy even to my earplugged ears.

Band members were still boarding, lugging their own stuff up the portable stairs. I was halfway, stuck behind a couple of leather-clad Whyte Noyse members and bookended in back by my roadie escort, when everything stopped. Something wasn't fitting into the hatch door. I nearly panicked, wondering if Jack would leap out of the concourse doors at any second. Since half the band wore shaded glasses, I put mine back on and scrunched down. I'd have to be careful as I climbed. I fiddled with my shoe, trying to pretend I wasn't hiding behind dark lenses and the metal sides of the stairs. I peeked over the railing to see if Jack had made it through customs and followed us, then I caught my breath.

It wasn't Jack I had to worry about. Standing outside one of the nearby hangers, directly under a light pole, was a rather disreputable looking guy in a duffle jacket. I lowered my lenses to better see over the top of the frame. As the man took a toke from his cigarette and pulled his hand from his face, I was sure. I'd spent agonizing minutes looking at that face. I folded up my own trench coat less than a month ago to make a pillow and try to keep him comfortable before the EMTs arrived at the London docks. He was Jestin Jones, the man I first knew as the smelly Welshman. Last I'd seen of him was at the London Docks when he'd been whisked away by an ambulance in a near death state. He obviously was alive and kicking. And he was one of Simon's henchmen.

FOURTEEN

I had to get Jack into this. The noise level was too awful to call him, and the riotous music would give my precise position away if he was outside the airport. He'd home in on my exact current location. The only recourse was to text him and hope he recognized the number. The burner phone was in my hands, and my thumbs were flying in seconds.

"Hey, no." Clive snatched the cell from my fingers. "I told your friend when she brought the other mobile phone for you that I keep all visitors' mobiles until the plane lands. We don't need any surreptitious tweets or embarrassing shots on Facebook or Instagram."

He turned off the phone and started to place it in his jacket pocket.

"No, please." Down below the rail level, I raised enough to peek over the bar and point out the now alive and smoking Welshman. "The guy over there? Standing in front of the hanger? He's wanted by the police. I have a friend in the airport who's connected with British intelligence. I was texting him to alert him to handle the takedown.

The roadie squinted one eye at me, then turned and followed the direction of my finger. Truthfully, the rumpled Welshman in his dull duffle coat looked far from dangerous. We watched him move around, then grab a clipboard when it looked like one of the actual working crew questioned his need to be onsite. The answer apparently satisfied the Welshman's accuser, or the poor crewman was too overworked to care, because he waved a hand as if disgusted and walked away. The Welshman leaned back against the building to finish a last drag on his cigarette, tossed the butt, and ground it under his heel.

I held out my hand. "Please. Believe me. I know what I'm talking about."

Clive shook his head for a moment, then said, "Okay, but I want it back right after. No mobile phones on the plane."

"Promise."

A second after I'd fired off my text to Jack, I returned the phone to Clive with my thanks. The gang above us finally managed to force their oversized container through the door with a lot of cursing and an abundance of elbow grease. I kept my head turned away as I made my way up the last few steps.

Clive hustled me over to a leather couch on the side of the plane where we could watch the Welshman. The roadie handed me a pair of binoculars, keeping a digital camera with a long lens for himself. I expected to see Jack but instead witnessed several airport security personnel scurrying over to the man. Apparently they asked for ID, because the Welshman patted his pockets as if searching for a wallet. He started to pull something from a pocket, then faked a move left and went right, tearing off around the corner of the building with the rent-a-coppers following close behind.

A minute later, an even larger crowd returned to view, with Jack now appearing in the frame as he restrained the struggling Welshman by holding the man's arms locked behind his body.

"Good show!" Clive yelled over the noise of the speakers. I think he snapped a couple of pictures too, but between the earplugs and the pounding bass coming from the speakers, I couldn't hear the clicks to be sure.

Clive slapped me on the back. "Good show," he repeated. I think he added something about being right back, and he moved toward the front of the plane. I wasn't sure what a roadie did, but Clive seemed to be "a man for all rock seasons," and I assumed he had plenty of tasks to check off his list.

The luxurious leather couch where Clive left me felt like a million-dollar hug. People continued filing onto the plane. The interior was predominantly leather, a buckskin color and blond on the scattered couches and captain's chairs. All of the wood surfaces were stained a honey-oak color.

The Whyte Noyse musicians and crew, dressed mostly in black leather and jeans, steadily loaded equipment, running in and out of the door or roving the cabin when their stuff was aboard. Everyone seemed friendly, nodding a greeting to me, which was about all anyone could accomplish in the heavy-metal haven. Several of the band members looked drunk or half asleep when they first stepped onto the plane but perked up within a minute or so. Despite the early morning hour for Brits whose biorhythms were set to Greenwich. The quick transformation left me wanting to do some head scratching.

In the front of the cabin, I saw a fully stocked bar and galley kitchen. The half wall hiding part of the kitchen boasted a lovely built-in cabinet, which obviously secreted a supersized television screen. A closed door led to areas presumably kept private. Everything was neat and functional. Not what I expected in a rock-and-roll party plane. Well, beyond the volume button stuck on ear-bleeding, of course.

The noise was getting old fast, and I half contemplated taking my leave and finding alternative passage. But not before the flight attendant closed and locked the hatch, making my decision for me. Everyone immediately found seats and buckled up. Clive came back and sat beside me. He still had the camera and continued to fiddle with the viewer. The takeoff was as smooth as any I'd ever experienced. As I felt the landing gear retract beneath us, the musical cacophony suddenly stopped.

"Will it come back on again?" I asked.

"Not until we start to land," Clive said. "Appearances, you know."

Ah, I did know. That's what he meant about not "grassing to the press." I looked around and saw the heavy metal rockers quietly talking and reading. The drummer had earbuds in his Kindle. I assumed he was listening to an audiobook.

"It's all a front?"

Clive shrugged. "The boys know how to party, but as we've gotten older, we've found we don't need to do so much of it anymore." He pressed a button on the camera and turned the view screen my way. "Got a couple of good 'uns, I did. They nailed that bloke good."

I peered closely at the takedown. Jack looked truly in his element. "I couldn't by chance get a couple of these, could I?"

"Sure. Give me an email address, and I'll send the whole lot to you."

I withdrew my wallet and found one of my business cards. "Thank you, Clive. I'd like to send them to my friend."

"The one what got 'im, eh?"

"Yes." *The one what got 'im,* indeed.

As soon as the flight attendant signaled we could move around the cabin, Clive unbuckled his seat belt and motioned me to follow him.

"Gordon made me promise to fetch you for him. He's a big art collector, and when Patricia told us who was doing a ride along, old Gord recognized your name right away." Clive stopped and ran a hand over his cheeks, his fingernails playing a scritchy refrain over the couple of days' worth of whiskers. He leaned toward me, brushing my arm as he said, "A bit o' warning, love. Gord's a great bloke, but he can get a mite...focused...you know?"

I could only imagine, and my face must have shown my guarded understanding, because he quickly added, "Nothing bad, see, but he gets fixated. It can annoy people. This isn't really a long flight, you know, and sometimes he gets on a subject. And if you wouldn't mind..."

Was he kidding? After they saved me the time and trouble of flying commercial? Not to mention giving me a way to sneak around any operatives Tony B had watching out for me.

"Don't worry." I placed a hand on his forearm as I spoke. "I've spent a lifetime around people who love art and want to talk exclusively about their favorite artists and works."

The relief on his face spoke volumes. He smiled and motioned for me to again follow him. But first things first.

"Clive, I've been traveling in these clothes for a couple of days now." Okay, so it wasn't consecutive time frames, but I wasn't skirting the truth by much. I looked down at my brave, trusty gray knit dress, then looked back up at Clive. "I'd really like to change before I meet new people."

"Sure, gotcha. The loo is this way." He motioned me through the door I had already guessed led to a toilet and dressing rooms and found instead it held a conference table and a couch I assumed pulled out into a bed. Alrighty, then. Not what I expected but then neither had much of anything else about this flight. Clive closed the connecting door, and I was left with the space to myself.

The bathroom was larger than a conventional airline toilet but not anything to get excited about. There were real towels with good soap—how nice—and I took my time luxuriating in the little niceties.

I pulled a sapphire wrap dress from my bag and thanked the heavens once again for giving me Cassie and her common-sense approach to life and travel. A few minutes to retouch my makeup and artfully toss my curls, and I was set to go. The gray dress went into a handy plastic bag my thoughtful assistant included and was zipped into one of the outer pockets of the bag.

I felt human again and ready to meet a rock star or four.

Clive was still by the door when I exited back into the public part of the cabin and walked me around to make introductions. I knew everyone's names and faces, but I had little opportunity to chat as the roadie systematically herded me toward the bass guitarist who sat near the galley in obvious anticipation of our meeting.

Clad in head-to-toe black, even his shoulder-length hair dyed an unrelieved ebony, Gordon Silver was the defining image of aging rocker. When he began talking I immediately understood what Clive meant and why he'd offered the subtle warning about Gordon's *focus*. "Laurel Beacham. I've been looking forward to meeting you. I want to add pieces to my collection, and I was wondering..."

And I went temporarily on autopilot. It was no problem, since he handled the monologue quite well on his own. From the way Gordon launched into his preferred topic and mostly kept his gaze slanted away from mine, I presumed some level of highly socialized Asperger's. Now in his late forties or early fifties, he may not have been actually diagnosed as a kid, but likely enjoyed a large family or friendship circle who helped him through support and acceptance and let him evolve out of the stereotype of the syndrome.

He tumbled headlong into an immediate waxing of affection for art—and particularly for his personal collection. "Acquired my first Constable when I attended an *Antiques Roadshow* event at Belton House. Still remember the gardens and the blue of the sky. Brilliant. The National Trust opened the grounds up to the *Roadshow* crew and visitors that day, and I stood there under the lovely azure heavens along with the rest of the hordes. Thousands of us came."

Backstories like these always made me smile, and I let him patter on for a while until I realized he was stuck in a circle. I prompted, "What did you take for appraisal?"

"Nothing important." He made a face, and I assumed his valuation by the experts came in at a disappointing level. He continued, "What's more important is what I took away. Wandered down a bit to do a lookie-loo, and that's when the paintings bloke, Philip Mould, took a turn inspecting the old paintings what people trotted out of their attics and grannies' lounges to bring along for the day."

He stopped and tilted his head, staring into the distance. I started to ask for his recollections of the paintings he saw there, but he cut me off. "Gorgeous stuff. Liked it all a lot. Studied music at the Royal Conservatory, and for the first time I saw music in something besides the art we all played on instruments. One painting in particular caught my attention because the blue above perfectly matched the one we were under that day."

Again he stopped and kept his attention riveted once more on a point to his right. It was just the couch Clive and I had sat on, but I felt he was instead seeing rolling green fields and lawns along with well-tended gardens anchoring a stately historic home, all under the fairest of British skies. I waited, contemplating his words about his musical studies. I'd always noticed a classical method below the Whyte Noyse trademark decibel-pumping rock standard, and now I understood why. This day was shaping into one of nonstop surprises and unexpected information.

After a few minutes, Gordon spoke again. "The killer for me was an absolutely brilliant Constable. A landscape that hooked me right here." He covered his head with his left hand and his heart with his right, but he stared at the couch as he spoke. "The genius of the man. I'd been to the Royal Gallery in London and seen Constable's work before, but until that day at the Belton House *Roadshow* event, I truly hadn't tumbled onto what his art really said."

The flight attendant came by with a tray. "I have cappuccino, Americano, and espresso. And I'll bring along pastries in a moment."

Gordon took a sip from his tiny cup of espresso and picked up where he'd left off. "Constable grew up in Suffolk, like me. But my father wasn't a mill owner. I know the country Constable painted. Even once he moved into London circles, he still went back to Suffolk, the home county, you know, to paint the scenes he'd known ever since childhood."

I knew how Constable's landscapes created a harmony between the nature he loved and the human beings he usually put in for perspective. Most of his landscapes showed peaceful scenes, with workers at the day's tasks in the distance doing jobs like cutting hay. "I always liked *The Hay Wain* the best, I think."

"Love that one." Gordon actually smiled directly at me for a second. "That's on the Stour River. And you know the house on the left side of the painting, under the trees? It's known as Willy Lott's Cottage."

"Anytime I see a Constable, I'm amazed at the way he could always capture nature in the tiny movements."

"Yeah, like the way the shadows ebbed and flowed across the meadows. Like the light was shifting all the time."

Before I could ask what pieces he owned, the rocker switched gears. "I got me a couple of Gainsboroughs too. Both of mine are portraits, but he really wanted to do landscapes. The people in the foreground are fine, yet unremarkable. The setting, though, that's the masterpiece each time. Gainsborough picked up the time of the year beautifully in each of the paintings I own. Both are great estates, with the owners all fancy dress in the close part of the painting, and the landholding sweeping back and circling behind. Summer in one, autumn the other."

"So, do you concentrate on English painters?"

"Pretty much. Would like a J.M.W. Turner, but I keep getting outbid anytime one becomes available. And you really have to have the right space and lighting and all for his work. But I segued out some." He ducked his head and grinned, looking almost like a mischievous schoolboy. "I always liked the Alice books by Lewis Carroll, and I heard about this artist—"

I laughed. I couldn't help myself. At Gordon's shocked expression, Clive hurried over. I spoke quickly. "I'm sorry. I figured you were going to say you added Quinten Massys to your collection. Though the artist is from the Netherlands, it's believed his painting *A Grotesque Old Woman* was the ideal for Sir John Tenniel's illustrations of the Duchess in *Alice in Wonderland*."

A huge grin spread across Gordon's face, and Clive took three slow steps back again.

"That's exactly what I was going to talk about," Gordon said. "Imagine using Leonardo da Vinci's work of grotesque figures to base your painting, *A Grotesque Old Woman,* as a means to give a social statement in the fifteenth century about women who try to look younger than they are."

Yes, the thought occurred to me about the pot calling the kettle black as Gordon sat there in his tight leather pants and pushed his salon-colored hair behind one ear. But I remembered I was a guest, and I knew Clive was counting on me to keep Gordon occupied. Somehow, I didn't think the rock guitarist would appreciate the irony.

My world began tilting though when he pulled a sheath of photos from a leather briefcase standing alongside his chair. He flipped through them and said, "Heard you were at the Browning event. Even saw snaps on social media. What did you think of their setup for the Sebastian exhibit? Getting one of his works is on my bucket list, but only one since he isn't a Brit. But the one I really want was stolen years ago."

He turned his hand to show the top photo, facing out, and I stared at a small archive print of *Juliana*.

I had to clear my throat a couple of times before I could speak. Wordlessly, I took the print from him, placing it in my lap so I could look down and no one would see the tears I knew shined in my eyes. "Yes, I think everyone is under the assumption this piece is in the private collection of some megalomaniac." Maybe the term was over the top to apply to Tony B, but my knees still tingled when I thought of crawling to escape from the gallery room. At the same time, my heart ached because I left without setting *Juliana* free.

I hoped I'd have another chance before Tony B decided to carry out his threat.

FIFTEEN

The ear-bleeding rhythms were cranked up again as we buckled up for landing in Florence. While the rock-and-roll appearances weren't anything I wanted to relive anytime soon, I did hope I'd see the band again. I had a chance to talk to the other members when Gordon finally decided our face time was completed, and the rest seemed like a bunch of regular guys with leather clothes and electric instruments. You know, just boys next door with a trillion rabid fans and the bank accounts to match.

Clive took over my care and maintenance when we landed, all with the band's blessing. He handled my luggage, returned the burner phone, and gave me the new smartphone Cassie had brought along, and he made sure his direct number was loaded in case I needed to reach him or the band later for any contingency. I knew part of my allure was the fact Gordon wanted me as his personal art listener, but I'd had worse gigs, and none of them kept me in the luxury of a private jet. I especially counted my blessings and wished for my very own roadie when I was ushered through customs in the blink of an eye. Then Clive shook my hand and gave me a wink as he turned to stride back to the plane. I headed for the taxi stand.

I texted Nico and Cassie that I'd safely arrived in Florence, then used the burner phone to do the same for Jack and Max. I didn't trust either of the latter at the moment and wanted to be able to rid myself of any inconvenient GPS tracking if I determined I should. I got immediate responses back, positive on the first two and livid abbreviated rantings from the latter micromanaging duo.

When the burner phone started buzzing with a call, I turned it off and decided not to wait to see what happened next. I dropped the now nonemergency phone into the closest trash bin. I'd call Jack later when he had the chance to cool down, but I notified Cassie in the meantime that if he or Max called to tell them I promised to stay in communication. Nothing more. I had a few things to do before I let those two spew at me with their expected rancor. At least the cab ride was short. The reason we'd wanted the Aeroporto di Firenze-Peretola was because downtown Florence sat a mere fifteen-minute cab ride away.

The first cabbie in line was a Florentine native who looked like he could have been Nico's much flirtier cousin. He opened the back door for me with a flourish, then stowed my rolling bag in the back of the small vehicle. A second later he was behind the wheel and firing off incoherent questions, a broad smile flashing across his face.

"English, please." I pointed to myself. "American."

"Ah, Americana." He nodded, then pulled out into traffic. "Destination? Address?"

I knew enough Italian to function, but playing dumb had always served me well. Since Nico was still working on lodging options to hide me from Tony B, I figured I may as well see if my cabbie had better options. With an exaggerated shrug, I shook my head in the negative and said, "I have to find something. Do you know a good place to stay?"

He pursed those beautiful lips, and I knew he was contemplating my clothes and designer accessories. "Four star?" he said, his eyes hopeful.

"No." I shook my head, frowning. I raised a hand and held my thumb about an inch from my index finger. "I'm on a budget."

"Eh...a budget," he said, disappointed. Turning his head to look at me again, he almost sideswiped another vehicle. I don't care what city in Italy I traveled to, I refused to drive myself. If it was that dangerous when a native was driving, I knew I had no hope of getting anywhere in one piece if I was at the helm.

Time to check what cash I had. "Give me a minute," I said, then held up a finger. "*Un minuto.*" I assumed that was right, because he nodded and turned all of his attention back to the road.

I unzipped the smaller side pocket of my luggage and found an envelope Cassie stashed inside. As expected, it contained enough euros to last me several days. And since most of Florence was accessible by a fifteen or thirty-minute walk, I could stretch this money further if I stayed out of any more cabs. "Something reasonable." My cabbie raised his eyebrows in a questioning way, and I held up my finger and thumb again. "Budget. Comfortable but cheap."

"Two star? Three star?" he asked.

"I'd prefer three, but it depends on the price." He acted like he didn't understand, but I figured he knew more English than he let on. Then I had a brainstorm that should have come to me sooner. "A *pensione*? A room is all I need. Please? Close to the Duomo? Or to the Via dei Serragli maybe?" The Palazzo Medici was on the Via dei Serragli, and I had no hope of staying there. But at least it gave him an idea of the area I aspired to and might give him ideas. Apparently, the clues worked.

"Across the Arno?" he asked.

"If it's close."

He nodded and made a quick turn.

I had contacts in Florence, but if I could use the taxi driver to secure my room, I'd be more incognito. Not a perfect plan, but it was a place to start.

At some point, when I had privacy, I needed to get digital face time with Cassie to explain the whole situation to her and get her focused on new tasks. While I needed to keep old loose lips from giving away my current location and everything else, she needed to be the go-between for Max and me. Nico and I had worked too hard to get me to Florence under Tony B's radar, and I needed to keep Max from telling anyone else. Cassie had turned into quite the charmer where he was concerned. I didn't particularly like talking to my boss on a good day—unless I had earplugs to combat the shouting—and this was far from the figurative blue skies kind of moment. Though the literal sky outside my taxi window was pretty close to perfect.

Ten minutes later we were on the Oltrarno side of Florence, and a short street past Via dei Serragli. He pulled up to a nondescript white-and-blue home. The place was small in comparison to its Medici-inspired neighbors. In fact, I think it was once a carriage house or something similar. But my driver opened my door, grabbed my bag, and motioned me to follow him to the front door, my luggage bouncing on its little wheels behind him.

I had no real idea what he told the severe dark-haired woman who greeted us. She thawed a smidgeon it when my driver started talking euros, and I pulled money out to pay him. He quoted another number, looking at the hotelier for confirmation. When she nodded, he flashed his white teeth at me and raised his eyebrows as if proud of the bargaining he'd accomplished on my behalf. The sum was less than I expected, but I also assumed it didn't include any meals. That was fine. A soft bed in a quiet house off the beaten path and off Tony B's or Moran's radar was all I asked. The driver left, and minutes later I was ushered up the narrow stairs and into my accommodations.

The room had a lovely view of the cathedral skyline over the intermediate rooftops and a balcony where I could gaze onto the *signora's* garden. She spoke to me in rapid-fire Italian, of which I knew enough to realize she was asking if the room was satisfactory. "*Sì. Buono.*"

I didn't try anything further. My mind was feeling foggy, and I didn't want to misspeak and risk accidentally saying something offensive. I passed enough euros to cover a week, thanking the heavens that Cassie had sent what money she had. The *signora* actually smiled then, but the facial movement was fleeting, and I almost missed it. She motioned that the toilet was down the hall, and then she finally left me alone.

I sank onto the twin bed, covered with a lovely rose and lace spread. The walls were white, and a crucifix hung over the plain wooden headboard. It was austere but comfortable. A tiny closet was in one corner, and an overstuffed chair upholstered in a muted floral stood in the other, with a pine chest topped by a wood-framed mirror filling the space between. Overall, acceptable. Close to the main part of Florence, and the perfect bolt-hole for someone who needed to venture out yet have a place to run and hide.

There on that lovely lace coverlet, I felt my body start to quiver. My gaze drifted to the window, picking out Brunelleschi's magnificent dome atop the Duomo. I stared hard at the sight, willing myself to calm, for my courage to return once more to the forefront.

I didn't know if it was a form of shock, a symptom of exhaustion, or a large measure of common sense that invaded my physical being, but I soon realized my mind and body were trying to tell me what my stubbornness attempted to ignore. I couldn't do this alone. Not here. Not now.

Tony B could have eyes and ears all over Italy, and we were already here because we presumed Moran had something in play in Florence. And despite all of my safeguards, either of them could play cat and mouse with me as long as it remained interesting, whether I liked it or not.

True, I had resources of my own, people who would keep me safe and work with me as I needed. But I'd acknowledged the risk of trying to reach out in any of those directions. Who was to say that any or all of my contacts hadn't already been compromised? Hadn't already spotted me on my journey in and left a friendly message to that "nice Tony B" who would have called earlier and asked to be alerted if the *signorina* arrived in the city? I already knew Moran's objective was stealing masterpieces, but I had no idea what game Tony B was playing at the moment beyond holding *The Portrait of Three*.

My body shook harder, and I hugged my torso, feeling aghast when tears splashed onto my skirt.

There was only one thing to do. Call the one person I could count on to back me against Moran or Tony B. Nico was out. He hated fieldwork and had reiterated his feelings on the subject back in the Miami airport. Cassie would be in Florence on the next flight if I called her, but an art restorer/personal assistant was not the skill set I needed.

I retrieved my phone from my bag and dialed. The call was picked up immediately.

"Where the bloody hell are you?"

I took a quick breath, then answered, proud of the steady tone in my voice, "Florence. Why would you think otherwise?"

"Meet me at Ghiberti's Doors in fifteen minutes," Jack barked.

"I'll be there in an hour."

He was sputtering as I cut the connection.

SIXTEEN

Before I met Jack, I needed to talk to Cassie. However, before I could talk to Cassie, I needed to make sure Jack couldn't storm the castle because I'd put him off schedule. I removed the battery from my cell phone. If he'd worked at superspeed, he may have locked onto my GPS position already, but I doubted it. I can remove a battery in record time, and I was primed to do so even before he gave his ultimatum.

So how was I going to call Cassie? Well, my very bright assistant obviously realized I might ditch my burner phone and included another something extra with all those lovely euros she added to my rolling wardrobe bag—one of the Italian-based phones we kept in the office. The foundation had phones for every country, and for a country like Italy that was particularly helpful. Without going into detail, my smartphone contract was supposed to enjoy worldwide coverage but such wasn't always the case.

I extracted the *always to remain secret from Jack* phone from my bag and dialed. I may not have been able to see her as we spoke, but safe audio was always better than risky video.

"It's about time you called," she huffed in greeting.

"Hello to you too. Or, I guess I should say *buon giorno*."

"Yeah, yeah. Quit being clever. I'm mad at you."

"I'm sorry, Cassie, but truly, this has been my first real chance to talk to you. Clive wouldn't let me have a phone on the plane, and I threw away the burner phone at the airport to keep Jack from tracking me, and—"

"I know. I know. Stop. It's okay," Cassie said. "But I have news, and I've been dying to tell you. Are you in a private place?"

I walked over and closed the drapes at the balcony door, suddenly paranoid. "Yes, super secret. Tell me what you have."

"Well..." Cassie launched into a lot of technical jargon about how she finally found a way into several of the corrupted areas of the flash drive I'd discovered last month in one of Simon's hidey-holes. She'd been mining the portions she could open, matching up stolen works of art against sheets from Interpol and the FBI. Not all of the art on the drive were missing. We had been operating under the assumption that whatever was still where it belonged was on a potential hit list for theft by Simon or, through his connection, by Moran. Until we learned otherwise it was assumed they still worked together. The inaccessible sectors on the drive worried us for obvious reasons. We couldn't try to put out alerts on things we knew nothing about.

"I got the one sector open, and I'm going to fine-tune my technique to see if I can get more sectors accessible by the end of the day. There is a clincher though." Cassie went silent then, and I was nearly biting my nails in anticipation. When she didn't speak right away, I thought I'd lost the connection.

"Cassie?"

"I'm here."

"Why did you stop talking?"

"I paused for dramatic effect."

I sighed. I couldn't help it. I'd had very little sleep in the past seventy-two hours, had to listen patiently to an overly enthused rock star art fanatic, and a moment before had pissed off a man whom I needed to work with—though we did always seem to get the job done better if there was friction between us. Maybe that was why I called him before Cassie, so I could put him off and wind him up in the process. Suddenly, I realized she was talking, and I hadn't been listening.

"Cassie, wait. I have jet lag on steroids. Humor me, please, and tell me what you said *after* pausing for dramatic effect."

She laughed then, and I knew I was forgiven for spacing out.

"I'm sorry. I know you must be totally wiped out. Do you have a nice place to stay?"

"Yes, a room in a private home. My taxi driver was very accommodating. I'll text you the address."

"No worries. I can get it from this call."

It seemed like everyone knew where I was except me. But I tuned back in when she started talking art again.

"It was the snuffbox that really brought it all together. Nico sent it to the office by courier and added a note to check out the mark on the bottom. He thought it was a forger in Florence and wanted you to have the information as soon as possible."

"Okay, let me find a pen and pad—"

"No, I'll email you." I heard her clicking keys and knew when I replaced my battery I would have email pings on my regular cell. I was wishing I'd asked the landlady for water. I hadn't realized how thirsty I was until I started talking.

"Are you listening, Laurel?" And I realized I wasn't—listening, that is.

"No, Cassie, I'm sorry. But I'm back now. I promise."

"You need to find an espresso."

"What I need is caffeine rocket fuel. Let me walk around while we talk. Maybe that will help. Okay, go."

"Well, the mark is one used by the particular forger Nico knew about, but more importantly, the forger's mark is forged."

"What?"

"Right. The forger's mark on the snuffbox is almost the same as the Florentine forger, but two things give its provenance major problems. One is there's an extra curlicue on the lower end of the mark. One never made before by this forger."

"But he could have gotten careless—"

"I thought of that, but nope. I called Nico." Cassie giggled. "I would say I'd awakened him, but I don't think he was sleeping, if you know what I mean. He apparently was 'entertaining' the rock group's publicist. To thank her for helping you."

Was the man a machine, for heaven's sake? I couldn't even

think about sex at the moment. If my body went horizontal, I would be comatose. Maybe that was it. They did it standing up.

"What did Nico say?"

"He gave me names and numbers, and I made a few calls. Turns out, several more forgeries with this same kind of new mark have been appearing on the scene lately, from small items like the snuffbox to paintings and sculptures. Each one a better copy than this particular forger had been known for throughout his career."

"So, he's been getting better?"

"No, he's been getting dead."

I must have heard her wrong. "Come again, Cass?"

"He died. Almost a year ago. Under most mysterious circumstances, I might add. And less than a month later the first of the forgeries with this new mark appeared at Sotheby's. In all, Nico's contacts told me about almost a dozen pieces that have now been discovered, and with the quality of the work, the fear is there are many more out there that people are taking as the real thing."

"And...the new forger...is taking the signature...of the dead forger?"

"Or using the dead forger to keep people from realizing someone new is in the game."

Yes, my brain felt fried and fuzzy, but this was strangely starting to make sense. "As long as people recognized the older forger's mark, any items discovered as fake would be attributed to a dead man, and the new forger could continue working merrily along. Is that the idea?"

"What I figure, anyway."

"Cass, if he's as good as everyone says, and as good as the snuffbox implies, why didn't he forge the forger's mark truer. Why the extra curlicue?"

"Ego?"

"Yeah, I could see that." Talking about forgers reminded me of the painting on the yacht. "Hey, I have an extra thing I want you to look into. Not as important as what you're doing now, but curious all the same."

"What is it?"

"A painting that was on the yacht called *Woman Dressing Her Hair*. This copy is a known fake, but when I looked at it something about it keeps nudging my brain."

"So what do you need from me?"

"See what you can find out historically about the piece. When it disappeared, why. Maybe who anyone believes might be the forger."

"I'll get on it."

"But don't let it sidetrack you from what you're working on," I said. "Jack would kill me if he thought I was slowing you down. We can talk about it after I get back to London."

"Right. Have you seen him yet?"

I looked at my watch. I had a half hour, and it would take me almost that long to cross the Arno River and make it to the Piazza del Duomo. Unless I hurried. No, he might see me, and him thinking I was hurrying to meet his mandate would never do. A stroll was positively a necessity.

Plus, it was much easier to watch for people following me if I wasn't running headlong into crowds of tourists. And there would definitely be tourists.

"I'm set to see him soon. This is good information, Cassie. Send anything you want Jack and me to see on my foundation email address. Email anything for my eyes only to my personal addy. I'll share this forger info with Jack and see what he's come up with to send your way."

My own final word reminded me. I had more for her to do in the interim.

"Speaking of which, while Jack and I are starting things going here, I need you to do some judicious charming of the Max Monster." I filled her in about the Tony B problem and gave her carte blanche to spin the story in a way that made Max understand his mistake without completely revealing Tony B's larceny. I knew I might need to tell Max everything later, and if I did, I would have Jack and Nico beside me to back up the story. But until then, I needed Cassie to stress to our boss that my current location needed to always stay confidential until this entire operation ended. Too many twists continued forming in our plotline.

"Also, remind him Nico saved him airfare to get me to Italy. That alone should send the man over the moon with happiness and get him to agree to most everything you ask."

"Will do. What should I tell him if he wants to talk to you?"

I thought over my current fiscal state and how Max ordered all of my monetary requests must go through my personal assistant, even though I was supposedly head of the London office. A glance at the mirror over the bureau revealed my face wearing its most evil smile as my blue eyes glowed. "Tell Mr. Max we'll use the same go-between procedure he authorized for my budgetary needs. If he needs to speak to me, he has to ask you to initiate the request."

"Feeling a little vindictive, Laurel?"

"Feeling a lot vindictive, Cassie. Talk to you soon. I'm behind schedule to face a volcano."

SEVENTEEN

As fast as I walked—okay, as quickly as I strolled—Jack still beat me to the east doors of the Baptistery. I figured he'd been waiting there the whole time.

The Gates of Paradise are the famous fifteenth-century doors of the octagonal Baptistery of Saint John, crafted in bronze by Lorenzo Ghiberti over a fifty-year time span. The doors on display are copies, but the original masterpieces—believed by art historians, my humble self included, as heralding the beginning of the Renaissance due to their masterful work of perspective—are now behind protective walls in the cathedral museum adjacent to the Baptistery. But no matter. One look at the copies was enough to take a person inside the vision as the images leapt out in a manner defining Italian Renaissance art. This was the beginning use of the three-dimensional perspective, and Ghiberti's *Gates of Paradise* gave the art world its new sense of depth.

Equally breathtaking, but for other reasons, was the thunderous look Jack shot my way when I caught his attention. My gaze made a quick sweep of the perimeter in case I needed an escape plan. The calendar showed it was past the height of the summer tourist season, but the crowds were still thick enough in the Piazza del Duomo. I could get away from him if I really wanted to. From the furrowing of his brows, I assumed he came to the same conclusion. Though his actual greeting surprised me.

"You have no idea how worried I was."

I couldn't win, whatever way I answered. A glib quip would sound crass, and a simple thank you would come across as stupid or sarcastic. I smiled and patted his arm, and it surprisingly seemed to work. He slipped my hand into the crook of his elbow, and we headed for the Giotto Bell Tower. Without another word of lecture, I might add.

"I know what you're doing," I said as we neared the spot to trade our euros for gaining entrance to the two-hundred-and-seventy-seven-foot bell tower.

"You do, do you?" Jack dropped my hand and pulled out his wallet.

"You don't want to be overheard when you read me the riot act and then try to find out how much I know that you don't."

He cocked an eyebrow at me, then he put a hand at the small of my back, and we walked to the entrance. "Or I'm going to throw you over the side once we get up there because I'm tired of you giving me a heart attack nearly every day."

I laughed. "I still have a portable chute in my purse. I may break a leg, but I wouldn't die."

"One more thing I have to thank Nico for doing."

The bell tower, like the dome staircase by the way, can feel somewhat claustrophobic, especially if there's a pack of people climbing along at the same time. For that reason, I was happy to see the closest tourists gamely attempting the trek were quite a distance above us. I shifted the Fendi on my shoulder and grabbed the handrail to start the circular journey skyward. "I take it Nico provided our reasoning for the split flights, and you disapproved."

"Hard to disapprove of a plan when one isn't given the option."

I straightened taller. "Max told me Cassie is my keeper now. I never received the memo I report to you as well."

He took hold of my arm and pulled me around. Though he was a step down, we were eye to eye. "This isn't about you spending too much money, Laurel. That's between you and Max. This is about watching each other's backs. I can't back you up if I don't know where you are or how you're going to get there until you've already disappeared."

"In that case, where did you go yesterday morning after you left the yacht?"

"What?"

Oh, good. He saw the trap he waltzed himself into. "You know, Jack, back in Miami? Before you met me outside Tina's condo building. The errand you had to leave early for, despite the fact you said we needed to talk?"

A French couple entered the tower below us, laughing and chattering as they mounted the staircase. I pivoted and resumed our trek. But I did say over my shoulder, "I do appreciate your choosing the bell tower instead of the dome. The double dome always feels a bit close to me, and this route saved us about fifty steps."

"It costs the same, whichever view I'd chosen," Jack said. "Figured there would be fewer people heading up the tower since the dome is the better bargain for the euros."

"Don't mention the extravagance to Cecil. If he's anything like Max, he'll give you a money monitor like Cassie."

"That's really bothering you, isn't it?"

"Wouldn't it bug you?" I looked back at him as the stairs turned.

He nodded, looking skyward as he spoke. "Probably. I'll speak to him on your behalf if it would help."

"Just the fact you suggest the possibility increases my distrust of you."

"But—"

"Max is the reason Tony B knew I was in Miami." My voice dropped to a whisper. "Trust me. That will be one of the first items discussed when we reach the top. Oh, and what about the Welshman at Gatwick?"

"Last I heard, he's not talking. But good catch on your part, spotting him."

"We Beachams have always been a sharp-eyed bunch. Hopefully he'll spill something on Simon."

I wasn't a virgin at climbing the Florence fifteenth-century version of a StairMaster, and I knew to pace myself. I also took advantage of the lovely little rest stops conveniently placed every couple of stories and remained grateful the crowds in the piazza hadn't followed us for our tower escapade.

"Could give one a touch of vertigo," Jack said at our final rest stop. I saw the way his hand clutched the railing, and I smiled. Big, tough Jack Hawkes bothered by a tightly wound staircase a couple of hundred feet high. I could have taken pity on him. After all, he'd probably had less sleep than I, and it had to affect the lug. Nah, no pity from me.

I clapped my hands. "Come on, Jack—last one to the top has to tell a truth the other person doesn't know." Then I took off like a shot. I wasn't going to lose after suggesting that kind of wager.

Views of central Florence unfurled from the windows at the top. Personally, I preferred the panorama of this tower as opposed to the top of the dome, though a host of visitors would likely disagree. Both views are awe inspiring, no argument. But here the sights were more spectacular to my mind due to its closer proximity to the ground, and the vistas included the dome as well. I stood at one of the openings and breathed in the majesty, putting one hand up to the rough wall to help contain the adrenalin coursing through my veins. I wasn't afraid of heights. On the contrary, I knew their genius for offering new information from a previously thwarted angle. We'd had so many things hitting us to this point, things that seemed to herd us from one exciting end of Florida to the other, then across the ocean, and now to the most singular city of Florence. I wanted the disparate parts to make sense. I wanted to hear what Jack had learned and to put his intel together with what Cassie sent. We needed to agree on a connection. The change in altitude couldn't hurt.

I let my gaze sweep again over the Florentine landscape below, wishing I had X-ray vision to penetrate the hidden sights under the terra-cotta roofs. I wasn't a voyeur. Rather, I wanted vindication of how our reasoning for coming here was sound. Cassie's data included the info on the forger brought back from the grave, and detailed bills of lading furnished by those whose imitations received the dreaded spotlight when the fakes were revealed. Each time, the stepping off point for all of the found frauds began in Florence, regardless of where the works were ultimately headed.

Jack arrived seconds before the French couple. I think he stopped to plan his argument since he knew I couldn't be beaten. I played the grownup and didn't mention the wager. Besides, it wasn't like I believed he would honestly answer any question I really wanted to know.

"It is nice," he said softly. He stood behind me and reached a hand to the stone opening, placing his above the one I used to brace myself. He leaned into me. "Play along. Make sure we look like a couple to anyone watching. Anyone who might be questioned as they leave."

I hadn't thought of that, but he was right. After zoning out with Cassie, I should have known sleep was more important than reconnaissance, yet here I was playing Miss Scarlet in the bell tower. Or, no, I guessed Mata Hari offered a better analogy, since Miss Scarlet was a killer, and the only person I'd thought of killing lately was Max. I pasted on my fake happy grin and said, "Yes, I knew we needed to come up here to see the city."

One of the couples who came ahead of us chose to leave right then. The other remained to take pictures and point at landmarks below. The French couple stood close enough to be conjoined, and I worried they might be a problem as they seemed more interested in the dark corners of the space than they did the city view. I inclined my head to the farthest corner from them and Jack nodded.

I pulled a guidebook out of my purse to use as a prop as we spoke. I briefed him on what information Cassie provided, then we walked back to a window and pretended to take pictures with my phone so we could scan the emails together undercover. When the French couple became the final hangers on, Jack pulled out his phone and said, "Here, let's get shots of you with the view behind. Make a perfect photo for my desk back home, love."

No way I could keep from raising an eyebrow, but I did control the laugh bubbling inside me as I moved to look thoughtfully out at the horizon. There was a lot of activity on the flat roof of one of the neighboring palazzos, but I couldn't get much detail without pulling out binoculars, and I'd left the mini-but-mighty lenses Cassie thoughtfully added back in my luggage at the *pensione*. Besides, most of the roof was covered with dark awnings. But I could see busy workmen flitting back and forth under the canvases. Probably nothing. But still...

I turned and smiled as Jack continued snapping digital photos. The French couple watched us and giggled, and I started to get nervous about the interest of the pair. Leaning close to Jack's ear, I whispered, "I'll note the characteristics of her face. You take his."

"No need." Jack's voice rumbled as he kept the volume low. "I've never seen them before. It's not likely they're from either camp."

"How can you be sure?" I shot back, stepping away to cross my arms.

Jack took two slow steps closer. "I know for the same reason I could track you on CCTV. I remember faces. It's a gift. Trust me when I say those two have no previous connection with Moran or Tony B."

I kept walking toward the other end of the space. "You've memorized every confederate either of them has?" I whispered.

"Yes. I've been following the careers of both men for some time. You're not the only one who knows every crook in the art world."

I stared into those teal eyes. "Yeah, but am I the only person right now looking at one?"

He opened his mouth, then shut it again without speaking. Instead, he started flipping screens in his phone until he found his own saved emails, and we resumed the charade of oohing and ahhing over emails as if they were photos of me and Florence. The French couple finally chose to leave, kissing and squeezing until they got to the edge of the first step. I could hear voices coming from down below and knew there wasn't much time before the next set of tourists arrived. I took the opportunity to give him the scoop on Max's role in Tony B kidnapping me.

Jack's face reddened. "Of all the stupid—"

I shushed him. "Max doesn't see Tony B as a hood. The things I hear and see in the field are quite different than what my boss sees behind a desk. We've all been at benefits together, and that's chiefly how Max knows Tony B. I knew info from the field, but I had no proof against the man before the last twenty-four hours. As irritated as I am with my boss, I can't blame him for answering what he obviously felt was a simple question. I don't doubt Tony B was very smooth."

"So Cassie has your back on this?"

"Everything from me goes through her to Max. And we'll make sure his knowledge of my location is at least a day late."

"Good."

"What info do you have from your sources?" I asked.

Jack tensed his shoulders, then let them drop and pulled me back to one of the openings. He flipped three screens very fast, but I recognized two sculptures and the painting as ones Cassie included in my email info dump.

"Are those the real works or the fakes?"

He sighed. "That's just it. These works were recently deemed frauds but were in place instead of the originals. And they're brilliantly done. If not for the cursed mark, they would likely still pass all tests. Which also makes the task of determining when the switch was made infinitely more difficult."

"Yet duplicates were forgeries and had the 'new' makers mark of the dead forger from here in Florence," I mused. The terra-cotta roofs below offered a lovely uniform pattern to rest my gaze and soothe the challenges to my brain. For the last twenty-four hours, I'd been thinking about all of the pieces of this case and how they did and didn't fit together. This new information made it more complex. Or something entirely new.

"So, are we on track for something?" Jack asked. "Or is all of this a means of diffusing our attention to the point where we don't see what we should?"

At least we were thinking along the same lines. I threw out the one connection I had. "The snuffbox. You and I were both after it for vastly different reasons, but it ties to Simon through Tina, Tony B through Tina, and Florence because the forgery looks to have been made here because of the mark and the shipper's bill of lading that Cassie wrangled from Max's original source. It's in the email. And the mark itself is one of legend. Who has appropriated the forgery mark of a dead forger? Or is it more than one person? We know Simon was aligned with Moran, and Tony B was seen with Rollie at the art fair. Is Tony B working for Moran or extra hired muscle? Or is it all nothing more than confidence men keeping their enemies close? And Tina told me she received the snuffbox from Simon, which makes a definite connection. But with Tony B ending up with it, was she a dupe in all of this or his latest conquest gone wrong? If the latter, was her murder to stop her from giving me the snuffbox, or to keep her from also giving me information at the hand off?"

"All brilliant lines of thought," Jack said, his face contemplative. "But it still doesn't give us clear direction. There's also the number in the safe-deposit box assigned to Simon in Orlando. No one has been able to crack that code either. Did he put the number into the box, or was it and the map placed there by someone else for him to pick up when he came to get the snuffbox from Tina?"

I hadn't thought of that. I knew this wasn't a competition, but I preferred to have already processed a possibility before Jack voiced it. There was another connection to all of these people and artworks. "This is the country where we first tried to get the snuffbox, and now we're led to Florence. And the Greek courier who originally was supposed to give me the snuffbox wasn't simply robbed like Tina, he had his throat slashed exactly like hers. But his death was in Italy. Coincidence? I hardly think so."

"You think if we find Tina's killer, we'll know who killed the Greek?"

I shrugged. "You were the one who said there was no doubt the man who confessed to the murder had been paid to be the scapegoat." Something else lay in all of this, but what? An idea teased my subconscious, but I wasn't sharp enough at the moment to latch onto the answer. Another missing link that eluded me. I shook my head. "Jack, I'm tired. I know I should see something here, a real connection to truly help, but I can't."

He looked at the time on his phone. "We've made progress, and you're right. Neither of our brains are rested enough for this kind of a workout. It's lunchtime, then everything will be shuttered for *riposo*. Let's follow local tradition."

Ah, *riposo*, siesta, a nap. Sounded beautiful. But food first. "There's a trattoria a block from here."

"What? You don't want to share *bistecca Fiorentina*?"

The enormous rustic Tuscan T-bone big enough to serve two. "If I shared a steak with you now, I'd be out before we hit the dessert course."

"Who said anything about sharing?" Jack laughed at what I knew was my startled expression, and I joined in as a party of four emerged from the staircase. The problem was, we were both close enough to exhaustion that we couldn't stop laughing once we'd started. Jack motioned for me to follow him back down, and we kept our gazes diverted from each other as we made the return trek. One shared glance and hysteria would start again.

Every table at the trattoria was filled. We needed an alternative, and Jack knew a stand-up sandwich and wine place on the way back to cross the Arno River. "It's a hole in the wall," he said.

That was literally the truth. The storefront had an opening at the top of the counter where orders were taken and filled. As we finished our sandwiches and wine, our glasses went onto the shelf along the side wall. Several empties already waited to be retrieved by the dishwasher. A convenient gelato vendor finished off our feast with dessert, the creamy chocolate and hazelnut *gianduia* for me and the decadent dark-chocolate *cioccolato fondente* for Jack. We continued moving out of the center of the city as we ate. Neither of us seemed to have the energy to talk, and I was getting too tired to walk, but we were in the pedestrian-only zone. Parking in Florence can be a nightmare, and buses and cabs must stay beyond the city center. Once vehicular traffic again shared our space, I searched in vain for an available taxi so I could return to the *pensione* for a nap. I was tempted to flag down one of the Vespas buzzing by and try my luck playing femme fatale to any young Italian male driver. The motor scooters zipped by constantly.

"The sound of those things is bloody annoying," Jack fumed. "No wonder people call them wasps."

"Regardless, I'm sure there's not a one of those grouchy old men who call them wasps who hasn't enjoyed riding a Vespa at least once."

"Always contrary, eh, Laurel?"

I smiled. "Since members of my family maintained that to be true, I won't bother arguing."

Suddenly Jack stopped. "Wait a second. Your family. The foundation."

I turned away from the street to look at him. "What about them?"

"The night we met, you were representing the Beacham Foundation."

"Yes." I frowned at the absurdity of the statement. "I'm always representing the foundation one way or another."

"It just occurred to me. That's precisely what we need."

"The Beacham Foundation?" I wasn't following him. "I think you really need sleep, Jack. You aren't making any sense."

"Not the foundation. You. We need to get the word out to everyone who matters in the art world that you are here. Let the city know you're here in a big way, and see who comes out to kidnap you again."

"Set myself up? That's your best plan?" I couldn't believe it. "Stake me out like a goat and wait to see who tries to snatch me up and run?"

Jack stared at me. "Staked like a goat? A tethered goat?" He blew out a long breath, then stood back and put his hands on his hips. "Personally, I was thinking dangle you like a sacrificial lamb, myself."

"And one is different from the other in what way?"

"Semantics if nothing else. And a dash of Madison Avenue. You're a beautiful woman, so..." He kind of shrugged his shoulders. "You know. Sheep are lovely, and—"

I couldn't help rolling my eyes. My grandfather had kept sheep on a marvelous place he had in Ireland. He'd kept goats there too. I knew the difference.

"Sheep are stupid. If I'm going to have to live by my wits, I'd prefer the smarts of a goat."

"You do know the animal analogy was an expression? Nothing more."

I ignored his question and smiled, giving a little dig. "So, I'm beautiful, huh?"

He didn't miss a beat. "Beautiful, long-legged, smart, and the biggest pain in the arse I know. You're right. A goat reference would be much more apropos."

We stared at one another. The more I thought about it—setting myself up, stirring the pot so to speak, not the sheep or goat thing—the better I liked it.

"I think your idea may be okay." No sense in letting him know after considering it, I thought it was actually pretty great. "I'll contact Cassie and find out what's scheduled in Florence this week and if we have tickets to anything." Unexpectedly, I yawned. "Sorry. I guess dessert was really a mistake, despite how I love gelato. All those carbs."

"Women. They blame everything on carbs," Jack said, disgusted. "You don't need—"

"Sounds like you've had some bad experiences with women," I interrupted. "You know generalizing by gender is the mark of a weak mind. Speaking of which, I don't know how I could have forgotten. An old friend of mine is holding a big art show here celebrating women." I frowned again, thinking. "You know, I believe it's actually happening tonight, but I'm not really sure where it's being held. I didn't pay much attention since I didn't think I could attend."

"You know Flavia Bello?" Jack looked surprised. Nice to know I could pull a few things out of my hat he didn't know about. "Her show's tonight."

"Yes. Longtime family friend. How do you know her?"

"We've met a few times. She's older than you, isn't she?"

"A few years." In truth, probably more than ten, but I doubted she would admit to it. "We met through our grandfathers. She sent me a couple of tickets I can print out. This is the type of event you had in mind, isn't it?"

"It's what we need, don't you agree? Get you out there in the art public's eye."

"Are we talking about officially attending this together? I'm okay if you want to stay more in the background." In fact, it would likely be better if I attended on my own. Working a crowd alone was one of my strong points. Jack would serve as quite a deterrent to getting people to open up, but if I made the mistake of insisting he not attend with me, I knew he'd remain glued to my side.

Or he would choose the moment to grow even more committed to remaining by my side whether I tried to psych him out or not. I was nearly able to hide my sigh of frustration when I heard his next words.

"Forget it, Laurel. We're going to attend this together," he said firmly.

It was time to throw down the gauntlet. "I'll probably get more action if I'm alone. The more action, the more possibility of leads. This is a system that has worked for me for years. Why screw up a good thing?"

His hands gently closed around my upper arms. "Because for reasons too numerous to list, we are now a team. Partners. Wriggle on the hook as much as you want, Laurel. I've always enjoyed a good fight. You know as well as I do we need each other on this."

I wanted to argue, especially with another animal analogy depicting me on his hook instead of the other way around, but maybe this time he was right about the team thing. Run the risk of being together publicly one more time. What was one evening?

"Okay, okay, point made." I wiggled out of his grasp and took a small step backward, not a defensive move but rather a strategic one. An empty cab headed my way. "I think it might be a night to get leads. With the list of donors Flavia sent, I have a feeling this is going to be the event of the year, even in a city known for its art events."

I held out my hand and whistled. The cab pulled over. "The event probably doesn't start until eight. I don't know about you, but I'll have to pull together some kind of outfit or get Cassie working on it. Frankly, I have no idea what I have in my bag to choose from."

I got into the backseat and started to shut the door.

"Laurel, what do you think you're doing?" He held onto the door to keep me from closing it.

"Let go. I'm going to my hotel to take a nap. I'll meet you tonight on the Ponte Vecchio. I'll get there early. About seven."

His brows moved dangerously close together. "Where are you staying?"

"It's safe. I'm fine. Cassie knows where I am."

"*Signorina—*" The poor taxi driver looked concerned.

I waved and smiled, as if to say, "Don't worry."

"Jack, you're bothering the driver. Find your own cab." Another car scooted around our cab, horn blaring, and almost clipped him. That was all I needed to get the door away from him and locked. I cracked the window. "I'll meet you on the Ponte Vecchio at seven-ish, and call before I get to the bridge tonight."

EIGHTEEN

Since Jack's win over the event protocol and my escape in the taxi shortly after meant we were tied once again in our private ego battle at one apiece, I figured I'd better do well on my end to prepare for the evening. Or I might not get away from him the next time. I may not have asked for a partner, but he was turning into something not at all bad. And our ideas meshed in a good way when he wasn't trying to control everything. Yet a lot of that control was due to the changing kaleidoscope this project seemed to entail. I understood. To be completely honest, it was nice having someone to worry over me. Just not too much.

His idea for tonight held promise, if indeed I was the connection we'd been looking for. It sounded conceited to think so, but if his plan worked and our being in the very public place smoked out a player or two in this farce, put a face to the threat, it was worth the effort. I still worried though. His rationale was valid, but it was he, after all, who was tied up in the Orlando airport. I could have easily caught the flight without him. Was it Tony B, since he'd spoken to Max the day before, or someone related to the painting Jack stole in Orlando earlier that morning? Or was it someone else entirely? We knew Tony B was responsible for the Miami car thieves in the Honda—at least he laid claim to the credit—so that tallied over to the side shoring up Jack's idea. But if his henchmen waylaid Jack and tied him up like a Thanksgiving bird, why didn't Tony B brag about the accomplishment too? It wasn't like the slimy bastard not to sing his own praises.

Too many things to consider and not enough sleep. My brain was exhausted. As the cab pulled up at the *pensione*, I passed over a few of my dwindling supply of euros to the cabbie and headed inside to call Cassie.

The balcony drapes were still closed, giving me a more secure feeling that my landlady likely hadn't poked around in my things while I was gone. Not that there was much problem with the little there to go through. All of the top-secret stuff stayed in the bottom of my Fendi.

The bed called to me. "In a minute, you wonderful little bed. I promise," I said. I dropped my purse on the dresser top and pulled out my Italian phone. Probably costing the foundation several times as much per call, but that was Max's problem. He put me with Jack and gave him a blank check. Of course, since I'd told on my boss for giving away too much info to the enemy, Jack was less likely to be quite so accommodating with the information Max thought he was cultivating. Not that I think Jack ever told Max the truth either, and vice versa. I was tired, and my brain was dithering again. Time to set Cassie with a new task.

"Hiya, Laurel." Cassie sounded distracted when she answered, and I could hear the sound of computer keys clicking in the background.

"Hate to bother you, Cass, but I need you to do something for me. I need to look fabulous tonight for an event. Big blowout. Got any ideas?"

I heard Cassie slow her typing. "You probably don't have anything suitable there. I put in a nice dress or two but nothing that says 'primo event.' Nico is here in the office. We're tag teaming on something I want to tell you about soon but not until we know more. We need a coffee break anyway. We'll go get some java and throw around ideas for tonight. When do you need it?"

Lovely, both members of my A-team would be on the hunt. "The event starts at eight. But I need to leave here before seven."

"Are you going anywhere until then?"

"Across the room to the lovely twin bed that's waiting to send me into dreamland."

Cassie laughed. "Sounds like the best plan. You've got to be operating on no reserves. Leave it with me, Cinderella. Your dreams are about to come true."

I laughed. "Sounds magical. You have my address, right? In case you can get things delivered here for me? Also, I have information Jack gave me. I'll text it to you in case it helps with whatever you and Nico are puzzling over today."

"Terrific. I'll let him know more intel is coming."

I awoke a few hours later to the sound of buzzing. I didn't remember where I was but automatically reached next to me for my phone. It was Cassie.

"Are you asleep?" she scolded playfully.

I shook my head before realizing I had to say it aloud. "No, I'm awake."

She guffawed. "Yeah, right. Well, this will definitely wake you up as nothing else will."

"Two espressos...in a skinny latte with a touch of vanilla and caramel can come through the phone?"

"Listen, and listen good, Laurel. The dead forger?" Then silence.

A dramatic pause was not the best thing in the world right now. I tried to be empathetic but couldn't quite manage it. "Yeah, Cassie?"

"He's not the only one."

"What does that mean?"

Cassie's impatient sigh came through loud and clear. "You know the copy Nico traced that was a forgery of the dead forger's work?"

"Yes, I remember."

"There are more."

"More forgeries signed in the dead forger's method?"

Again, a sigh. "No, Laurel, wake up. There are more forgers' marks being reused. At least that's how it appears. Nico's found several others in more recent use on a few paintings and additional metalwork. Each time the marks are a shade different than what the original forger always created as a signature. And all the forgers who authored the marks are dead. We don't know what to make of it yet, but Nico is still searching. Some old research published in an obscure journal caught his attention and detailed facts and figures about the commonality of forgeries, and typically what forgers looked for before they copy pieces. That led him to lesser-known artwork where he discovered the provenance and authenticity of the pieces also tie back to Florence. But while the bills of lading are dated prior to each of the late forgers' demise, the items all arrived in their current locations within the past few months. We thought you'd want to know what he'd found as soon as possible."

Sure, but what is the information telling us conclusively? I didn't say this aloud. It would have sounded negative, and my dynamic duo didn't need anything slowing them down. However, there was one part of this information that leapt front and center into my mind. I rolled over and stared at the plastered ceiling. "You're right. Somehow it's hard to grasp, but if you and Nico have found this—"

"What's stopped others?"

"Yeah, what's stopped others?"

"As much as Nico hates to speculate..." Cassie paused a moment, as if working this carefully. I figured he might be close by. "When persuaded, he admitted this is probably the work of an organization. Too well executed and too well hidden to be done solo or by an amateur. He immediately qualified this and said we shouldn't do or say anything until he'd conducted more research to verify his very preliminary theory."

I thought back to Jack's and my recent discussion.

"Jack said duplicates were found to be great fakes. I'll get the information to you and Nico. It might help the research. I forgot to send it to you earlier when I sent the other data."

"Sounds great. No worries."

"Thanks for getting in touch. You and Nico know what to do."

"Yes, we'll keep looking."

Seeing my reflection in the mirror, wearing a camisole, reminded me that I had a ball to go to tonight. "By the way, fairy godmother, did you and Nico have any luck securing me clothes for this evening?"

"Oh, we did indeed. Check with your landlady. If you don't have boxes downstairs yet, you should very soon. Enjoy! And that's an order coming from your financial watchdog."

"Why do I get the feeling Max is going to replace you in the role?"

Cassie giggled. "Nico promised no slip-ups this time. I think he's taking great pleasure in this new challenge to his computer skills."

"You two are scaring me."

"A warning never to cross us, boss." Cassie laughed then added, "Be sure to send me that info Jack had on the duplicates. Don't get excited about an extra Christmas downstairs and forget all about us slogging away here in the trenches."

"Never." Thank goodness she said that. I'd already forgotten again. We signed off, and I let my thumbs fly over the text screen. I was really missing the laptop I lost when the Honda guys stole our luggage with the rental Mercedes. I needed to at least see about getting a tablet to use if this phase of the job lasted much longer.

I sent the text and considered my next option. Clothes, no contest. Although I could have slept longer, within minutes I was dressed in a pair of designer jeans and pink silk overtop, and downstairs hoping for coffee while I searched out my new wardrobe. For the price of the room, I never expected any food served, but coffee would have been a godsend.

No fragrant hint of the wished-for aroma, but I found several boxes of various sizes stacked on the large round table in the entry. A white embossed card with my name printed on it stood propped on top. Inside, a note Cassie asked the store to add read:

Enjoy yourself tonight, Cinderella. Hope the shoes fit. If not, don't leave them behind. They're my size, too.

Now for the hard choice. Coffee, food, or boxes with the names

Armani and La Perla? The packages won hands down, and within minutes I was back in my room, boxes and tissue strewn all over.

A stunning black sleeveless knee-length sheath that offered new meaning to the concept of the little black dress, and a luxurious silk shawl in ivory with silver Lurex accent thread embroidered throughout added the finishing shimmery elegance. Silk stockings, a pair of barely-there heels, and a perfect clutch covered the essentials. Exquisite and understated matching silver earrings, necklace, and bracelet rounded out the ensemble. Plus undergarments to die for. The goodies covered my unmade bed.

Leaving everything where it was, I grabbed my bag and scooted down the street to the nearest coffeehouse and ordered an Americano and a couple of *bomboloni*, quickly scarfing down the Italian donut holes while standing like every other patron around me. I had a few tasks of my own to complete before I met with Jack.

The smell of a bakery reminded me of France, and France reminded me of Rollie, since that's where we'd first met. Briefly, I wondered if he would be at the evening's event. For a second, I wanted to call Flavia, but I knew she'd be too busy with last-minute details to talk.

First, I'd see if I could find a place to print out the tickets for tonight. I'd discovered no hookup at the *pensione*. I also wanted to rent a Vespa and drive around the city, but I didn't have time. Maybe tomorrow I could drop in on some markets. If we'd come the last weekend of the month, I could have hit the huge Mercato delle "Pulci," when the stalls overran the famous flea market and spilled out from the Piazza dei Ciompi into the surrounding streets.

A brisk walk and a few minutes later, I walked through the famous lobby of a hotel I had stayed at many times with my grandfather and father. I recognized the receptionist, who had grayed but changed very little otherwise.

"*Buon pomeriggo*, Lorenzo. Do you remember me?"

Lorenzo gave a small bow. "Of course, *Signorina* Laurel. I was sorry to hear about the passing of *Signor* Beacham. He was a fine man."

I knew he was talking about my grandfather, rather than my father, even though more than a decade had passed since Grandpapa's death. "Thank you, Lorenzo. I'm not staying, just in and out of the city this trip. But I was wondering if I could very quickly make use of your computer facilities?"

"*Sì, sì.* It is my pleasure to help." He gestured to someone behind me, telling the clerk, apparently Benni, to help with my computer needs.

"*Grazie*, Lorenzo." I pressed euros into his hand.

He bowed again as I followed Benni to the computer facilities. Within moments, I had the tickets printed, Benni tipped, and was back out on the street.

I called Nico. He answered on the fourth ring. "Nico. For a moment, I thought you were letting me go to voicemail."

"Believe me, I thought about it." He sounded distracted and not himself.

"What's up?"

"I am not sure. This counterfeiting thing may be bigger than I thought. Jack's information provided another avenue, but my careful digging has come up with nothing."

"Carefully? No one can spot what you're doing?"

"Who do you think you're talking to, Laurel?"

I sighed. "How big?"

"Big. And I'm not sure who, what, or where. There's literally no chatter to be found."

"Then how do you know it's big?"

Nico sighed impatiently.

I could hear his busy brain telling him to stop explaining and get back to detecting. I fully expected the conversation to be shut down in typical Nico fashion—a quiet, polite hang-up.

Instead, he began saying, "Number one, the why is money. Number two, the how is someone somewhere is apparently convincing and organizing great forgers to create these masterpieces. Forgers are not known for working well together. It's a solitary occupation because they prefer it that way. Which is how

I know this is big. Lots and lots of money to be had in counterfeiting masters well, and there is a lot of money rolling around. Unfortunately, the organizational details remain completely blank. I also have not figured out what marks a masterpiece as worthy of imitation in the eyes of these people. This is where you say, 'Good job, Nico,' and trust me to know what I am doing."

"I trust you. I always will." For Nico to talk at such length on the telephone meant something absolutely out of the norm was going on. "Who and what could convince good solitary forgers to band together?"

"Exactly my question. All of them I've found so far are good. Better than good actually. A big operation."

"Moran big?"

"Definitely, but I have found nothing connecting his name nor any of the others to this enterprise. Not his grandson, Tony B, or anyone else. And before you ask, I checked for that dilettante idiot, Simon, too. Everything came back nada. A mystery I know I'll eventually solve, but it is going to take time."

Good. Not about the time, but I didn't even wince when he mentioned Simon's name. "You'll get there—you always do. How's Max?" Might as well get the bad news out of the way. I didn't really want to know. That's why I hadn't asked Cassie.

"Strangely silent."

"That's a first. What do you make of it?"

"Not worrying about it at this point. Too many other things to do."

"Jack had some things he wanted to take care of today. Do you know anything about what he's doing?"

"No, not this time. He keeps me no more apprised of his plans than you usually do."

I smiled at the verbal poke. "But you have talked with Cassie," I said, curious as to what he would say.

"Do not remind me. The woman is in almost the same wheedling class as you."

I could forgive him his woman rant. "Why, Nico, are you saying I have competition for your attentions?"

"Let's say if I don't speak with either of you again today, it will be a good one."

"All right, all right, I get the message. When you or Cassie gets the chance, I could use more cash. She enclosed what euros she had in the office when she packed my bag, but I want to stay off credit cards if I can to avoid the tracking risk. Paying for cabs and lodging and food adds up quick. Plus, I want to go exploring a few hours around Florence tomorrow, play tourist. To see what I can see."

There was a pause, then he said with a fake Cuban accent, "What are you up to now, Lucy?"

I laughed at his Lucille Ball reference.

"Don't worry, Ricky," I said. "I won't make you and Fred have to come and get me."

Nico returned, "Seriously. Be careful. We know one forgery has come from Italy. Florence may be the origin or at least a major stop along the line. The people responsible for this aren't about to let anyone snooping around come between them and their money."

"I told you, I'll behave like a tourist. Don't forget I still have your magic escape bag."

"Laurel..."

"I promise. No risks, only touristy fun. Would you let me know where the nearest Vespa rental place is with regard to my housing and arrange for a rental? I'm in the mood for something hard and fast that doesn't talk back."

NINETEEN

A quarter to seven in the evening, the *signora* who ran the bed-no-breakfast knocked on my door. "A cab is here, *signorina*."

I looked around the room making sure I'd forgotten nothing. I hid my Fendi inside my luggage and hoped my landlady remained as disinterested in my things as earlier in the day. Now, my taxicab chariot awaited, and I would soon come out in my "Florence debut."

I walked down the stairs, breathing deeply and visualizing calm success for the evening. The heels felt like a dream, as did the various silks rubbing against my skin.

The leather clutch in my hand held all the necessary accoutrements for a woman in my position: the invitations, pink lip dew, compact, comb, tissues, mints, both telephones, mini-flashlight, and my favorite traveling set of various sized tools—AKA picks and weapons. I wasn't planning anything heavy duty, but I wanted to be as prepared as possible.

It wasn't completely dark yet, and my euros were disappearing faster than planned. I had the cab drop me a short distance from the bridge to save part of the fare, and I walked to the rendezvous point to meet Jack. It always amazed me how sturdy heels could feel when they appeared as light and unsubstantial as a cloud. If Max kept up the austerity plan, I might be able to drop my gym membership. I slipped the battery into my phone as I neared the bridge to give Jack the heads up. He didn't answer. I didn't know if I should be concerned or if he was still miffed at how I'd run away from him again.

The Ponte Vecchio was packed with people. Most of the excruciatingly expensive shops were closed, but a few of the lights were still on, showing jewelers catering to select clientele. I passed a shop I remembered from a trip with Grandfather, where he knew the owner and had a special necklace and earrings made for my grandmother. The older jeweler was gone now—he was a contemporary of my grandfather—but his son and grandson still kept the family business alive.

The sunset view of the Arno about midway down the bridge was breathtaking. I smiled at teenage couples more interested in viewing each other than watching the shifting light over the water. Their loss. I loved the romance of the bridge.

My mind was lost in the movement of the water when I felt Jack behind me. He didn't say anything. Didn't touch me. Yet I knew it was he. I didn't want him to know I was so aware of his presence and pretended to remain captivated by the view.

"You really shouldn't stand out here in the open," he finally said.

I made a slow turn to take in the almost wall-to-wall experience of humans around us. There was no point in arguing. I knew where his remark came from. I looked at him and smiled. "Hello, Jack. Ready to put me on display?"

He should have been on display himself. He was magnificent in a black tie and custom Armani tux. A silver-tipped ivory rose, matching my wrap, graced his silk lapel.

"You've been busy." I smiled and tilted my head.

He held out another ivory rose, this time long stemmed, and said, "A beautiful rose for a beautiful woman."

I shockingly felt my skin heat at the hackneyed phrase and tried to stop the blush. I quickly looked down as I took the rose. "You must have spoken to Cassie."

He held his hands up in a *what can I say?* gesture. "She told me your colors, but the beautiful part comes from me."

"A compliment twice in one day. Thank you, Jack. It's lovely." I sniffed and found the flower smelled equally terrific. "Do I need to be worried about a tracking device?" I teased, peeking into the bloom.

I looked up in time to see his freshly shaved jaw tighten. "No. No tracking, listening, or any other gadget tonight. I trust you to stay with me. Be my partner." He took my arm.

Someone had his knickers in a twist again. He smelled wonderful. Clean with a faint afterthought of a woodsy cologne, Bulgari Man, maybe, that my nose picked up even over the floral aroma of the rose. Time to lighten the mood. I pretended to pout as we headed for the cathedral side of the bridge. "The whole time? What will everyone think?"

"Does it matter? We're trying to set in motion a series of events that will get us somewhere in this hurry-up-and-wait investigation. I'm sick of being on the outside looking in. Don't worry, I'm not going to stop you from talking to your friends."

We took our time getting to the gallery. I could tell he was still on edge, but the conversation stayed light, and he kept any further orders to himself. Since we had no idea what to expect, there was no way to plan. I decided to enjoy the city.

He apparently had other ideas and broke the silence. "What's going on in the Cassie and Nico world?"

"You spoke with her earlier."

"For color combinations. She was busy and said you would fill me in on their work."

In other words, she was letting me pick and choose what he needed to know. Good girl, but under the circumstances I figured I'd better play completely fair. I delayed answering by sniffing the rose. Jack brought a halt to that ploy by placing a hand over mine and pulling the flower away from my face. "Laurel, spill."

I did a smoothing move down my dress. "Not until I have your solemn oath to tell me what you did today."

"I slept. Tried to find out something more about the snuffbox without success. Got in touch with a few of my contacts to discreetly inquire if they had heard anything at all about forgeries. Your turn."

"Had they heard anything? Information on Tony B or Moran?"

"No. I'm hoping this little get-together will bring someone or something out in the open. Nico, Cassie?"

"This might be bigger than we had originally thought." I quickly ran through the little I'd been told. "Often, as I'm sure you know, the social world is the first place to start checking out anything trending in art—good or bad. Tonight we should work on forming or re-forming social contacts, play the game, as it were. If Florence is the key and it's as big as Nico thinks it is, we need to immediately create a reason for our presence here separately."

"You've read my mind. The tickets indicate Beacham Foundation, and I'll make sure everyone knows I'm your plus one. Nothing official, but wherever you go tonight, I go as well."

"I'm still not sure our being known as working together is a good idea."

"But it is safer, Laurel. We need to see what happens. Play up your relationship with Flavia as the reason for the last-minute decision to show up tonight. Our joint interest in the art world is our common bond."

"I guess that's plausible. The guilty parties will see us as trying to catch them in our semi-official capacities, even as we have innocent excuses for being there."

While I still didn't fully trust him and he irritated the heck out of me, Jack, his contacts, and his brawn and ease with a gun had proven to be helpful a few times already. His idea didn't seem to be asking too much, even if it was a change in Nico's and my original plan. After all, it didn't take much of a stretch for me to catch on to the staked goat analogy, so my subconscious obviously agreed with the idea. My conscious mind kept warning me to watch out.

"Okay, casual but cautious. You point out your bogeymen, and I'll point out mine. We'll see what transpires."

"Deal."

My mind started fast-forwarding to find any hitches we might need to anticipate in the plan. "If anyone asks, where do you want to say we met?"

"We'll stick to the truth as much as possible. Giovanni

Nicoletta's *castillo* is where we met, and since then we've kept in touch."

Silence lasted about a minute. "I can do this if you can."

"Shake to seal the deal?" Jack smiled wryly and held out his hand.

My much smaller hand slid into his smoothly calloused palm, and we shook on it.

Before he released my hand, he said, "A deal is a deal, Miss Beacham. I fully expect you to honor your word." He said *word* like it meant a vow.

I pulled my hand away. "I expect the same from you, Mr. Hawkes."

The look he shot my way was every bit as suspicious as the one I sent back at him.

TWENTY

Too busy thinking, I hadn't paid much attention to where we were going. Jack kept my arm secure in the crook of his elbow, and my feet followed his lead, but my heart double-timed its pace as my vision finally filled with our destination. The entrance had been retooled. Huge pots of shrubs and flowers, probably hired for the event, rested in front. But the building was the same.

"La Galleria del Giardino della Vita," I breathed.

"Not anymore. The new owners renamed it."

"I thought it had been made into a bank after Andrea Tessaro died."

"That's true, but several years ago the bank moved, and the people who purchased the property wanted to bring back the art. They have big dreams," he finished a bit sardonically as we climbed the steps, my hand on his proffered arm.

I looked at him questioningly. "I'm not sure what you mean."

"Its new name is La Galleria del Sogno Infinito."

"The Gallery of the Infinite Dream," I repeated as we walked into the lobby, and I was transported back in time. The simplicity of the entry, now filled with a long centrally placed table and surrounded by people dressed to maximum effect in a variety of colors and textures, remained as I remembered. "It hasn't changed."

His very British sarcasm knocked me out of memory lane. "Whatever changes the bank made, the new owners apparently restored it to its former glory."

"You know, if I knew you better, I might think you had a grudge with the new owners," I murmured.

We reached the table, and he handed over the invitations while I picked up a couple of brochures. A few seconds later we arrived in the main section of the gallery, moving slowly but steadily with the rest of the crowd. Again, the place was as I remembered it.

"That's just it. No one really knows who the new owners are. They've applied for and received the proper permits, but as far as putting a real name or names to the buyer, there's nothing to report. A company called Ermo Colle purchased it, and their front man is an Italian exporter/importer who has fingers in lots of distant and varied company pies but no real stake or public connection to any of them."

"Ermo Colle? I think *colle* is hill, but *ermo*?"

"Solitary, lonely. Actually a Greek word. Goes back to a nineteenth-century poem by Giocomo Leopardi, and the gallery's name is taken from the poem's title, 'L'Infinito.' Leopardi was a gifted student who outpaced his instructor and resorted to long hours of self-study. Before he even reached age twenty, he had compromised his health from spending every waking hour hunched over books. 'L'Infinito,' his best-known work, is a poem beginning with a solitary or lonely hill the poet can't see because his sight is blocked by a hedge. The challenge required he use his mind to open up a vision of the limitless world for himself."

"I had no idea you possessed such an interest in poetry, Jack."

He grimaced as we moved into the main salon and took two glasses of Franciacorta, a sparkling wine from the Lombardy region. One of my favorite Italian wines, but not one I expected to be served at a Tuscany region event. I hadn't bothered to check, but the tickets to this party must be pretty steep or the owners cut a great deal with the winery to be able to serve this vintage en mass.

"I'm not. When I take on a project, part of the investigative research I do includes finding out as much as I can."

"You? Or a team?"

"I'm assuming from your reaction when we walked in, you visited this gallery during Tessaro's time. You must have been a kid."

Okay, he was obviously changing the subject to keep from answering. No surprise there. I decided to play along and explore his non sequitur for a moment. Maybe he would return the favor and give me an ounce of new data. "Yes, I was here—"

"Jack! I had no idea you were in Italy." A tall, thin red-haired man, with the same type of public school accent Jack had when he employed the full Brit, greeted him with a smile and handshake. "You remember my wife, Milli." Milli and Jack briefly hugged. "Tell me you haven't been in Florence long, or I may be offended."

Milli had a friendly, well cared for, middle-aged Italian vibe and wore a spectacular Valentino that flattered her figure and her skin. Though well turned out, she appeared several years older than her husband, who had the English fuddy-duddy formal thing happening.

"Hamish, I had no idea you were still here. Continuing to plug away at teaching art students to appreciate their masterpieces' British counterparts?"

A teacher? No way could a teacher afford Valentino.

"You know me, Jack. Never say never. Someday the ungrateful whelps will appreciate quality when they see it. Besides, I'm saved from teacher purgatory by the two English and five American transfer students I've got this semester."

We all laughed. University professor. Still not enough for a designer gown—this year's line, if I wasn't mistaken. Must be family money on one side or the other. My guess was on the wife's.

"Hamish, Milli, please let me introduce my friend and companion, Laurel Beacham. Laurel, this is Hamish Ravensdale and his wife, Milli. Hamish and I went to school together."

"Nice to meet you," I said.

"Went to school together? Modesty doesn't suit you, Jack." Hamish looked over at me. "He saved my life from the cruelties of English schoolboys more times that I can count." He pretended to flex a nonexistent bicep. The loose, expensive material of his suit didn't tighten. "Never had much bravura or stamina as a kid. Jack, on the other hand, had enough for all in our year."

"Hmm, Jack as the overly protective type. Not hard to see him in that role." I lifted my eyebrow and eyed him over the rim of my glass as the others laughed.

"See you've come up against his white-knight side," Hamish said.

I nodded. *White knight, my ass. More like control freak.* But I judiciously kept my thoughts to myself.

The resonance of tinkling glass and a microphone slowed conversation until everyone turned toward the sound.

"Mi scusi, mi scusi..."

The rest of the brief introduction gave a potted history of the gallery, thanked the many people, especially the donors of special pieces, who had made this venture possible, hoped everyone had a wonderful time, and explained in synopsis fashion about what we would be viewing—the same rhetoric on the brochures as well as Flavia's email—women artists and women subjects beginning with the Renaissance through the Baroque period with a few noteworthy current women painters and paintings.

He turned the microphone over to a woman who had entered the room from a side door.

Flavia. From the distance, she didn't appear to have aged. I hadn't seen her in person in probably five years. She basically thanked all of us for coming and told everyone to be on alert for several unexpected and exciting surprises throughout the gallery, specifying a few of them to whet our appetite. She also mentioned a private bar for everyone's pleasure—not free of course—and the very great need to continue to provide revenue for the important artistic exposure of women artists. Especially in Florence, considering the historical significance. In other words, she meant that historically women were used as art subjects to display their husband's prominence, magnitude, and wealth, while women artists were typically not appreciated and their art dismissed as of lesser importance.

She finished speaking to scattered applause and slipped out again through the same side door. Strange. I expected her to mingle with the wealthy crowd. Maybe a problem existed elsewhere only she could handle.

Patrons ebbed slowly toward the rooms of displayed art. Hamish continued talking to Jack. His wife, after a smile to us and a brief word in her husband's ear, moved to speak to another couple. I took advantage of the men's conversation to observe other people. I saw faces I could put names to but not as many as anticipated, and none I considered important to our current interests. I made a point of speaking to them, though, since the whole exercise was for me to be noticed.

The main salon looked basically the same. Hamish's voice became an inconsequential murmur as I lost myself in thoughts of the last time I'd been here fifteen years ago.

As far as current events ran, I had not really kept up with what was happening in Florence except in a very superficial way. I hadn't heard the gallery reopened under another name or of Flavia's connection to it. I did find it strange she hadn't said anything in her email. She knew all about what had happened here those many years ago with the theft of *The Portrait of Three*, not simply from a newsstand point of view, but from a shared emotional viewpoint with my own. Her family attended the gallery event that fateful night as well.

"Ready?" Jack's voice was as clipped and steady as his hand on my arm and refocused my attention. I realized Hamish had moved away.

"Yes." My mind continued operating on two levels—past and present, but I needed to focus on the here and now. I sternly reminded myself this night had nothing to do with what happened fifteen years ago and pushed those thoughts out of my head as we moved from the salon into the main hallway. Various rooms branched out to other rooms.

I didn't know what Jack had in mind, but I was having a hard time keeping my time frames straight. Surreal. Forget the art, the hordes of people, the food, and the drinks. The halls were as I remembered them. Like my child's brain had somehow taken an adult video. Was this what the owners planned, or something else I needed to figure out in this mess?

"No. I'm looking for connections where none exist," I said softly, angry with myself.

"What?" Jack moved to face me. "Do you have an idea?"

I shook my head. "Too many thoughts at one time. Seeing the building is triggering old memories. I was reminding myself to stay in the present."

He gave me a grim look. "It's a historic building."

"Exactly," I said. "It's expected that when they remodeled, they returned it to its former appearance as much as possible. My thoughts are dead ends."

As we strolled through and admired the exhibits of women's artistry and their roles as subjects from the Italian Renaissance to the present. And I did what I do best and put aside my personal issues. As we lingered and moved on, more and more people joined the masses, many of them familiar faces. See and be seen would sum it up well. Jack and I momentarily split up, came back together, and kept tabs on one another throughout the evening.

On my way back to Jack, after a short departure to visit with an old donor of Beacham's, someone grabbed me by the waist and whirled me around, briefly hugging me. "Laurel!"

Rollie. Dressed to the nines in a navy velvet suit with silk lapels. His hair, longer than the last time I'd seen him in person, fell over his shoulder until he flipped it back.

"Nice to see you," I said, giving him a warm smile, playing the game.

"Is that all you have to say? It is nice to see me?" He reached out and straightened a lock of my hair. His smiling eyes were as I remembered them. "I've missed you, Laurel Beacham. I thought we had a friendship. How long have you been in Florence?"

I forced myself to not ask if he'd enjoyed his flight from Miami. Instead I replied, "Here for one night. As a favor to Flavia."

"She is a friend?" His teeth were straight and white and shone like the sun. Such a gorgeous man with such dubious family connections and an utterly horrific taste in friends—maybe. "Longtime. Almost like a sister." My smile was slipping, and I wanted to get away before my expression gave me away. I held out my hand. "Now, I really must be off. I'm here with a friend." "Oh, is that the way it is blowing? I get the photograph now." "Picture, Rollie. You get the picture." After all I'd learned about him, I wondered if his struggle with English was fake or real.

"*Sì*, picture, *sì*." He held my shoulders and kissed me in continental fashion. "As always, a pleasure to see you. You are such a beautiful woman. You remind me of someone—did I ever tell you that?" He shook his head. "No, I don't think I did. *À bientôt*, Laurel."

He'd see me soon? Not if I had anything to do with it. I watched him walk away, greeting an older woman affectionately. What did he mean I reminded him of someone?

I ran Jack down as he laughed with another man, and I indicated we needed to talk. He introduced us and quickly made excuses to allow us to break away. "What's up?"

"Rollie."

"Here?"

"Yes." A passing waiter swanned by with a tray of full glasses, and I accepted one to keep my hands busy.

"He talked with you?"

I briefly described the conversation, leaving out the "remind me of someone" part.

"Did you—"

"I played the game like you said to do. Acted like nothing was wrong, didn't object when he hugged me. So on and so forth." Jack's eyes narrowed. "I told him I was here with someone else."

"You didn't mention my name?"

I shook my head. "No. It literally didn't occur to me to do so. I think he approached me because you weren't around." I walked away. He caught up with me, and the game continued.

When I'd had enough, I extricated myself delicately by mentioning the ladies' room, and Jack politely, albeit reluctantly, let me go with a promise to have a fresh drink for me upon my return. White-knight, control-freak syndrome style.

He was nowhere in sight when I returned to the spot where I'd left him. I drifted and smiled and became generally bored with our great idea.

The crowd was getting heavier than I'd expected, and the jostling became more full-bodied than I liked. When my clutch was knocked from under my arm and skittered on the floor under the Giorgio and Valentino gowns, I called the game and decided to make it an evening.

It took some time for my bag to finish its football scrimmage and get returned to me. I didn't want to appear gauche and look then to see if anything was missing. I did the mental weighing bit, also giving the bag a thoughtful squeeze to determine the clutch felt as if everything was accounted for.

I raised up on my toes, trying to spot Jack to give him the "let's leave" signal. But when I did see him, it was because he appeared at my elbow and pulled me back down to normal height before whispering, "Quick. Look over there."

He inclined his head, and I gazed toward the north end of the room. I didn't recognize anyone or see anything amiss and whispered back, "What do you mean?"

"The blonde with the short hair and the killer black dress. It's your friend Tina."

I laughed and patted his arm. "Oh, Jack, I have to learn when to cut you off. How many drinks have you had tonight?"

"I'm serious, Laurel."

Suddenly, I saw that he was. The laughter died in my throat, and I looked again at the blonde across the room. "Tina's dead. The homicide detective confirmed it."

"Did you see the body?"

"The news al—"

"Did you see the body?" His gaze bore into mine, and suddenly those lovely teal eyes gave a hint of menace.

I swallowed hard. "Thankfully, no."

"Then I guarantee you the woman over there is Tina Schroeder. And since I don't believe in reanimation or reincarnation, I'd say something more sinister is going on."

As Jack talked, he'd been pulling me toward the north end of the room. "Look past the makeup. It's quite different, I know. An expert job. Like the hair. But bone structure never lies."

"What are you?" I twisted to face him. "A kind of human face-recognition software?"

"Yes. That's precisely what I am." His voice held a tinge of steel. "No joking here, look closely. Don't let the professional camouflage fool you."

I did as he asked, attempted a mental strip of the carefully applied makeup—managed by a professional or über-practiced hand. And like dawn breaking, I suddenly saw what Jack had been saying. My hand shot to my mouth to hide my shocked words as I whispered, "Ohmigod, you're right. I would never have seen it if you hadn't pointed her out to me."

At that same moment, her gaze locked on mine, and she straightened. Her look said it all—she knew that I knew.

In the next second, a waiter passed between her and us, and she deposited her glass on the departing tray. I watched Jack break away and head in the same direction as the waiter, and I knew he was going to grab the glass for a fingerprint comparison. Time to confront Tina. I turned to again face her direction and realized she was gone.

Unfortunately, I had a new problem. A smarmy voice spoke from behind me. "I didn't think he was ever going to leave."

I whirled. "Tony B—"

"Miss me, Laurel?" He reached for my arm, but I sidestepped him, staying out of range.

"No, there are so many old friends here tonight, I hadn't even had a chance to think about you," I said, opening my clutch and letting my fingers search for one of my picks, never taking my eyes off the snake.

He shifted to outflank me, keeping an eye on Jack's progress.

"Looks like you have a new friend. First at the Browning. Now here. Interesting."

I slipped around an older couple, both short enough that I could still see Tony B. They were carrying on a spirited conversation in Italian and didn't seem to realize they were the net in our game of verbal badminton. I risked a step back, throwing out a quick volley to keep his mind occupied. "Did you know Tina Schroeder is still alive?"

He offered one of his nonchalant shrugs. "I never said she wasn't."

And he hadn't. That was true. I'd assumed he was keeping the information from me. He was using it to his advantage, to let me be part of the ruse.

"Who really died, Tony B?"

He tsked. "Is this the kind of conversation we need to be having in such an opulent setting?"

I thought about *The Portrait of Three*, their theft from this very place on a night like this one, and the fact that the current... No, not owner. I couldn't even pretend to go that far... Curator. Yes, curator worked. The fact the current curator was on the premises, in a building I'd already noted was eerily restored to exactly the appearance of the previous time. Well, I wasn't born yesterday.

"You're here to return the paintings."

"The new owner wants to be able to see the beauties every morning."

The new owner. Ermo Colle. Who was that really? But then I thought about how Tony B worded his remark. He hadn't said he was returning the originals. I figured I'd better keep my epiphany to myself.

I saw Jack looking for me, Tina's glass safely tucked into the pocket of his jacket. "Over here," I called gaily, forcing a smile. "Look, Jack, it's Tony B."

"*Touché*," Tony B said, taking a step back and to the side as Jack began shoving his way through the crowd. "But I leave you with one last bit of advice."

"Why would I ever want advice from you?"

"Because we go way back. And this advice is very important. That man is not who he says he is. You're headed for a huge disappointment. But don't worry. I'm doing you a big favor. Wait and see."

"Well, the joke is on you, Tony B. He won't tell me who he is. How can I be disappointed?"

In that instant, the crowd did its conjuring trick, and Tony B disappeared like Tina had. A moment later, Jack was again at my side.

"Are you okay?"

"I want to leave, Jack. This isn't fun anymore."

TWENTY-ONE

The party was over as far as either of us was concerned, but we stayed alert and made the circuit to get out of the building, on the off chance we saw either of our unwelcome fellow attendees. The emotional toll was more than I anticipated. As we finally exited, Jack pulled out his phone and sent a couple of texts. I tried to wait patiently in the overly lit area, but when I could no longer ignore the feeling of being watched from every direction, I said, "I feel like a target here."

"Sorry. Let's go." Jack tucked my free hand back under his arm and held tight, like he'd done ever since he came up on me with Tony B. For once, I didn't feel controlled as much as grateful. I wanted him close.

When we got a good distance from the building, he explained. "My texts let people know we were leaving and who we discovered at the event. They'll check out the rest of the gallery opening, but I don't think they'll find anything. I also think we can safely assume we made an impression tonight."

I started trembling and pulled the shawl tight. He removed his jacket to place it around my shoulders. I wasn't cold, and both of us knew it, but I appreciated the gesture and said so. "Thank you, Jack."

He nodded and pulled me down onto a short wall that ran along the street. Then he asked a bit hesitantly, "I did get back in time, didn't I?"

I took a deep breath and tried to smile. "Don't worry. He was just playing mind games."

"Those can often be more serious than physical torture."

No kidding. "It's been too many unknowns. He was counting on that."

He turned brusque. "You need to eat."

"I'm not hungry."

"You're always hungry." He opened the coat I wore and pulled a flask from an inside pocket. "Here, drink this."

"What is it?"

"Brandy. A couple of swallows will take care of the sick feeling, and then you'll be ravenous."

"How did you know?"

"Signs of shock are easily recognizable."

We try to fool ourselves, but I apparently wasn't fooling him. I followed orders and learned he knew what he was talking about. I felt better almost instantly.

He stood up and pulled me back to my feet. "Come on. I know a place close by."

In the tiny restaurant, after Jack palmed euros to the *capo cameriere*, we were led to a secluded table in the back corner. I surrendered his jacket and asked to be excused. Jack shot me a look.

"I solemnly swear I only want to use the restroom. I'll be right back. This ladies' ritual is part of getting back to normal."

Jack reluctantly pointed the way. "I'm tempted to go with you. You have no idea how tempted."

"I promise I'll return. Besides, you were right, I'm definitely up for food."

"Laurel, I—"

"I promise. I really want to pull myself together." Translate: fix my appearance and call Nico in private.

Once in the bathroom, I picked at my hair to get it looking in better shape. When I reached in the clutch to grab my gloss, my hands found something else instead, something I hadn't put in there.

A woman's compact, fourteen carat if I wasn't mistaken, and I knew I wasn't. This was an old one, probably from the 1970s. My mind immediately went to a bomb threat, but I dismissed the possibility as absurd. It would have already gone off. I opened it, and a sweet smell filled the air, the comfortable aroma acquired by good face powder when kept on a shelf for a long time. A piece of folded paper sat atop the old puff. I almost didn't want to pick it up but knew I had to. I placed the compact on the marble counter, reached for the paper, and carefully unfolded it.

It was a faded color photograph, easily from around 1975. In the background, the ocean met the beach. Three people stood in the foreground: a handsome late-twenties, maybe early-thirties male facing the camera, and two women slightly younger than the male. The women were arm in arm, facing mostly away from the camera and at him. I could see a portion of their profiles because one was standing slightly behind the other, but not by much. The women weren't wearing tops—their backs were bare, as was the side of one woman's breast. I wondered if it was Nice or somewhere else on the French Riviera. I looked at the photograph as long as I could before turning it over.

Then I called Nico.

"I thought I made it clear. No more calls today."

"Quite bitchy, oh surly one. You picked up."

I filled him in on the latest development with Tony B, leaving out references to Tina as well as who I believed the three people were in the photograph. I wanted to keep my team focused. They had too much to consider and puzzle out at the moment, and I didn't want to feed them more information unless I felt it was pertinent. I also skipped over my exchange with Rollie. The photo in my hand told me I needed to further contemplate his remark about reminding him of someone.

"Anything else?" His tone indicated boredom.

"For a few minutes, at the gallery, I lost visual contact with my clutch purse." I quickly cut off his objections. "I know, I know. Stay with me a second. It's all about continuity. I came into the bathroom a moment ago to restore my appearance, and I found a piece of paper I didn't put in my purse. On the paper were these words: codes are often based on memories." My words met with silence. I could hear his brain ticking away. "I thought that was worth the call."

"All right, I see this was a necessary call. Are you sure you are telling me everything? I mean it, Laurel. It might be important."

"I'll think everything through again, and if something occurs, I'll get back to you."

"Good. Think hard and fast. I may be on to something, but I'm not ready to go there yet without more information. As soon as I am, I will get back to you."

At this point, I wasn't even tempted. Not even to help the case. "Hey, before I let you go, is the Vespa ready for tomorrow?"

"Check your email. I sent you the details."

"Thanks, pal. I could really use a break."

"Yeah, right, like scouting around for information is not your real plan. Pull the other one."

I laughed. "Get some sleep, oh grumpy one."

"I thought I was surly."

"Surly, grumpy, one and the same."

"May I remind you some of us do not have time for sleep."

"My violin cries for you."

I hung up, smiling, but the humor faded fast. What the heck had I walked into?

Maybe it would be a good idea to spend my Sunday scouting in Florence. I hadn't lied. I definitely needed fun time, and if I could combine it with finding helpful information, all the better.

Water and a glass of red wine graced my place setting when I slid into the chair on the opposite side of the table from Jack. The waiter came to refresh the wine, and I saw Produttori del Barbaresco on the label. Jack hadn't skimped. Wines made famous by an Italian vintner in the Piedmont area. No cheap Chianti for our Mr. Jack Hawkes, but a 2007 Nebbiolo.

"You aren't going to make any friends with the locals if you buy wine from outside Tuscany. Especially if we drink it while we're eating the famous local beef."

"If they didn't want to sell it, it wouldn't be available."

"Yes, but Chianti is pretty much a ritual with Chianina beef. You know what the locals say, Jack, 'si sposa bella.'"

"Yeah, yeah, 'they marry well together.' I like cheap as much as the next man. However, I saw this and couldn't resist. I'm in love with this wine. I don't need to see my meal marry to have a Tuscan experience with my food." He took a long swallow, and as I watched his throat work, I felt an unfamiliar twinge, which I summarily dismissed. We needed to have more fun. Maybe I would invite Jack to join me in my Vespa adventure.

A plate of antipasti and long bread sat in the middle of our table, along with a container of the house olive oil dressed with herbs.

We stared at each other over the table. Jack said, "I've waited, but it hasn't been easy. I'm starving."

We fought over who got to the bread first. I won. Unfortunately, he proved right. I too fell in love with the wine.

Jack took the opportunity to order both the wine and our dinner. Fortunately for my waist, he hadn't ordered a traditional Florence dinner with a series of never-ending courses. The three-inch grilled steak came back glorious. In true Tuscan fashion, the beef was cooked over a hot flame, and as we sliced the tender steak, the inside was *sanguinoso*, flavorfully rare.

"Magnifico." Jack barely breathed the word. I think I groaned with my first bite. I didn't want to think about the diet I was going to have to endure after leaving Florence, even without all the courses.

As we ate strozzapreti gnocchi with spinach, and finished off the magnificent steak, I briefed him on what had happened with Tony B and Tina. We more thoroughly covered the incident with Rollie, and I left out all the other parts personal to me.

"You never spoke with Flavia?" Jack placed his napkin on the table and relaxed back into his chair, sipping his coffee.

"No. If I did get close to her, I'd get stopped by someone and lose the opportunity because she'd already be gone when I looked again. I'll give her a call tomorrow. The whole night felt off. Weird. But I was right, you know."

"In what way?"

"No one of significance approached me until I was away from you. All the action occurred when I was alone."

Jack gave me the look. "I admit I can't be sure what's going on with any of the people who set off our internal alarms tonight, but as you pointed out the last time we talked, there's quite a lot going on none of us can explain."

"Anyone on your end find anything yet?" I ate the last bite of tiramisu, one of my favorite desserts in Florence. Nothing like the version I'd been served in the States, although I liked it there too.

Jack frowned. "Moran continues to remain invisible and off the known grid. Nothing on Simon. Still not sure where or how Tony B fits in at this point. As you said earlier, Tina links both Simon and Tony B. And based on the art fair, Tony B's linked to Rollie, we think, but in which way and to what camp? We still don't know who killed the Greek or came after you." He took another sip of coffee.

"What we can genuinely conclude is we have nothing much at all except the bill of lading from Florence for the forged snuffbox now in our collective possession and a number from the Orlando safe-deposit box we can't decode but which is labeled 'Miami.' Also, a chain of supposition on Nico's part about forgers and artwork."

Artwork. *The Portrait of Three. Juliana.* She was as beautiful as I'd remembered her. The way she glowed as though she had an inner fire, tempered by the sweetness of her smile and the clearness of her eyes. The artist had loved her. Anyone with half an eye could see the evidence. She'd had the same emotional effect on me yesterday as she had when I was a child. I'd wanted to be like her and everything I envisioned she was. I'd wanted so much to be loved as she was loved. The thick feeling in my throat when tears threatened began building. I could not tell Jack about the paintings, about how they were at risk, without crying, and I was not going to cry again in front of Jack. If we tried a rescue now, we wouldn't just be splitting our focus, but calling Tony B's bluff on hiding or destroying the paintings. We didn't have the manpower to try it now, as much as I would like to. I kept silent. We had to stay focused on the case.

Rollie's odd "you remind me of someone" statement. Tina's total makeover and disappearance. I stopped for a moment and contemplated her return to the living.

"Tony B has to be behind Tina's faked death. He's the one in this mix to have the connections to either make the police department cover it up or substitute another body. Probably the latter, since it would be more expedient. And he had the snuffbox. Was my knowing about the snuffbox the reason for her disappearance and the murder cover-up, or a coincidence?"

Jack nodded but remained silent. The look on his face said he was quietly brainstorming, but he still paid attention to my words.

"Funny how Tony B didn't mention the fact the snuffbox was missing from his safe when he waylaid me at the party." I played with my napkin as I mused, "Could he not know that I took it?"

"Good point," Jack said. "We'll have to keep that possibility in mind. Either way though, the micro-drive with the plans wasn't inside. Tony B bragged to you too much about everything else he had control over. If he had the plans, I have to believe he would have slipped in a hint. I don't think he could help himself."

I shook my head and tossed the napkin on the table. "He didn't say anything along those lines." Another thought hit me, and I stared off for a moment into the distance.

"What are you thinking, Laurel?"

I held up a finger for another moment of silence. "What if this was all a misdirection scenario on Simon's part? What if he planted the Miami reference in the safe-deposit box to lead us there, and if I hadn't run into Tina, he gave her instructions to find me. She's the one who first said anything about the snuffbox. I only brought up Simon's name."

"Awfully subtle plan to count on your friend Tina to carry out." Jack frowned. "I think if I were Simon, I would want a more direct route of getting a message to you, if my plan was to send you scurrying in the wrong direction."

I rubbed my temples. "You're right. My mind is working overtime, and that's probably the worst thing I can do until we learn more."

He leaned closer. "If hearing what I did yesterday morning would help at all, I was following Melanie." He waggled his eyebrows. "I planted a tracking bug on her when I was in her office."

"You bugged her like you bugged me in London?"

"Same bug, same method. Melanie was happy to put the business card into her purse. She wasn't as smart as you were to recognize the card for what it truly was."

"I'll take that as a compliment." I smiled. "But I knew you were following me because I put an audio bug on you."

He put a hand to his chest, and joked, "A woman after my own heart."

"Forget the accolades," I said. "Tell me what happened yesterday morning."

"She had an early breakfast with a couple of men who looked like donors. Flirted shamelessly with them, and when she finally got up to leave they each handed her envelopes that I presumed held checks."

I could have made a hooker joke there, except I wanted to at least pretend to be an adult. Yet temptation was a difficult thing to keep tamped down. "I cannot believe you would voluntarily spend time with that woman. Let alone spend a weekend in Austria with her."

"We all do what we must for the good of queen and country."

"Oh, come on, Jack." I crossed my arms.

"Okay, then. We all make mistakes." He shrugged. "But at least I left things on good terms with her. Not like some people I know."

I knew the zinger was directed at me, and I had a strong suspicion he was fighting hard not to mention Simon. I didn't play along.

"Tell me you followed her into the alley and watched her kill the Tina impersonator. Please tell me it's true."

He laughed. "That's one secret I would not have kept from you. Miss Melanie did nothing more than schmooze rich old men in a restaurant a block away from Tina's condo. She had the opportunity, and likely the motive since I believe she's trying to ingratiate herself with Tony B as well. But she isn't the murderer. When I picked you up in Bricknell, I'd seen her drive off in a cab heading the other direction. The murder had already been committed, and I was irritated that I'd wasted the morning and learned nothing."

The compact almost shouted at me from my clutch, but I kept its identity a secret. I wanted to tell him in that moment, except there were too many missing pieces to consider. Was it a possible misdirection, or something to keep me too occupied to see other clues? I'd told Nico what he needed to know, but the rest? The photo needed to stay with me for a while. Jack would come to the same quick conclusion I did if he saw the people in the shot, but not yet. Tonight, it was mine. Maybe I'd tell him later. Or maybe Nico would tell him about the message.

No, I would show it to him tomorrow. He'd waited a day before telling me info I wanted to know. I deserved at least this evening to process my feelings about the compact and the photo. I needed to talk to Margarite, and I couldn't contact her without Jack's assistance. But he would expect to know why, and I needed to be ready to tell him.

What did Tony B mean about Jack not being who I thought? And what was this big favor the thug was doing for me? An overwhelming part of me wanted to dismiss the whole thing as a made-up drama, a mind game Tony B was chortling over. And I could have easily tossed the worry aside if...if I just knew something—anything—concrete about Jack. I told myself that's what Tony B was counting on, expecting me to use my own fear against myself.

"Jack, where are you from?"

He laughed. "England, of course. I presumed Hamish made that abundantly clear tonight."

Yes, Hamish did. Question was, who were Hamish and Milli? They left me with more questions than comfort. "But where? What part of England?"

"What is the big deal?" He smiled at me, pretending humor, but then I saw his jaw tighten. No more answers would be forthcoming tonight. His streak of honesty was spent.

The waiter appeared to refill our coffee cups, and Jack settled the bill. By the time we were back out on the street, an after-dinner walk sounded like the best idea in the world. We would grab separate cabs later.

The streets were still active with pedestrians, and the traffic hadn't eased up too much. October was a beautiful time of the year in Florence, and while I quite enjoyed the air, the ambience, and its historic loveliness, my mind remained busily at work.

I'm doing you a big favor. What the heck did he mean?

Something about the rooftop activity I'd seen earlier from the bell tower continued gnawing at me, and I told Jack about the palazzo and how I wanted to get a closer look at it from street level.

"What were they doing? Why the curiosity?" Jack asked quietly.

"A feeling I have, really. I couldn't see anything. But a lot of the roof was covered with awnings. Why have a rooftop area if you're going to block out all the sun? What if they were trying to block out voyeurs instead?"

"Good point. But if so, why pick a location in such close proximity to the bell tower and dome?" Even as he fired questions, we began heading that way. "If someone is hiding something, a place on the edge of town or in the Tuscan hillside would offer privacy without the need for awnings."

"Maybe the location is key. Like it's temporarily convenient." I shrugged for what felt like the millionth time that day. "Or maybe I'm grasping at straws, and the place belongs to someone who loves fresh air but who sunburns easily."

Jack offered me a genuine smile. "Or maybe they're having renovations done, and the workmen don't want to be in the hot sun? I'm happy to play along. We're not in any hurry, and the place you're describing isn't far. I see no reason not to check it out. Your intuition is one of the things I like best about you."

There were others? Sometimes the guy really surprised me.

But that was nothing compared to the surprise we both had when we turned the last corner before the palazzo. We saw the house. A second later, we realized Rollie was heading our way.

The well-lit street made it easy to identify him as he spoke angrily and gesticulated with abandon to a swarthy man with an ugly scar down the left side of his face. Scarface frowned as he listened and kept pace, but never answered back. In that instant I realized Rollie was probably chewing him out for something. Luckily, instead of facing forward, Rollie stared at the other man and missed seeing us. Beyond the surprise at chancing upon him in that location, I was frozen by the sheer disbelief at how he acted. The charming young man was gone, and this was a Rollie unlike anything I could have ever imagined.

Jack reacted quicker than I. His arms wrapped hard around me as he pivoted to slam us into the hard stone of the closest building. His forearms took the worst brunt of the collision, but as my head tried to catch up with the movements of my body, Jack's lips covered mine and coherent thought became impossible.

Everything that happened earlier in the evening faded away as Jack's lips moved over mine, hard yet soft with a proficiency denoting a lifetime of experience with the opposite sex. Somehow my fingers buried themselves in his hair, the texture as silky as I'd imagined and the length long enough to hold tight as the world disappeared and only the two of us remained. I could hear nothing except Jack's heartbeat thundering against mine, smell nothing but his woodsy, unique scent, and feel nothing but the hardness of his body in the fine material of his tux when he pressed against every part of me. Secure in the strength of his arms as they tightened around my own smaller body, offering refuge.

I'm not sure how long we stood fused together before he finally raised his head. Reluctantly, I opened my eyes, not ready to focus. We stood that way for several long moments until I realized two things: he was as affected as I was by what had happened, and two men walking by conversing in rapid French reminded me where we were and why. Jack moved his arms up to frame my face and shield my profile. From Rollie.

Jack had made the best move he could, hiding me to prevent detection. Making us appear as lovers. While I appreciated his quick reflexes, I had to be smart. I couldn't let anything happen between us.

I'm doing you a big favor.

I deliberately lowered my gaze, removed my hands from his hair, and pushed on his chest since I couldn't step away. "I appreciate your good reflexes, Jack." I hoped a compliment with a little bravado would put us back on partnering terms. The crazy feelings were nothing but an extension of all the weirdness and adrenalin from the gala, the lovely dinner, and the sudden heightened risk of exposure mercifully averted. That was it. "I was shocked when I saw Rollie. Your ploy was perfect. Thank you."

He obligingly moved back, stood for a second and blinked a couple of times. Then that slow smile spread across his face, and the Southern Charmer accent was back. The one he employed the first time we'd met. "Why, my pleasure, miss," he said in his familiar Clark Gable *Gone With the Wind* impersonation. "Anything to help a damsel in distress."

I laughed. I couldn't help it. "My hero. Would you also like to help this damsel break into the little ole palazzo right down the street, kind sir?"

"If you have the means, I have the muscle."

I pulled a hand out of my clutch, holding my favorite set of picks and the mini-flashlight.

TWENTY-TWO

I waved the clutch at him. "Those of us representing the Beacham Foundation are ready for whatever challenges come our way."

We walked a bit farther and ended up across the street from the palazzo, protected from direct view by a huge urn and a potted tree, and stared at the outside of the building. No one appeared to be inside, but we weren't taking any chances. It was too much of a coincidence to think Rollie and his companion weren't coming from there when we saw them.

While we watched and waited, Jack filled me in on something else he'd observed.

"The guy who was with Rollie is connected to Tony B."

"Are you sure?"

He turned my way and cocked a dark eyebrow. "Remember what I told you earlier today?"

"Right." I sighed. "You know everyone. You've memorized everyone."

He chuckled. "You sound envious, Laurel."

"I sound tired of everything continually changing at a moment's notice. What do you think his being with Rollie means? I'd assumed Scarface was in trouble about something."

"Possibly." Jack trained his gaze back onto the palazzo. "Scarface, as you call him, is a Sicilian who actually got his facial disfigurement when a political kidnapping went awry."

"So what is his expertise?"

"Whatever anyone will pay him to do." Jack looked my way again. "But he's never been connected with Moran."

This left more questions and no answers. "What's your best guess? Moran hired Tony B and now he's sent Rollie to get things working the way he wants? Or Rollie is branching out on his own, hired these thugs without adequate due diligence, and is angry things aren't done his way?"

"Both are possibilities, as is a third option. The possibility we talked about weeks ago in France. That they're a part of the new underground group we've heard warning chatter about, but we can't get intel on yet. The one we believe is actually spearheading the huge art heist."

"But you still have no substance about the organization, right?"

"Right. Like I said, it's conjecture from clues we've picked out of chatter different intelligence sources have heard."

I hugged my clutch, thinking. "No." I shook my head. "It doesn't make sense. Moran wants Rollie to take over operations. It's Rollie who says he doesn't want the job."

Jack whirled and clasped my shoulders. "When did he tell you this?"

"A couple of weeks ago, when we first met. Before he and I left for the festival in Le Puy-en-Velay." I frowned, thinking back to what Rollie had said that day. "It was when he was still trying to make me believe the family business was an architectural firm. He said his grandfather was disappointed in him for not taking on the duties of the family firm."

He let go of me and turned back to stare at the palazzo as he spoke. "Yeah, I see what you mean. But it still could have been a ruse. He was lying, after all, about the type of business. The whole thing could have been a way to impress you. If he actually wants to be in charge and Moran won't give him the reins, he could have thrown in with Tony B on the promise of a seat of command. Realizing later he should have better picked his partners in crime."

We both seemed to have run out of ideas. There were city noises and strains of conversation periodically riding the wind but nothing that set off alarm bells for either of us. Everyone passing by seemed to be heading in a particular direction. No one took notice of the palazzo. The building was going slightly to seed after five hundred-plus years, but the bones were good, and someone had cared for it through the centuries.

After a good twenty minutes, we'd exhausted our patience and moved to investigate getting inside the palazzo via a side door along a darkened section of the block. The lock was tricky at first, but perseverance and determination triumphed. Jack left my side, motioning me to stay put, and took a quick walk-through. While I resented his highhandedness, this was not the time for argument. I removed my heels and stockings as a matter of caution, and hoped my feet had healed enough from the previous day's urban hang gliding. I knew wearing shoes was smarter for protection, but while neither of us really thought anyone was inside, high heels are never suggested for discreet breaking and entering. Even these ultra-light cuties made their share of noise as I walked. Jack made another quick sweep of the area and came back to my side. "We were right. No one is here. Go ahead and wear your shoes."

"No. Thanks for the concern, but this is much safer in the long run." I hung my heels on my necklace to keep my hands free and followed Jack into the darkness. Something about the blackness around us made me whisper, "Flashlight, or turn on the lights?"

"Let's take a quick jog upstairs first using the flashlight. I've got a funny feeling about this. Something feels fishy."

So he was sensing it too. Another setup? I hadn't wanted to voice my thoughts. I was beginning to feel like Polly Paranoid—envisioning scary scenarios with no facts to support the suppositions.

I flashed the light over the walls of the ground floor, and the frescos made me stop and catch my breath. These were no forgeries, but fifteenth- and sixteenth-century works created for the family who built and used this once grand abode as their home. They had likely delighted every family who lived here since. My hand itched to take pictures, to document how the wealthy lived and what they saw every day five centuries ago. The hallways were narrow, and the walls that weren't frescoed were most often covered in marble.

The past opulence had to have been breathtaking, and the ambience was still enough to make me stop in my tracks until Jack hurried me along. As we neared the main entrance and the staircase, I tipped my light upward to the high two-story ceilings. The ornate chandelier once held candles but had been electrified sometime after the turn of the last century.

We mounted the stairs. Within minutes, we traversed the first and second floors and took a closed staircase up to the covered roof. No one jumped out and said "Boo!" though I probably would have wet myself if it happened.

Jack returned to my side, and I said, "I vote for the lights. There's too much to see and look at with a flash. But let's hurry."

He reached out to the switch we found, and the rooftop illumination blinded us for a moment.

Instead of the usual paraphernalia, like chairs, tables, loungers, and potted plants, the space was packed with unopened crates and boxes, all wrapped in heavy plastic. "We don't have time to check these out. There are too many," I said.

"Agreed. But we can open a couple."

"Do we want anyone to know we've been here?"

"At this point, I don't think it matters. We've got to get something going. Besides, they won't know it was us, will they?"

I couldn't argue with his logic, but I wanted to badly. Something about this whole thing stank.

"Do you have the wicked sharp thing you used to cut me down in Orlando?"

The clutch was open in a second, and I slapped my favorite weapon in his hand like a surgical nurse. He approached the nearest crate and cut through the plastic like it was cotton candy. He quickly pried the lid, took a look, and slammed it shut.

"Wait a minute. We're in this together," I protested.

"Trust me. You don't want to see."

I ignored him and lifted the lid. What little bits remained

somehow identified the contents as human. I stared into the crate, fixated. "Why isn't there a smell?"

"They're using a type of chemical to break down the body and prevent odor. This didn't happen very long ago."

I pulled my gaze away from the grisly remains and looked around the roof. "Do you think all of these contain dead bodies?"

Jack replaced the lid, closing the deceased back in the coffin crate. I stepped away and took a deep breath. Seeing a human being dumped in a crate and left to rot on a rooftop filled me with a sense of unspeakable horror. He checked more crates while I spent the time picking my jaw off the ground and looking around fearfully for any sign of new trouble. As he moved closer again, he said, "If this is as big as Nico speculates, people become expendable pretty fast." He opened several more and shook his head. "Let's get out of here and recon through the rest of the place."

"More bodies?"

His face was grim as we walked to the door. "No, only saw the one. Most of the others hold artwork. Ready for shipping. Multiple copies of the same works. And that crate over there—" he pointed "—guns. I don't know if they are for sale or for security, but we can't waste time looking through the rest right now. What I've seen is enough to keep me awake all night."

I turned off the lights, and he followed me as we walked down the stairs to the third floor.

"I'm not sure I understand. A body and guns? What's going on?"

"Probably someone who crossed whomever is in charge. Nico's right. This is much more extensive than anyone has imagined. C'mon, let's get busy."

It became clear the second floor served as a studio. Different rooms became galleries for different mediums, and the entire space was wired with full-spectrum lights. Canvases of all sizes and shapes, wood, clay, metal pieces and all the tools associated with such things. Even jewelry and unfinished silver and goldsmith work littered the various rooms. All in differing stages of development.

Several top-floor rooms contained labs where it looked and smelled like chemical processes were taking place. Varnishing? Aging? Murdering? Creating mediums to mimic old art?

"But why do all of this in a historic palazzo in the middle of the most historically artistic place on the planet?" he asked. "Counterfeiting great works in the very heart of the city defined by the Italian Renaissance? Who would do that?"

"Someone with the bravado to pull it off. The ego to enjoy the juxtaposition," I responded, feeling the anger boil up inside me. "Someone who wants to flaunt his thievery right under the noses of the people committed to the celebration of true art and beauty."

"The irony would give his ego a boost every time he walked through the door," Jack said in agreement. "Another reason this is probably tied to the marked counterfeit masterpieces we've uncovered."

"But who? Moran? Or Tony B?"

"Tony B doesn't have the financial wherewithal for an operation of this scope," Jack said, authority in his voice. He shook his head. "Though he'd like people to believe otherwise. The man could be a general contractor-type for an organization, but as the leader...no. That doesn't mean I can't see him ordering the death of someone, then stupidly believing he could hide the body in a crate on a roof filled with similar crates of evidence proving criminal activity."

"I agree with your low opinion of his abilities and intellect."

"I thought you might."

So if Moran was running things through Rollie's presence in Florence, why hire a thug like Tony B, who didn't seem to try to curb his goons, and who possessed a vicious streak of his own that was almost tattooed to his face? Granted his record up until this weekend had always appeared fairly clean, but no one changed so quickly without a trigger for the switch deep in the DNA of his black little soul. Jack's words left a lot to think about, but the minutes were skittering by madly. We didn't have time to do much more than view and speculate as we rushed through the huge and intricate spaces, through the many rooms, and progressed down to the first upper floor.

There, paintings covered the walls, and all manner of works were displayed. The floor held a sense of the temporary, a sort of waiting in the air as though each and every object was impermanent and could be moved elsewhere at a moment's notice.

"This is where everything must cure," Jack said.

Of course. The creative process had several steps before a piece fully became whole. The canvas, the wood, the clay, the metal—each had to dry at individual rates.

"Look, Jack, this is a Poussin. I'd swear to it." I ran across the room. "Over here is what looks like a Turner and a Cézanne. I need more time—"

"Our time's run out, Laurel. We have to get out of here."

While I'd been focused on the art, Jack paid attention to our surroundings. He stood at the doorway waiting for me, and I made my way toward him. He dowsed the light. I passed him and turned on my flashlight to lead the way, but he whispered urgently, "No."

I clicked it off. He pulled me back toward him and put his mouth near my ear.

"Listen carefully. No matter what happens in the next few minutes, I want you to quickly and quietly find a place to hide and figure out a way to get out of here that doesn't depend on returning to the ground floor."

I slowly nodded, knowing he would feel the movement. "But what about you?"

"Forget about me. You are not to try to find me or help me. You may be putting both our lives in jeopardy if you do. We each need to take care of ourselves from this point forward until I get back in touch with you." He gave me a small shake as if for emphasis. "Play tourist. Have fun. Understand? Don't let anyone prove the real reason you're in Florence."

I again nodded and reached with my free hand to touch where he held my shoulder. "Be careful, Jack."

A soft kiss warmed my ear before he whispered, "I'm counting on your creativity and deviousness to get you out of here safely. Don't let me down."

I squeezed his hand and took off. On the second floor, I'd noticed an architectural structure in the far eastern room that seemed familiar to me, but I hadn't quite worked out how. I wondered if its counterpart was on this floor and raced in silence to further investigate.

Yes! The same. I skimmed my hand over the wood, searching for the irregularity I knew I would find. With a touch, a short door matching the wall paneling popped open. One step inside, and I used the small metal knob to pull the door closed behind me. I switched on my flashlight and knocked away cobwebs. I hated spiders, but evidence of their habitation meant no one used this recently. It wasn't just a space. There was an actual, very narrow, stairway. It went upward or down to the ground floor. I picked the downward option. Jack said not to return to the street level, but I couldn't bear to go up to the roof with what waited up there. Plus, the Fendi with all my emergency tools to safely climb down the palazzo's façade was still in my closet at the *pensione*. Ending up a greasy spot on the pavement, or if not a greasy spot at least broken in some way, was not part of my game plan.

Halfway down the stairs it sounded like all hell broke loose below me. No shooting. A lot of yelling and furniture movement. That kind of drama. And even scarier when it was sound alone and I couldn't follow the action.

I proceeded quietly until the stairway ended, and I stepped down to the very narrow enclosure. My fingers quickly identified the way out. I did not want to be trapped.

Because a narrow band of light lit up my space, I reasoned the paneling on the ground level in the room must have a decorative feature keeping the two pieces from sealing. After switching off my flashlight and sticking it in the clutch, I discovered I could see into the room if I stretched taller on my toes. I carefully pulled on my shoes and found I was now at a perfect height to see.

We hadn't fully toured the bottom floor, but I could tell this was the equivalent of a formal living area. It seemed packed with men—the noise level was atrocious—and the furniture could only be described as askew.

Jack stood in handcuffs, expressionless, and surrounded by men speaking Italian. Most wore uniforms, several dressed in suits, but all were either talking with each other or into cell phones. With this many people talking at once, in a language not my own, it was difficult to catch what was being said.

But not impossible. Something about how great a day it was with the apprehension of a famous thief they had been pursuing for months.

Say what?

As I nearly disregarded Jack's warning and stepped into the room in his defense, Tony B sauntered in from the entry. All conversation stopped, and the men came to attention. Even the ones on their cells stopped talking.

The next thing I heard was Tony B speaking Italian and calling Jack a hardened criminal. Hoping he'd be kept locked up until Jack was an old man.

Bastard.

The man who I assumed to be head of the team was part of the *carabinieri* contingent, or military police, with half the backup his men, and the others uniformed local *polizia*. How did Tony B get both military and civilian forces to work with him?

The top man nodded. He thanked Tony B for helping in the capture of a man who had eluded authorities for years. Tony B nodded and stood, waiting with a bored expression. What did the guy want? Flowers?

The head *carabinieri* quickly gathered everyone together to leave, and two uniforms manhandled Jack in a way I hated to watch. They hustled him out of view and, I assumed, out of the palazzo.

Tony B was left alone in the room. He strode toward a bar in the corner and poured himself a drink. The hood took a long swallow. He contemplated the empty glass for a moment, then slammed the glass against the wall. It shattered, and the shards showered to the floor.

Seconds later, he left the room, clicking off the light as he passed the switch. What sounded like the outer door echoed closed, and I heard a lock set.

The darkness gave me a kind of safety zone to contemplate what I'd seen. I now understood Jack's warning but not how he knew what was coming. Or why. My brain was too full, and I knew if I didn't move soon, the panic would start. Something I could not risk.

I focused on my breathing. Told myself to consider Jack. He'd said I could put him in jeopardy. Well, I could put both of us in jeopardy if I was discovered, but right now his predicament seemed far worse than mine. Remembering his warning helped me stay in that tight place until a full thirty minutes passed. I opened the door of the crawl space, then crouched to wiggle out.

Jack said to have fun and play tourist—I presumed to show I couldn't have been a player in this drama. Pretend and act carefree. But how? I didn't know what any of this meant, but I knew I wouldn't be able to casually dismiss seeing him dragged away, cuffed by police in a foreign country, and taken to a jail cell in who knew what kind of condition.

I didn't know anyone to call to help Jack.

I took a deep breath. I had to get out of here without being seen, return to the *pensione*, and call Nico. Possibly Max as well. Someone had to figure out what to do.

TWENTY-THREE

I hung up from my third call, frustrated. My little bedroom—so lovely earlier in the day—felt like it was closing in on me with every unsuccessful, long-distance, middle-of-the-freaking-night phone call. Since my return, I'd talked to Nico, Cassie, and yes, even Max. All three said the same thing, "Come home."

No way. I used the anonymous Italian phone to call Jack's cell, but after the umpteenth time hearing his voicemail kick on, I squeezed the phone between my hands and allowed the tears to flow. I'd never felt so powerless in my life. It was a totally foreign and completely miserable feeling.

Then Nico called back. "Tell me what you want for me to do. I will do it."

I hadn't had any options a moment before, and his words threw me off-guard a second. But no more than a second. "Find Tina Schroeder for me. Find where she's hiding."

"The dead girl?" His voice was incredulous. "I imagine she's in the Miami morgue."

Past time to fill him in on the rest of the previous evening's surprises. After a fast wrap-up, I said, "There's no doubt in my mind Tony B is behind her bogus death and sudden rejuvenation. See if you can get any intel on where the thug would hide her in Florence. I'd say to check her passport too, but I doubt she's traveling under her own name."

"Who do you think really got her throat cut? I assume there truly was a body since the news organizations reported on the mugging."

Given the lack of a hue and a cry over Tina's disappearance, I had little doubt. "It had to be her mother, Phyllis, who died in that alley. Tina was the family's meal ticket, and I've been checking my phone for either a memorial service or even an offered reward for information on the murder. Nothing. Not a damned thing associated with Tina's name except the flash reports from the newspaper websites. The dead body had to be Phyllis."

"And you believe Tina can help you find Jack?"

I took a long deep breath before answering. "I believe if I find where she is that she'd better tell me something, or she and her mother may be able to share a grave."

Nico chuckled. "Got it. I'll get information to you as soon as possible."

"Thank you."

Even better, I knew since he didn't hedge at all that I could count on something soon. One of the things I liked best about Nico, if he couldn't do something, he would say so. If he expected he could, then you should believe it as well. Still, he didn't end the conversation without a warning.

"From what you said happened at the palazzo, Jack apparently knew something was up. Tomorrow, do exactly what he said. Play tourist, act carefree, and do what you are told for once. We don't need to lose you as well."

I bristled, but then I remembered Jack's hand over my mouth and agreed with Nico. "Yes, I'll ride my Vespa, and I'll be a good girl."

He snorted, then asked, "How do you think he knew what was going down?"

I'd racked my brain over this very question and decided there was one possibility. "We both felt leery of the place as soon as we got on the roof, but I think if Jack had actually known something was going to happen by then, he would have warned me. I believe he must have set motion detectors when he did the recon of the outside of the building when we first arrived. Maybe with audio capability to hear chatter before they stormed the place."

"Notice a receiver in his ear?"

"I didn't think to look. I should have planted my own sensors too. Sloppy, I know. I was lulled by the wine and great dinner." And maybe the kiss—but I wasn't going to mention that to Nico.

"Good enough. I will get on this and let you know something as soon as I can."

When our call disconnected, I scooped up the Fendi and dug around for my cache of business cards. The one for the Miami detective was right behind the one for the CIA guy with the New York accent. I held a card in each hand and contemplated my next move. Miami PD likely had a more vested interest in news about Tina, but the CIA possessed the international reach this problem needed. Equally important, however, was the fact the CIA guy was already pursuing the human trafficking case. He would not likely be as tuned in to what was happening in Florence. Pros and cons weighed, my decision was much easier.

"Roblo." The detective answered on the second ring. Thanks to the magic of time zones, it was barely dark in Florida.

"Detective, this is Laurel Beacham. You interviewed me at the Bricknell condo where a woman identified as Tina Schroeder was killed on Friday morning. Are you still working that case?"

I could hear the suspicion in his voice when he dragged out his, "Yes. Who is this again?"

Briefly, I identified myself and gave him a synopsis on what had happened since he and I met in the lobby of Tina's building. After I finished, there was silence, then I heard a squeak and assumed he leaned back in his chair. A sigh followed.

"I guess I have to believe you since we've held back the information that the body wasn't who we'd originally believed. To weed out the nut job callers," he said. "So much for my plans to watch the Dolphins play the Broncos tonight."

"That's the beauty of on-demand streaming, Detective. Always ready later when you do have time to watch."

"Yeah, I'll remember that."

"I'm inferring from your tone that this is a new and interesting development?"

"Did you really have any doubt?" He chuckled, the sound warm and deliciously deep. "Nothing like answering the phone just before I'm set to get off duty, to learn the puzzling murder case we've been pursuing all day has developed into a fleeing suspect instead. Who is actually alive and attending parties in Italy." Then his voice moved a shade sharper in tone. "You guarantee this is her? I mean, we already figured out we had the wrong identification. Our corpse is someone decades older—"

"Likely her mother," I interrupted.

"Hmm. Okay. That helps." He stayed silent for a moment, and I waited. If I tried to talk him into anything, I risked any advantage I had in piquing his curiosity. It was his job on the line if I wasn't right, after all. Another minute into the wait and he asked, "Do you have any proof I can take to my superiors?"

I thought of the glass Jack had slipped into his jacket pocket at last night's event and wished once more that I'd tried to stash it in my clutch at the restaurant. "We had fingerprint proof, but it went with my partner."

"The one taken away by the Italian police, who you believe are following the orders of the man responsible for Tina Schroeder's getaway?"

I smiled. "Couldn't have said it better myself. You catch on quick, Roblo. I like that in a detective."

He chuckled again, and I imagined his head shaking as he said, "Let me see what I can do. Is there anything else you think might help me?"

I provided Nico's direct number and explained what I'd tasked him to do since we'd last talked. Then I also gave Roblo the CIA guy's direct line. "He's actually working on a human trafficking job we turned over to him, the FBI, and Interpol. But Jack seemed pretty chummy with the three of them, and you might get help there too. But it may be extremely limited due to their current workload."

"No doubt. Who is this Jack Hawkes guy anyway?" he asked.

My mind raced over the possibilities: spy, recovery agent,

military intelligence. Or, like I'd heard last night, a thief who'd been highly sought by the Italian police. I could have said any or all of these options. Instead I replied, "When you find out, I'd appreciate if you'd let me know." Then I said good-bye and disconnected from the call.

As the scene shifted to the possibility of action, I could only wait until these new feelers found something for me to use. That still left me with an excess of energy in the middle of the night and no way to expend it. Not being able to contact Jack also made me think of the photograph and how I didn't know of a way to reach Margarite.

I was going to tell him about the photo tomorrow. Then I looked at my watch and corrected. *Make that today.*

The photo was another wild card. Someone had to have added it to my bag while it was getting kicked around the gallery. Margarite was obviously the older of the two beautiful ingénues in the shot. If the photo was hers, and she wanted me to have the picture, she could have easily given it to me on the yacht. Did she pass it to me this way because the other woman in the scene, my mother, was also topless? Did she think it would offend me? If so, she obviously had never heard about any of my college exploits.

The man who stood talking to the enigmatic Margarite and my mother resembled Rollie. The man was older than the women, yet still close enough to their ages to have had an assignation with either of them. Or not. And why was that the first thing to pop into my head?

Rollie. I mentally ran through his error-filled conversational snippets. Had he really made a mistake with the way he used "photograph" for "picture," or was the slip actually his clever foreshadowing of a plan to secret the compact and its contents into my possession?

Was I meant to focus on the photo? Or the brief message on the back?

Maybe Nico could locate a phone connection to the Folly Roost or find its sailing itinerary somewhere. He needed to run an exhaustive check on the yacht, in case it tied in some way with Jack's background.

In contemplating timing again though, the photo had to have occurred during my mother's and father's engagement period. Given Margarite's story on the yacht, I couldn't imagine Grandfather taking such a strong interest in my mother's extracurricular activities otherwise. My darling grandpapa was a bit of a prude about keeping the family name pristine. My father's antics after Grandfather's death would have absolutely killed the dear old man if he hadn't already been deceased. As much as I loved my grandfather, and as much as I knew he adored his daughter-in-law, if the scene in the photo happened while my father and mother were dating, I knew in my heart Grandfather would have ended the couple's contact. On the other hand, if an engagement was already public, that would be the leverage my wonderfully sneaky grandmother could use to keep my grandfather from any act to rock her son's happiness. I loved both my grandparents and still missed them every day, but they were truly a pair.

No time to get maudlin.

Did Grandfather know about the photograph and that Moran—or someone who looked very much like him, a son perhaps?—smiled and spoke to the two women that day on the beach? Was Moran's connection, even if fleeting, Grandfather's true worry about the sojourn the two women took in the sun? It seemed impossible now that Margarite revealed the story a couple of short nights ago.

My mind backtracked through every moment of the last couple of days and came back time and again to the fact that nothing made enough sense to be conclusive. Yet if I had to make a leap of faith, I would jump toward the idea that Rollie planted the compact. I had no real facts to back up the idea, other than the knowledge he actually was on the spot and Margarite remained unseen if she attended the gallery gala. Yet in the tangled web of my thoughts, Rollie made the most sense.

But that still doesn't answer why.

I realized I would be beyond senseless soon if I went another night without enough sleep. I crawled into bed and fought the covers and my demons the rest of those predawn hours, with terrible dreams of Jack calling for help and Tony B laughing hysterically. Despite my good intentions to rest, I rose early, bathed, and dressed in the same jeans and top I'd worn the day before. It seemed like years ago. My hair went into a tight ponytail, and I was ready.

I grabbed what was left of my euro stash and an emergency credit card, and stuffed the money and my phone in a pocket. Nico hadn't sent new reserves as promised. I needed to call later and remind him. No matter. I had to do something fast, or I would go crazy.

My landlady met me downstairs with a key. She was dressed all in black and held a lace scarf in her other hand. Loosely translating her Italian, but mostly following her hand movements, I determined she was going to Mass and lunch somewhere with friends. I took the rounded silver key she pushed at me and nodded understanding. "*Grazie.*"

A nearby bar offered my best source for a quick cup of coffee, and as I walked, I called Jack again. Same answer. Straight to voicemail.

While I drank coffee, I searched my email and found the directions Nico sent for the Vespa place and quickly ran it down. Jack told me to play tourist, and this was the next best thing. If questioned later as to why I didn't wonder about my partner's absence, I could point to the rental receipt that showed a lone reservation made by Nico the day prior and claim I'd never intended to see Jack the day after the event.

Papers signed, international driver's license copied, and I was the proud possessor of a tiny blue scooter for the day, with no real idea where I was going. Nevertheless, I felt relieved Nico paid the entire day's fee. I had options, even if they had little substance at the moment.

A display of baseball-styled caps that carried the rental company's logo stood at the end of the counter. I asked the price, and my attentive clerk, Enzo, flashed a gorgeous smile and said, "*Signorina,* is yours."

"*Mille grazie.*" I put a hand on his forearm.

His smile broadened when I put on the cap there in the store. He reached up to reset it and let his fingers touch my cheek. Bless his heart. He had no idea I was more interested in hiding my face in public than I was in knowing him. I'd have to remind Nico to send Enzo a big tip as compensation.

The bigger problem with wheels but no destination is that it gave me more time to think about what little I knew of Jack and our current predicament. I honestly knew nothing for certain about him. He could be a thief—I'd certainly accused him of being one often enough. But there was more to him, and a lot more to find out before I could decide one way or the other. Unfortunately, the GPS on my phone provided a roadmap of the city, but not one to Jack's soul.

Florence is approximately forty square miles and divided into five main districts pretty much identified and named by nearby churches. I'd spent a good amount of time in the city with my grandfather and my father on art trips or short holidays. Flavia and I had also come to Firenze together on a quick backpack tour the summer before I left for Cornell, even though she was already out of university. Our family connections always kept us fairly close, which was one of the reasons we were all together in Florence the night *The Portrait of Three* disappeared.

I headed toward the Viale Giovanni Amendola, planning to ride for a while. The noise and traffic helped me shut my mind to anything but the sights around me as I played tourist. I eventually exited the roadway, parked, and began walking. Somehow I ended up almost back to the spot where I began. I grabbed another coffee and called Flavia before I thought twice about what to say to her. Did I want to leave it at a quick hello? And why hadn't she tried to call me?

Suddenly thunderstruck, I felt gut punched. Why hadn't she told me about her connection with the historic gallery? She gave me the new name in the email and left it at that. The frightening realizations continued to grow. How Tony B was at the gala. How Tina disappeared.

A chill ran through me, and I moved to end the connection before she answered. But the call went straight to voicemail. She would see that I'd phoned. To cover, I said, "Wanted to let you know I'm in Florence. Great event last night. We'll get together next time."

It seemed prudent not to request a return call.

The brave little Vespa sat waiting at the curb, but even it looked sad. The buzzing scooter hadn't done its magic. I just felt stung.

The Vespa ate up the miles back toward the city center. At the first public spot offering me a park-and-leave option for the scooter, I took it. I loved the little wasp, but for what I needed to do now, I would accomplish much more on two feet.

I left my hair in its ponytail and pulled my cap brim down lower over my brow. A good trek later, and I had eyes on the palazzo. A huge truck sat out front.

This could be a simple pickup, or something much worse. I took off at a fast walk toward the bell tower, wanting to run but unwilling to risk the attention I might receive if anyone currently monitored the area. At the ticket booth, I was one euro short of the price. I whirled around to beg a euro off a passing tourist, when the ticket taker asked, "*Signorina,* you are back today? Alone?"

He remembered Jack too. So much for my disguise. I turned and smiled. "*Sì.* I wanted to go up again." I pointed to the top of the tower, then held up my right index finger and thumb pinched together. "But I am short."

"*Sì.*" He waggled the fingers of his right hand in a gesture that told me to hand him my euros. He counted the money and stuffed it in his cash drawer as he handed me a ticket. "Enjoy."

"Oh, *grazie, grazie.*" The feeling of relief was incredible. I raced to the top much faster than the day before and shot over to the window I'd originally used to spot the palazzo.

Nothing. Everything on the roof was gone. No awnings, no crates. Even the lights we used had been pulled loose and dangling wire remained. I felt sick.

How would Jack and I be able to prove what had gone on in the palazzo with no evidence?

As I stood there, I watched the huge truck that had been outside, and which was hidden from above by the height of the palazzo, suddenly appear below as it turned and rumbled away. With the strict rules governing what vehicles could be on these streets, and the allotted usage times, perhaps we could use the information to track the truck and its owner.

If I'd ignored Jack's instructions and called Interpol last night, could they have gotten a warrant in time? If they believed me. If Tony B didn't have someone there on his payroll as well. No, I knew a search warrant that quickly without preliminary work was a ludicrous thought. Besides, admitting I knew anything about the palazzo to authorities could risk making Jack's situation worse. I didn't know how, and I could only rely on his warning in the dark, but the facts didn't change. And from the looks of things below, Interpol would not have arrived in time with a warrant, and the Florence police would have likely held it all up since they'd raided the place last night and left it intact.

My brain started making lists and plans. Things I needed to accomplish once I had more information.

The walk back down was infinitely slower. My brain couldn't stop running through all the loose ends. When I suddenly recognized the replica of Michelangelo's *David,* I realized I'd traveled all the way to the Piazza della Signoria without any conscious memory of the walk. How could I be so stupid? The tourists were legion around me, and anyone could have grabbed me as I meandered around brainless as a zombie.

To spend the rest of the afternoon gazing at the lovely public statues was my preference, but I needed a less open place where I could think in peace and more relative security. After the ugliness of the night before, I also needed to see something truly beautiful.

Bird droppings, colored red and purple by the grapes and berries the local birds devoured, decorated this outdoor copy of *David*. Two pigeons roosted regally on the shoulders of the statue. I had mixed feelings, half-mirth and half-irritation at the almost blasphemous treatment of the publicly accessible copy. Then realized I could see the original in its own perfect, protected setting. I changed idea into direction and headed for the Accademia Gallery.

Another short walk, this time with my mind kept firmly on my task, and I reached the Accademia. When I saw the ticket taker, I panicked again, until I remembered the lone credit card in my front pocket. I needed to risk the chance that someone could track me here. I'd be gone before they had time to try anything.

I entered the hall leading to what was likely the world's best-known sculpture. The crowd was typical for a weekend viewing, but I didn't have the sense of claustrophobia I normally felt when too many bodies tried to enter the same space. I took my time and looked at the double row of unfinished Michelangelo sculptures standing guard along the walls leading into *David's* octagonal space. The struggling sculptures stopped in mid-movement, showing the art trying to break free of the marble. Michelangelo said he didn't create his sculptures, that God had put them inside the rock, and it was his job as an artist to help them break free. No explanation was given about why those prisoners were left half trapped, but their place in history remained as secure as the half-completed gatekeepers standing watch in the anteroom of the masterpiece.

I wondered who guarded Jack, where he was, and if his would be a story where the man became a strong beacon or a prisoner trapped forever by the circumstances that made him.

Some of my tension rolled away as I let the light-beige and eggshell palate of the hall wash over me. I stared at *David* and wondered for the millionth time what it would be like to create something like this. A classic masterwork for the ages. Even in the use of symbolism by making the right hand larger to denote the hand of God and his power in our lives. A masterpiece, a message, a metaphor.

From my Sunday school years, I recalled David was a lad in his early teens. Maybe fourteen? But this was no high school freshman on the pedestal before me. Michelangelo captured more than the beauty and confidence of youth, but also the resolve to make the right thing happen.

What was the way to make the right thing happen for me, for Jack, and for this mission that seemed to change constantly? I drifted backward to stand next to a wall, out of a straight line of sight as new arrivals entered.

It was known that Michelangelo dissected cadavers to get a greater knowledge about human anatomy. This would have been a punishable offense a generation or two earlier, but to him and other great renaissance masters, their art wasn't simply about beauty. It included the science and nature beyond the art and splendor as well. They believed there were an infinite amount of parts that made up and celebrated life, and the masterpieces they produced proved up their theory.

What did I need to strip away to see the true measure of what seemed an insurmountable task? What did I need to dissect to see the truth?

Tony B definitely had to be part of Tina's great illusion, as well as the puppet master behind last night's *carabinieri/polizia* raid. I knew without a doubt he'd intended for me to be led away in cuffs— either with or instead of Jack. I was tired of his taunts and the way he bullied his way to upset my plans—our plans. How badly were we upsetting his plans that he remained focused on toppling the two of us?

I contemplated the statue's slingshot and wondered again about Jack and his resolve last night to protect me. I hugged my torso and told myself Jack was the underdog hero in this, and for once I had to listen to him and let him work with whatever pitiful pile of rocks he had for his personal slingshot. Let him rocket his humble weapons on his own. But like *David,* I knew Jack had an inner resolve, even if he wouldn't answer any of the personal questions about himself I hurled his way. As hard as it was to trust him in the little things, I realized in that moment I'd always been able to trust him when my safety was at stake.

I pulled out my phone to text Nico and asked him to find an Italian lawyer completely unaffiliated with the foundation. We could at least see if Jack had legal representation already. And if Nico couldn't do that, I said to find a good, reputable private investigator operating in Florence to provide us with updates as the proceedings progressed. I sent the text and heard an immediate *ping* nearby.

Nico pushed at his phone screen with a finger as he walked closer, then opened his arms and drew me into his embrace. *Thank you* seemed too little to say, so I quipped instead, "Thought you hated field work."

"I do." He released me from the hug and used a finger on my chin to tip my face upward. "But I do not mind doing pickups. Especially for beautiful blondes who are easy to track by GPS. Let's go collect your things and get back to London."

I pulled away from him and stood tall. "First, you're going to tell me how to find that little bitch, Tina. We aren't leaving Florence until I have the chance to question her."

"Or beat the information out of her?"

"I'll point out her physical flaws." I smirked. "That will hurt worse than my fists."

TWENTY-FOUR

Nico hustled me out of the Accademia Gallery and raised a hand to stop me every time I tried to speak. Outside, he scanned the periphery and kept a hand on my elbow as we hurried through the crowds. We walked a couple of blocks before he slowed his pace and asked in a soft voice, "Why do you think she remains in Florence?"

"Has Tony B left the country?" I asked.

"No. I find no property recorded in his names or that of his wife, and he has no hotel room booked in his name. But according to his passport he is still in Italy. When I checked his cell phone records, his calls showed he was in Florence and busy online until last night and is currently en route to Pisa."

"How—" I waved a hand. "Never mind."

We were nearing the start of vehicular accessibility, and I turned on the next cross street to more easily find a taxi. "We'll head for my *pensione* and get my things. It doesn't have any internet facilities. We'll go and camp out in your hotel room while we make plans."

"I came straight from the airport."

"Then we know what our first order of business is."

"Right. Secure a hotel room."

We were close enough to the traffic to hear distant engine noises when I spotted our tail, dressed casually in jeans and a dark brown leather jacket. He followed from the other side of the avenue. I remembered him from the Accademia Gallery when Nico's phone pinged and I'd shifted my gaze his way. I used shop windows to follow his progress, making sure before I spoke. When

Nico pushed me into a cigar shop a moment later, I knew my observant geek noticed the shadow too.

Nico ask the shop owner if we could exit out his back door. "No," I said. "I have a better idea."

Minutes later, we departed from the store with a small bag that held the lighter we purchased as a cover. I'd pocketed the euros Nico gave me and briefed him in the store on where the Vespa was parked. At the next corner, I took the bag and waved gaily as he frowned and took off at an angle toward the location of the parking area.

He'd made me promise, actually *made me hold up a hand and swear*, that I would stay close to other people as I walked and keep my eyes open to dangerous traps. Like I didn't have sense enough to do that myself. But I didn't argue. He was concerned, and I understood why. And though he wasn't happy about it, once he'd listened to the quick plan I sketched out, he agreed it was our best option.

When we split up and I was the person followed instead of Nico, without any hesitation from the shadow I might add. It meant our suspicions were valid.

I arrived unscathed at the outer end of the pedestrian zone. My watcher's duties apparently were to pursue rather than intercept. I was relieved by this revelation but not particularly reassured about my future safety. When I arrived at the road I recognized as the one leading to the parking area, I pretended to window shop and drifted down the sidewalk in the direction toward where I'd left the Vespa. I wanted to give Nico time to move the scooter into position to watch for us. We'd decided not to call or text when he was ready, in case my shadow got too close at the wrong time. Once enough time elapsed, I quickened my pace and noticed my "friend" doing likewise.

The blue front fender of the Vespa peeped out from the cover of a shrub, and I assumed Nico was ready for the second phase of our plan. I watched for two empty cabs coming at the same time and hailed the first one.

As expected, the other cab was quickly flagged down by my tail.

I gave the cabbie the address of the *pensione*. I was paid up for several more days, and I intended to leave today without a good-bye to my landlady. I wanted her to be able to honestly say she expected me back at any time. A look at my watch made me send up a quick prayer that her priest was long winded and her lunch a lengthy affair. We were working on instinct and serendipity and had to take every advantage.

The taxi soon pulled to the curb in front of my *pensione*, and the other cab drove on, but stopped where someone in the backseat could easily observe my destination.

As I paid my fare, I asked, "Can you come back for me in thirty minutes?"

He cocked his bald head to one side. "Thirty *minuti*?"

"*Sì*." I racked my brain for the Italian word for return, finally remembering, "You…" I pointed at him. "*Ritorno* here…" I pointed down, toward the spot the taxi occupied in the street. "In thirty *minuti*." I felt like such an ugly American with my disjointed words and sign language.

"*Sì*." He nodded and gave me a wide smile. "*Sì*."

I thanked him and climbed from the cab, walking casually toward the front door despite a desire to run. My taxi pulled away. I hoped I would see him again soon, as promised. The other cab remained parked in its nearby location.

Palming the key, I turned slightly when I got to the door and used my body to hide the fact I was unlocking the entrance. A neighbor standing outside was surprised when I called a greeting and waved, pretending I was happy to see her. When I actually opened the front door, I extended my charade, remaining on the stoop for a moment to talk nonsense at the empty foyer. As if carrying on a conversation with my landlady before finally crossing the threshold. Once inside, I bolted myself in and raced up to the nearest window.

A tiny break in the curtains allowed me to watch for six and a half minutes until the other cab pulled back into traffic and drove away. I stayed rooted to my spot and was rewarded with the sight of Nico and the Vespa emerging from an alley across the way a moment later. He would tail the cab to see if that gave us a location for Tony B's headquarters in Florence.

I hurried upstairs to pack, and was back in the foyer again, my luggage sitting beside me when my patient cabbie returned for the second time.

The next phase of our plan called for me to ride around in the taxi until Nico called for a pickup from the Vespa place. Another forty-five minutes and he was sitting beside me and giving our cabbie directions in Italian to the hotel he'd chosen.

"Find out anything?" I asked quietly in English after our driver pulled back into traffic.

"A business first," Nico said. "It was a converted palazzo too, but on the other side of the city and in a rundown area. No sign outside, but there were a lot of trucks, as if they used the building for storage."

Generally, addresses with red numbering signified a business in Florence, whereas residences used either black or blue, so I understood how Nico reached his conclusion. "Without a business name, we don't know who operates out of the place."

"I sent the address to Cassie and told her how to research it. She will send back info when she has something."

"You two work well together," I said, proud of my team.

"She is very smart. Her brain—" He made a curve motion at the side of his head with an index finger. "You see behind her eyes. She is working. Puzzling it all out."

I'd better watch out, or my assistant could stage a coup. She already has Max and Nico behind her. I smiled at the thought. Cassie was one person I would trust never to betray me. Unlike my current reticence about my old friend Flavia.

"That reminds me." I took a minute to sketch out my concerns about Flavia and reiterate what Jack told me the previous evening about the gallery. "When we get a chance, we need to check on everyone associated with the Florence gallery, but especially Flavia." Instinct told me she was connected somehow with Tony B. His appearance at the fundraiser alone was enough to fuel suspicion. But I wanted to know if she was also involved in the forgeries, and if she could have set up the police raid when she disappeared behind that door at the gallery. I would have never thought Flavia could be crooked, but her not contacting me at all left little doubt. Even if she'd missed seeing me at the event, the bar code on my ticket proved I was there, and she hadn't tried to phone or text me later.

He nodded, pulling out his wallet as the view of our hotel filled the windshield.

"But we got off track," I said, stepping from the cab after he opened the curbside door. "I take it you went somewhere else after the warehouse?"

The cabbie passed him my luggage, and Nico extended the handle. "Yes, we went next to a villa on the outskirts of the city. There was a high wall, and the house was at least three stories, but I couldn't find any trace of guard dogs."

"So you think—"

"That is where your friend is staying, I believe."

I barely acknowledged the sumptuous lobby. My mind was too focused on the possibility of interrogating Tina. Nico got us checked into a suite, and I kept silent until we entered the elevator alone with my one piece of rolling luggage.

"Was the wall electrified?" I asked.

"I saw no evidence. What I could see was razor wire across the top of the wall."

I grinned. "I can get around that."

"I know you can."

"Like his office in Miami, he counts on his goons for protection instead of gizmos. Tony B needs to join the twenty-first century and amp up his security." No dogs. No perimeter electric hazard. A sense of calm filled me. "How many stories did you say?"

"Mostly two. There is a small third story, but I seriously doubt

Tina is there. My guess is the balcony bedroom near the southwest corner. At least, I would start there."

"Because?"

"I saw a young woman walk past the open balcony doors while I was scouting out the area. She didn't appear to be a servant."

Our floor dinged, and Nico rolled my bag down the hall. I instinctively noted where the staircase was located, not for fire safety as much as general escape. The keycard produced the necessary green light, and we were inside.

"Why didn't you think she was a servant? Was she young? Beautiful?" I asked.

Nico set my bag on the luggage rack, then walked over to the table and pulled out a chair. He lowered himself elegantly into the leather seat and took a moment to pinch the crease in his tan slacks, pointedly ignoring me until he was ready. Then he looked up and smiled. "Yes, she was young, and she was beautiful."

I was about to ask if she resembled the picture that first appeared on the internet in connection with the murder in Bricknell, but I stopped when Nico added, "And after she removed a chin-length blond wig, she pulled out the clips in her dark hair, and the long waves fell to the middle of her back."

TWENTY-FIVE

By nine in the evening, Detective Roblo's plane landed at the Galileo Galilei Airport in Pisa, and he would soon be en route by train to Florence. It was the cheaper way to get into the area, and I felt sorry for him having to take the longer route. Originally, we'd planned to wait for him before approaching the villa, had even promised him we would when he returned our call during his layover at Heathrow. Then he called from the train departing Pisa, pleased to inform us he'd connected with local authorities and made sure Tony B stayed under surveillance as we directed our investigation toward the villa.

I choked out words that sounded something like "Oh good lord" and tossed the phone to Nico. When he disconnected, I was already changing into my black Lycra catsuit.

He shifted rapidly through screens on his phone and said, "I take it you believe our detective was a little naïve in thinking he could trust the *polizia* in Pisa."

"No, right now I'm thinking *we* were beyond naïve and way over into *stupid* to trust a detective from Miami understood how dangerous Tony B is." I finished pulling at the neckline to get the material to lay comfortably over my shoulders. "Can you track the thug's movements?"

"He's currently using his phone. Given what the detective said, and based on the cell towers triggered by Tony B's call and his movements, I can deduce that he's heading back this way from Pisa at a significantly higher rate of speed than the posted limit."

"Shit." I added a utility belt around my waist. "Can we get to the villa ahead of him?"

"It will be close."

With the right tools, I can get into anything, and I'd spent the afternoon acquiring whatever I needed to break into the villa in the event a worst-case scenario occurred. Currently, we were well past that point.

Half an hour later I had Nico planted along the inside of the villa's perimeter wall and was scaling the building's rock face like Spiderman. A fanny pack of chalk powder kept my hands from slipping from the stone façade. Nico had a rope and grappling hook if he had to ride to the rescue, but I preferred to try the stealth approach.

Each move offered its own risk and reward. I couldn't climb close to Tina's room, because the wall below it was a bank of floor-to-ceiling windows and a French door with patio access. I had to move over about twelve feet to start my climb, then once I reached the second level take a horizontal path to get back to the balcony. Anytime a hold slipped, I grabbed another handful of chalk. I knew my suit would look like a panda by the time I reached my objective, but I carried a set of wipes tucked into my bra to return my suit to its black beauty at the proper time.

I heard movement and shouts inside the villa, and engines revving in the garage. Time was ticking away fast for us to pull this off. But at least all the activity kept them from noticing me attempting to sneak inside.

When I reached the balcony, I slid my left foot over to balance on the railing. Then I carefully dragged my right shoe left to meet its mate. Every nerve ending in me wanted to leap off and run into the room. My endless planning and training was the saving grace that held me back. I couldn't stop a quiet thump when I hit the stone deck, but reassured myself I was the only one who heard the sound.

In seconds, I removed the wipes and dusted away the chalk from my suit in case I needed to move farther into the house and hide in shadows. I knew Nico would be watching to see me when I hit the light from the room, so didn't bother to wave or give him any kind of high sign. Focus was the key, and I was giving it my all.

Under the glare of every bedroom light, I saw Tina flitting from one end of the room to the other. She was packing her clothes and sorting through papers. Some of the pages were packed in a file case. Others were shredded. I couldn't help wondering what was too sensitive to simply throw away. Bills of lading? Counterfeit provenance on the marked masters we'd already discovered? And what part had she played in this terrifying farce of fakes, guns, and dead bodies?

I unsheathed the knife hanging on the opposite side of my belt from the chalk pack and pulled the flexible plastic tie cuffs from my bra. I waited. Whenever she shredded documents, Tina had to turn away from me. If she grabbed a larger than normal stack, I planned to use her action, along with the grinding noise of the shredder, to cover my entrance. I'd almost given up hope, when she grabbed the last stack. She scanned the top couple of sheets, then grasped one side tight in one hand and used the other to fan through the pages from the opposite corner as if she were viewing a flip book. Satisfied, she moved to the shredder with the ream of paper.

My knife was at her throat in seconds.

"Put your hands behind your back."

"Laurel, I—"

"Now!" I let the knife scrape her skin. She didn't need any more persuasion. A second later my free hand held her wrists together. With the knife between my teeth, I had both hands free to restrain her with the zip tie cuffs. I shoved her toward a chair. She missed the seat and landed in a heap on the floor. I pulled another zip tie from my bra and bound her ankles together, then flashed the knife. Her eyes grew wide as I asked, "Who killed Phyllis? You or Tony B?"

"Are you kidding me? Who cares?" She started crying, and her face mottled in red splotches as her angry words spewed. "You know what my family is like. You saw how I was pimped out to any feeble old billionaire Phyllis could sink her tentacles into. You have no idea the kind of humiliation—"

"So now you pimp yourself out to Tony B?"

Her tears stopped in an instant, and she sneered at me. "You have no idea what you're talking about. You're completely off-base."

"Why did Tony B have Jack arrested?"

"Because he could," she snapped at me.

"What is he afraid of? Why is he after Jack and me?"

She started laughing then, and I wondered if mental illness was also a gift from Phyllis. When she stopped, she said, "He isn't afraid of anyone. You have no idea the scope of what and whom you're dealing with, Laurel. You have no idea who you're dealing with when it comes to Tony B."

"No, he has no idea who he's dealing with when he messes with me. Especially if he thinks he can get Jack arrested and assumes I'm going to walk away."

"This is so much bigger than you. You can't imagine." She laughed again and nodded. "Why don't you ask Tony B for yourself what he thinks?"

I felt the gun barrel at my temple. It was the Miami office all over again. I'd never heard him coming up behind me. Before I could step away, his arm looped my waist and tightened like steel, holding me tight against him, unable to move.

"Yes, Laurel." I heard the glee trapped in Tony B's voice. "Why don't you ask me yourself if I'm afraid of you? Or of Jack."

The only chance I had was to use conversation to try to throw him off-balance and buy time. My knife was useless with his gun to my head. I asked a question he wasn't expecting.

"I really want to know what I did to piss off Moran."

"Huh?" His grip around my waist loosened for a second, but not enough for me to risk trying to break free. He said, "How should I know? I don't give a rat's ass what that old man wants. My concern is about what's going to make me rich and give me power. You've messed up things for months and never even knew it. Letting too many people know Tina isn't dead is the latest. Now you've even brought in a Miami detective to arrest her and take her back to Florida. That's it. That's the last kink you're ever going to put into my plans, Laurel Beacham."

"Who wanted Jack arrested? You or Moran?" I pushed, ignoring what he'd already said.

He whirled me around to face him, stepping back to aim the gun at my heart. "What's this Moran shit? You think I work for that creaky old bastard?" He spit on the floor. "You don't know anything." He wrenched the knife from my hand. "I should have killed you in my office right away, but I wanted to show you the damned Sebastians first. That's my good nature biting me in the ass again."

"At least tell me who you're working for. If it isn't Moran, is Rollie trying to take over?"

Tony B laughed, but there was no humor in the sound. "You spend too much time thinking, but you'll never get it. You wouldn't believe who's in charge of this thing if I told you."

The room was warm, even with the balcony doors open, and the stocking cap made sweat run into my eyes. I thought of how brave Jack had looked, standing in the palazzo as the *carabinieri* marched him away, and hoped I could stay half as strong. The fact that Tony used military connections instead of the more local *polizia* scared me. Who did this thug have in his pocket, and how far would he go?

Tony B kept whining on, but I'd stopped listening. I looked over my shoulder at Tina, still on the floor, her hands cuffed, forgotten by the man she'd decided was her savior as he went on with his monologue and power trip. Nevertheless, she smirked at me. She might be tossed aside tomorrow, but right then she was on the winning team.

For the millionth time I wished I'd listened to Jack as he'd lectured in the Town Car. If I ever had another chance I would—

CRASH!

The window behind us shattered, cutting off my thought. Tina screamed. Tony B wheeled around to shoot. I saw the grappling hook lying atop the glass and a figure at the end of the balcony. As Tony B aimed, he loosened his grip enough that I could pull free. He squeezed off his first shot. A cry for Nico lodged in my throat. But it wasn't Nico. Jack was knocked against the balcony railing and crumpled to the floor.

Tony B aimed his gun at Jack's head.

"No!"

I high-kicked his gun hand, and the Beretta flew from his grip and skittered across the room. My next kick slammed his chest. He staggered, caught off-guard, and I smashed his nose with my fist. Blood spurted through his fingers as he held up his hands to protect his face from another blow. I aimed my next kick for his balls but changed direction when I noticed Tina scooting toward the gun.

"Oh, no, you don't." I dove in the same instant she scuttled closer to the weapon. It was a photo finish. I came away with the gun in my hand.

"Over there," I shouted at her, my adrenalin level likely through the roof. "Next to your favorite asshole." She didn't move fast enough, and I shot wide to get her attention. "Over there, I said. The next shot won't be a miss."

She got as close to Tony B as a second skin. I kept the gun trained on both of them and walked backward, crunching glass, to check on Jack. I felt tears on my cheeks, and that made me even more livid. Appearing weak in front of that rat bastard Tony B was the last thing I wanted.

As I got next to Jack, he raised up. The relief I felt was almost overwhelming.

"Jack, are you—"

He grabbed the gun from my hand and jerked my arm, then kicked my legs out from under me. I hit the floor of the balcony as a flying object slammed into the balustrades where I'd been standing. Simultaneously, I heard Jack fire a shot over my body. When I looked to see what had flown toward me, I discovered my knife.

"Why aren't any of his men coming to find out what happened?" Below us I could hear Nico hollering for us to send down the rope, but my brain wasn't working well enough yet to comply.

"Everyone's gone." Jack's voice was weak but steady. "Tony B sent them away, planning to take care of you himself. That was our tip-off to move in. All the cars leaving, but you and Tina still inside." He used the railing to pull himself to his feet and held his ribs with one hand as he moved closer to our captives. He waved the gun toward the grappling hook and rope, and said, "Hang this on the rail for Nico."

I moved then, finally realizing things were going to work out in our favor. But while Jack was mobile, he wasn't unscathed. "I take it you're wearing a Kevlar vest." I tossed the end of the rope to Nico.

"Yeah, no blood, but at least one broken rib. Probably two."

"Where have you been? And how did you know to come here?"

He kept the gun trained on Tina and Tony B. "The first question would take too long to explain. I'll just say it was a good thing this asshole tapped military connections. That helped me tremendously." He took a couple of shallow breaths, then said, "Regarding your second question, I was in Pisa keeping an eye on..." He motioned the gun toward Tony B. "I picked up enough conversation. Saw the quick move out and knew something was happening back here."

"I'm glad you did." I moved next to him and put an arm around his waist. He was flagging fast.

Nico came up behind him and took the gun. In the distance we could hear the bebop of Italian sirens. "Get him out of here," Nico said, then aimed at a spot near the ceiling and fired. Plaster flew as the bullet buried itself in the wallboard. "I will take care of this, Jack. Hurry."

"But you'll be arrested," I said. "I'll tell them I shot him."

"I am Italian—you are not," Nico reminded, speaking quietly. "Take off your gloves and bury them in your chalk pack to hide the gunshot residue. I'll be fine. Max will get someone good to represent me."

"No."

Jack squeezed my arm and spoke softly. I hoped it was to keep the other two from overhearing what was said. Not because he was more hurt than he admitted. "Help me get off the balcony. That's faster than going through the house. Then stay here with Nico as a witness."

Nico started to argue, but Jack cut him off, "He already has gunshot residue on his skin. If you don't stay and back up his story as self-defense, Tony B could twist it around with Tina's help."

As we reached the balustrade, I leaned down to pick up the knife, but Jack stopped me. "Leave it. And make sure you and Nico say Tony B threw the knife at Nico, not you. It needs to be a self-defense plea, even though I hit him in the shoulder."

I nodded and climbed over the railing before giving the grappling hook another good tug and reaching a hand out to Jack. He clasped my fingers, holding onto the railing as I guided his hand toward the rope. Then we descended in a kind of reverse piggyback style so I could keep Jack from an accidental free fall.

The sirens were close by the time we hit the grass.

He gave me a careful hug. "Thank you. Now, get back up there."

"In a minute." I pulled my cell phone out of the side pocket of the fanny pack and started thumbing through my contacts. "Do you have a passport?"

"Yes, I have a passport. I'll get away. Don't worry."

I held up a finger for silence as my call started ringing at the other end. "Clive? Can you hear me?"

"Laurel, love, are you ready to fly with us again? We're leaving Rome in a few minutes and heading back to England," the roadie replied.

I smiled. "Not yet. I have more business to take care of first. But I have a friend who could really use your concierge service."

"A friend, you say?"

"Yes, and you might recognize him. You snapped enough pictures of him at Gatwick," I said.

"That bloke? The one what got 'em?"

"Yes, the very one. His name is Jack Hawkes," I said. "I'm giving him this phone. Call the number when you get to the Florence airport so he'll be able to find the right gate."

"Will do. Gotta go, Laurel. Still a few things to do before takeoff."

"For me too, Clive. And thank you."

I cut the connection and handed the phone to Jack. We could now see the flashing lights coming up the road.

"You heard what I said."

"Yes."

"Be careful," I warned. "And you'd better be in London when I get back there. Any more disappearing acts and I'll get seriously pissed off at you."

He gave a tired laugh. "I'll try."

"Do better than try. You want me to trust you. Give me a reason to. We have a lot of work ahead of us, and if I lose Nico while this all gets dealt with, I'm going to be counting double on you."

I knew he hated being told what to do, but I didn't care. When he gave me his stubborn-jaw look, I reflected it right back at him until he said, "I'll do my best."

Squad cars filled the circle drive, producing a carnival air as Jack disappeared into the shadows. I scrambled back up the rope and slid next to Nico as Detective Roblo entered the bedroom. Five more Italian officers following close on his heels.

I pointed to Tina. "Glad you could make it, Detective. There's your dead girl, alive and breathing."

Too many hours later I finally returned to the hotel room alone. Jack and Clive both texted me when their plane landed in London: Jack to say he was home and feeling fine, and Clive to tell me that Jack needed medical attention.

I set Cassie to work making sure the big lug saw a doctor. The objective was both to take care of Jack and to keep her busy enough to not worry as much about Nico. I was worrying enough for both of us.

Nico was allowed to call Max. He told me to leave after my interview was over. I wanted to stay, to camp out, to yell, and to scream—but I did what he asked since it truly was for the best. Max would take care of things. He was good at dealing with these kinds of messes. Primarily because it gave him terrific ammunition to use when he wanted to yell about something later.

In all, we'd made a good second step. We'd found the snuffbox and learned Simon had possession of it at some point after the Greek was killed. We still didn't know the significance of the number from the safe-deposit box, but we did have it in our possession. When our searches eventually turned up the mystery it could unlock, we were good to go. I had to believe that anyway.

Tina awaited extradition to Florida as an accessory to murder, and Roblo was set to escort her back on the first available flight. Tony B was fighting extradition at the moment, probably because they wanted to charge him with Phyllis's murder, and he faced a death penalty risk in Florida. But I really wondered if the killer wasn't actually Tina. I still remembered her "Who cares?" and shivered a little at the memory. I said as much to Roblo, and he agreed, then he added, "I think she would have done anything Tony B told her to do. She saw him as a means of getting away from her mother's control, and had no idea she was simply repeating the process with him instead. She said when she told him at dinner Thursday evening she was meeting you in the morning to hand over that art object, he got angry and set everything in motion. She was mad at you for being the reason she made Tony B angry."

Made me think I was lucky I hadn't met up with her the next morning. There may have been two bodies dumped in the alley. I needed to take a lesson from Jack and put bugs on more people next time—even the ones I thought were too clueless to matter.

The detective also let me know Tony B wasn't leaving it to his lawyer to do his fighting. With the knowledge Jack was free, the thug realized he didn't have the clout he'd originally thought, and

Roblo said the slimy toad was making quiet noises about trading information for a suspended sentence. I wondered who Tony B was turning on, but it certainly didn't surprise me that he chose this route. He had to know about the counterfeiting operation, something intriguing enough for Italian officials to try to keep him. His suggestive actions also put a finer point on what Jack and I had already decided—he wasn't in charge. I wondered if any evidence he gave would be the truth.

Who would Tony B finger as the top man? I thought about Jack and my rooftop excursion, and the dead body, the guns, and the counterfeits in triplicate we discovered there. Had Moran branched out into more than masterpieces? Or was it like Jack suspected, and Rollie was spreading his wings? But the fact that Tony B scoffed when I mentioned Moran at the villa implied he wasn't working with the mastermind. If so, someone or group with no affiliation to Moran had this process in play. Someone who would be harder to catch because he or she was an unknown. That's what Tony B implied, but his words could have all been bravado.

Roblo promised to share any information he could with me, and I urged him to push the interrogations extra hard. I think he was feeling guilty about Tony B getting tipped off by his coordinating with the Pisa police. I forgave Roblo for the misstep as soon as I saw Jack on the balcony. Though I wasn't going to admit it to either of them. I needed all the intel I could get, and Tony B might actually let something important slip. I also needed to learn what Jack discovered when I thought he was in jail but was actually staking out Tony B's Italian organization.

Yes, Mr. Hawkes had a number of things to explain when I got back to London. I counted on the hope at least some of them offered a lead to our next piece in this puzzle. Not that I'd forgiven him yet for keeping me in the dark when he was already freed from custody. I was definitely holding him to an explanation.

I hung the Do Not Disturb sign on the door and slid out of my black suit. The last thing I did was look at the picture of my mother. The very image of a lovely ingénue. I smiled at how much I favored her, but I knew I didn't possess her innocence. I stared at Margarite. I pondered the man who looked like Moran and let my thoughts drift for a bit. Then I turned out the lamp.

All the information in the world could wait. If I wanted to solve anything in the future, I had to catch up on about twenty-four hours of sleep. Starting immediately.

RITTER AMES

Ritter Ames lives atop a high green hill in the country with her husband and Labrador retriever, and spends each day globe-trotting the art world from her laptop with Pandora blasting into her earbuds. Often with the dog snoring at her feet. Much like her Bodies of Art Mysteries, Ritter's favorite vacations start in London, then spiral out in every direction. She's been known to plan trips after researching new books, and keeps a list of "can't miss" foods to taste along the way. Visit her at www.ritterames.com where she blogs about all the crazy things that interest her.

Henery Press Mystery Books

And finally, before you go...
Here are a few other mysteries
you might enjoy:

KILLER IMAGE

Wendy Tyson

An Allison Campbell Mystery (#1)

As Philadelphia's premier image consultant, Allison Campbell helps others reinvent themselves, but her most successful transformation was her own after a scandal nearly ruined her. Now she moves in a world of powerful executives, wealthy, eccentric ex-wives and twisted ethics.

When Allison's latest Main Line client, the fifteen-year-old Goth daughter of a White House hopeful, is accused of the ritualistic murder of a local divorce attorney, Allison fights to prove her client's innocence when no one else will. But unraveling the truth brings specters from her own past. And in a place where image is everything, the ability to distinguish what's real from the facade may be the only thing that keeps Allison alive.

Available at booksellers nationwide and online

Visit www.henerypress.com for details

DOUBLE WHAMMY
Gretchen Archer

A Davis Way Crime Caper (#1)

Davis Way thinks she's hit the jackpot when she lands a job as the fifth wheel on an elite security team at the fabulous Bellissimo Resort and Casino in Biloxi, Mississippi. But once there, she runs straight into her ex-ex husband, a rigged slot machine, her evil twin, and a trail of dead bodies. Davis learns the truth and it does not set her free—in fact, it lands her in the pokey.

Buried under a mistaken identity, unable to seek help from her family, her hot streak runs cold until her landlord Bradley Cole steps in. Make that her landlord, lawyer, and love interest. With his help, Davis must win this high stakes game before her luck runs out.

Available at booksellers nationwide and online

Visit www.henerypress.com for details

NUN TOO SOON

Alice Loweecey

A Giulia Driscoll Mystery (#1)

Giulia Driscoll has just taken on her first impossible client: The Silk Tie Killer. He's hired Driscoll Investigations to prove his innocence and they have only thirteen days to accomplish it. Talk about being tried in the media. Everyone in town is sure Roger Fitch strangled his girlfriend with one of his silk neckties. And then there's the local TMZ wannabes stalking Giulia and her client for sleazy sound bites.

On top of all that, her assistant's first baby is due any second, her scary smart admin still doesn't relate well to humans, and her police detective husband insists her client is guilty. About this marriage thing—it's unknown territory, but it sure beats ten years of living with 150 nuns.

Giulia's ownership of Driscoll Investigations hasn't changed her passion for justice from her convent years. But the more dirt she digs up, the more she's worried her efforts will help a murderer escape. As the client accuses DI of dragging its heels on purpose, Giulia thinks The Silk Tie Killer might be choosing one of his ties for her own neck.

Available at booksellers nationwide and online

Visit www.henerypress.com for details

DEATH BY BLUE WATER

Kait Carson

A Hayden Kent Mystery (#1)

Paralegal Hayden Kent knows first-hand that life in the Florida Keys can change from perfect to perilous in a heartbeat. When she discovers a man's body at 120' beneath the sea, she thinks she is witness to a tragic accident. She becomes the prime suspect when the victim is revealed to be the brother of the man who recently jilted her, and she has no alibi. A migraine stole Hayden's memory of the night of the death.

As the evidence mounts, she joins forces with an Officer Janice Kirby. Together the two women follow the clues that uncover criminal activities at the highest levels and put Hayden's life in jeopardy while she fights to stay free.

Available at booksellers nationwide and online

Visit www.henerypress.com for details

MACDEATH

Cindy Brown

An Ivy Meadows Mystery (#1)

Like every actor, Ivy Meadows knows that *Macbeth* is cursed. But she's finally scored her big break, cast as an acrobatic witch in a circus-themed production of *Macbeth* in Phoenix, Arizona. And though it may not be Broadway, nothing can dampen her enthusiasm—not her flying cauldron, too-tight leotard, or carrot-wielding dictator of a director.

But when one of the cast dies on opening night, Ivy is sure the seeming accident is "murder most foul" and that she's the perfect person to solve the crime (after all, she does work part-time in her uncle's detective agency). Undeterred by a poisoned Big Gulp, the threat of being blackballed, and the suddenly too-real curse, Ivy pursues the truth at the risk of her hard-won career—and her life.

Available at booksellers nationwide and online

Visit www.henerypress.com for details

CPSIA information can be obtained
at www.ICGtesting.com
Printed in the USA
BVHW04s1219260718
522666BV00011B/178/P